WEST COUNTRY MURDER

A totally gripping crime mystery full of twists

DEREK THOMPSON

Detective Craig Wild Mystery Book 2

Joffe Books, London
www.joffebooks.com

First published in Great Britain in 2022

© Derek Thompson

This book is a work of fiction. Names, characters, businesses, organizations, places and events are either the product of the author's imagination or are used fictitiously. Any resemblance to actual persons, living or dead, events or locales is entirely coincidental. The spelling used is British English except where fidelity to the author's rendering of accent or dialect supersedes this. The right of Derek Thompson to be identified as author of this work has been asserted in accordance with the Copyright, Designs and Patents Act 1988.

Cover art by Dee Dee Book Covers

ISBN: 978-1-80405-080-4

*This book is dedicated to Jenny Coralie,
Richard Coralie and Reece Coralie.*

PROLOGUE

The body stopped twitching while he sat beside it, eyes at the window, watching for the best time to slip away. A relentless August sun had turned the inside of the car into a greenhouse, but that wasn't the reason for the breathlessness, or the sweat clinging to the living and the dead.

A gloved hand gingerly searched a pocket for house keys, fearful even now that the victim might recover. Finding those was easy, unlike the car keys — no way to search across the body without leaving contact traces.

He wiped the passenger door and then released the catch, bringing in a welcome rush of air and the sounds of summer. One door manually locked and wiped clean, just the driver's side remaining.

From the outside he could have been sleeping, only he wasn't. The door slammed shut and the body slid towards it, head lolling like the deadweight it had become. No time for regrets and still so much to do.

CHAPTER 1

PC Marnie Olsen took another sip from her recycled coffee cup as a cool breeze billowed the edge of the festival tent. She leaned towards DS Craig Wild and whispered.

"Remind me again what we're doing here?"

Wild shushed her and tilted forward in his chair, muttering over his shoulder. "It was your idea, remember? Stop being a copper twenty-four-seven. Do something cultural, you said — try the local literary festival."

A nearby punter shot him a loaded glance. Fat chance of that working. Wild stared back like an angry shark.

Marnie carried on, oblivious. "No, I mean why *here* — for the past fifteen minutes?"

Up on the podium, Juliette Kimani continued to hold court beside an artistically stacked pile of books. Wild estimated she was in her mid to late forties, maybe younger if she'd had cosmetic surgery, and something of a big-ticket author.

Marnie leaned in again. "I'm going to slide out quietly before I fall asleep. Maybe I can catch a pickpocket or something. Give me a buzz when you're free."

He waved her away. A hand shot up near the front of the audience and its owner launched into a vacuous question about motivation.

"Well, of course," Juliette simpered. "I would encourage everyone to write the novel they want to read, only not too similar to any of mine!"

Polite laughter rippled around the tent. A well-rehearsed skit, Wild reasoned, and probably instigated by a plant in the audience. The questions that followed were predictable, everything from 'where do you get your ideas' to 'would your publisher read my book'. Juliette responded to each question as though she had all the time in the world, but Wild had clocked her looking to the lackey waiting in the wings with a plate of cling-filmed sandwiches.

"Okay, there's just time for one more before the break."

Wild creaked his plastic chair to grab her attention and raised a hand. Sometimes the old ones were the best.

"Yes, the man at the back holding a red baseball cap."

"How do you stay relevant as an author?"

She smiled for an instant and then swatted him like a fly. "That's a very intriguing question. I stay relevant by remaining authentic."

He watched a sea of heads in front of him, bobbing gently like seaweed in an ebb tide. He decided that every one of them was a budding writer, and what she'd said made no sense at all. Then he realised she was still talking.

". . . And I write about what affects me personally. Those of you who've read about my daughter's inspirational journey will see a resonance in my next book — but I can't say too much about that until my publisher gives me permission! Okay, let's take a quick break and I'll sign some books. If there's any time left over I'll answer more questions."

Wild wondered how she made it all sound so fresh, when she'd been in the writing game for, well it must be a good twenty years or more. The new face of literary Britain, they had called her. And perhaps she had been just that.

He joined the line to get his copy of *Junction Street* signed. It looked a little worn, as he'd found it in the charity shop. Maybe it would be worth a few quid with a signature — especially to Americans. They'd buy anything.

The line shuffled along, five people ahead of him gushing with praise and exchanging similar pleasantries with the author when they reached their turn. Juliette sprinkled fairy dust on every one of them and they floated back to their chairs. As Wild stepped up to the table his mobile rang so he answered it. Juliette waited patiently, unlike the people behind him.

"Craig, it's Marnie. You'd better get out here right now."

He held on to the phone and looked down at Juliette in her marginally more comfortable chair. "Sorry. Some other time." He abandoned his place in the line, tucked the unsigned hardback into his rucksack and left the tent to a chorus of polite discontent.

Marnie was still talking. "I'm with a body, or I'd come and get you. Head out to the car park in the main field. I'm near the end fence. I'll wave."

He grimaced. Fields seemed to be very dangerous places in Wiltshire. The literati swarmed past him for their culture fix. Somewhere behind him he heard a jazz trumpet launch into life. New Orleans meets Mayberry. He followed Marnie's directions until he saw the slow waving arm, simultaneously attracting his attention while trying to be inconspicuous.

She stood beside a Mini Cooper, while an ashen-faced couple leaned against a nearby fence. Wild noted how the man's pallor matched his linen suit, giving him the appearance of human laundry. He spotted the vomit on the grass a few feet in front of him. The man's partner — judging by the way their hands were fused together — looked away as Wild appeared, as if she could somehow unsee whatever had required Marnie's attendance. He chewed on the thought. Good luck with that.

An adult male lay slumped against the driver's door, inside the car. At first glance he might have been sleeping. At second glance the drool soaked into his T-shirt, the total lack of movement and the unnatural tilt of the head as the body had fallen to one side were a *dead* giveaway. As Wild surveyed the body under glass a fly crawled up the face and entered a nostril. There was no reaction.

"Doors are locked," Marnie explained. "I did try knocking on the glass." She glanced at the couple by the fence. "They think they saw him here half an hour ago and assumed he was having a nap. This time they looked closer. I happened to be walking past. Is he . . . ?"

Wild nodded but his attention was elsewhere, on the traces of foam at the mouth and the blue tinge to the lips. He spotted the coffee cup in its holder with a logo from one of the festival tents. That, and the absence of a key in the ignition.

"Find me a rock, will you. And get details from the witnesses."

"Already done."

He was about to send Marnie off on a geological expedition when she bent down and passed him a fist-sized chunk of rock that already lay at her feet. He walked round to the passenger door, Marnie following him like a police probationer. Then he raised an arm to move her away and swung hard at the window. The glass resisted but the car alarm made its own protest. Four more blows and the glass finally gave way.

People began to drift towards the car at the sound of the alarm. Marnie went into action, warrant card extended as if it were pepper spray. It had the same effect.

"If you could all stay back please. And if anyone noticed this car earlier, can you wait over there and we'll come and speak with you."

Wild tapped shards of glass away with the rock and then reached in to pull the door release. Once inside, he leaned over to the victim and eased his legs open to reveal a car key between his feet. A lucky guess. He bleeped the key and the alarm stopped shrieking.

Marnie spoke through the driver's closed window.

"Shall I ring DI Marsh, as Senior Investigating Officer, and then get the team in?"

He nodded. They'd wait a long time to get the victim out otherwise. And little inconveniences like it being the weekend wouldn't stop the DI from parachuting in on his — and Marnie's — investigation.

The body was very warm and very dead. He eased back the victim's jacket and carefully lifted out a wallet, which helpfully contained a driving licence and the usual detritus — gym membership, shopping receipts, and thirty quid in cash.

Marnie tapped on the glass so Wild obligingly lowered the driver's window.

"The witnesses are asking if they can leave. We have all their details and the DI said for you to hold the fort till she gets here . . ."

"Fine. Everyone can go, except the puker and the woman with him. Tell them we'll sort out appointments for formal statements." He looked over at the mass of cars around them. This would be a nightmare to evacuate. "Chase up two more uniformed officers pronto and then once I can get his driving licence picture copied we'll circulate. Other people on site might have seen something."

As he leaned back he spotted a paper bag under the passenger seat. Inside was a copy of the same hardback he'd brought along, only this one was signed. "Lucky sod," he said without thinking and then he glanced back at the corpse. "Then again, maybe not." He took out his ever-present notebook. Time to get busy so the DI's opinion of him remained in the temperate zone.

* * *

In the space of half an hour everything changed. The Scene of Crime Officer arrived, gave him and Marnie the third degree about what they'd touched, and then set to work beneath a plastic canopy erected around the car. Dr Bell arrived for a preliminary examination of the deceased, along with an ambulance — the sort that didn't need blue lights or sirens.

Marnie, meanwhile, had recorded all the car index numbers in the immediate vicinity, so some unfortunate soul would be tracing them later on the Police National Computer.

Wild liaised with one of the literary festival officials, who gave him access to a photocopier and a printer. Grateful that the event didn't have to be abandoned, they also loaned him an unused exhibitor tent as a temporary base of operations. A suspicious death, a free coffee voucher and the chance to work with Marnie again on a case — this was rapidly turning into Wild's best day off in years.

CHAPTER 2

Wild rested some papers on a plastic table, noticed the wobble and fixed it with a discarded coffee cup crushed to order. And to think his ex-wife, Steph, had criticised his DIY skills. He pressed on the tabletop a few times, like lazy CPR practice, and then sat back with a disproportionate sense of satisfaction. Still no sign of DI Marsh.

"Oh well," he said to an empty tent as he checked his watch, running a fingertip over the scratch. "Crime waits for no one."

He heard Marnie outside. "You can go in."

Juliette Kimani appeared through the gap between the tent flaps and stalled, mid-tent, when she saw him.

"Excuse me . . . didn't we meet earlier today?"

He smiled, sharing her awkwardness. "Yeah, I was in your tent then. I asked the question about staying relevant."

She flicked an index finger like a percussionist. "The man with the baseball cap. You abandoned my signing line as well — every writer's nightmare!"

He smiled again. Very observant. "Yeah, couldn't be helped. Please have a seat." He waved a hand towards the chair facing him and carried on talking. "You've probably heard by now that unfortunately a man died here today.

We're trying to trace his movements. He had a signed copy of your book in his possession. Perhaps you remember seeing him?" He showed her an enlarged copy of the victim's driving licence photo.

She lowered her gaze, blinked a couple of times and swallowed. He understood — not every day you saw a photo of someone who had since died. She stared at it again and squinted.

"Hmm . . . to be honest, I might well have seen him. I've been here for two days." She looked up and coughed politely. "After a while the faces start to blur. Although it's just as likely that he bought a signed copy at one of the festival bookstores."

A part of him inwardly recoiled at *bookstore*. "As part of our investigation we will check for any bankcard transactions."

She threw him a smile. "Let's hope he didn't pay by cash then."

He didn't react and she quickly got the message.

"Sorry, that was inappropriate." She changed tack. "By the way, would you like me to sign your book now, seeing as I'm here?"

He blushed and reached into the bag by his feet, planning to compare the signatures once she'd gone. "Thanks."

"I have spare copies of some of my other novels — I'd be happy to send them to you at the police station." She paused. "Or maybe you need permission from your superiors?"

He passed his copy across and she signed it with a flourish.

He added, as he received it back, "I really enjoyed it." He made a couple of notes, aware that she was trying to read them from her side of the table, and then closed his notebook. "Would you say this guy . . ." he patted the picture, "fits your usual readership?"

She looked puzzled. "Because he's young and white, you mean, whereas I am . . . neither?"

He lurched back like she'd shot him. "Christ, no, I didn't mean it that way. I s'pose I think that literary fiction is a bit, you know, high brow."

She folded her arms. "Not too high brow for police officers though! Like I say, I don't recall meeting him so I wouldn't know his intellectual capabilities."

A voice in Wild's head screamed 'stop digging this hole'. She stared at him pointedly and he found something else to talk about.

"Is this something you do regularly — these book fairs?"

"The literary festivals?" she corrected him. "Where I can, yes. Some I commit to every year, so I stay connected to my readers. And of course my publisher is very keen if I have a new book coming out!" She lowered her gaze. "Although I took a break when my daughter became seriously ill."

He felt the tension, as if she was willing him to intrude on her private life, but he let it go. He could always check online later.

"Okay," he tapped his notebook. "I think we'll leave it there for now. Thanks for your time. We might need to speak with you again." He stood up and leaned across the table to shake her hand.

Marnie appeared on cue to see her out. He'd spotted her at the entrance, listening in. She didn't speak until it was just the two of them. "The Support Officer is checking the bookstores."

"Shops," he insisted. "They're shops. Or pop-ups at a push. We're not in Massachusetts."

She sat in the empty seat. "They're removing the body. So far, no journalists lurking. Strange really, I would have thought this was a major local story."

"Yeah, great headline opportunity: *Man Turns the Final Page*."

She smiled and countered with, "*Body found at Lit. Fest: The End*."

He put his signed copy away. "So, how are the troops getting on?"

She read his tone. He wasn't expecting much. "We noted every car reg. in the field . . ."

"Any that hadn't left already."

She nodded. *Touché, DS Wild.* "Okay, those we had access to. And the staff at the coffee tent didn't recognise the victim, but to be fair . . ."

"I know, hundreds of people and nothing memorable about any of them. What else?"

"It is definitely the victim's own car and the home address is out of county — in Lincolnshire."

His brow furrowed. She shook her head slowly.

"It's in the north-east, Wild."

"Right, gotcha. It's a long way to come for a literary festival."

"Yes, especially as he only bought the one book. SOCO found a festival programme in the glove compartment, although there's nothing marked in it."

"I'll talk to the DI about me and Ben Galloway visiting Juliette Kimani tomorrow morning. Maybe we can jog her memory." He could see Marnie crestfallen at the realisation she wasn't on the invite list. "Listen, if it was down to me, when Ben Galloway transferred . . ." He hesitated and switched tack. "Incidentally, when you first said the victim's car was locked, did you check the back of the car?"

Marnie paused to think about it. "No, why?"

He shook his head. "Shit, that's a lost opportunity." He met her blank stare with reason. "In some modern cars you can still lock the door by pushing down the button and holding the handle outside when you shut it. So someone could get out, and still lock it with the key inside."

"Sorry, never knew that. Guess I still have a lot to learn."

He tried to soften the blow. "You weren't to know. Someone locked me out like that once — *for a laugh* — when I left my key in the car. Fortunately the boot still worked so I had to crawl in through the hatch." He stopped talking and got out his phone to find the number he wanted. "Hello? It's DS Wild." The SOCO didn't appreciate being disturbed. "Can you make sure you dust the driver's door handle for prints, and the passenger's . . . right." He let her enjoy the moment and waited for her to end the call.

"Good news, Craig?"

"That depends on what you're looking for. No prints on either door handle — not even a partial. It's suspicious as fuck. And no gloves in the car so unless he was a reverse Houdini act, something's not right here."

No sooner had the thought left his mouth then the tent flaps rustled and DI Marsh stood in the opening like an apparition. "I hope I'm not interrupting a private conversation. Wild, can you go grab me a coffee and bring another chair, and then the three of us are going to have a little debrief. Well, after DS Wild tells me why Juliette Kimani has already been allowed to go home."

CHAPTER 3

Wild never bothered with satnav. Not when he had Ben Galloway to navigate for him. DC Galloway seemed to have really shaped up in the past month or so. Maybe that was because, according to the rumour mill, his transfer had been approved. Not that DI Marsh felt the need to keep Wild in the loop about it.

"Isn't this a long shot, Skip?"

Wild winced. He'd given up trying to educate Galloway on the proper use of names, but it still rankled with him.

"It *is* a long shot — we have nothing else at this stage. The victim seems to have led an exemplary life. We basically know sod all about him. No criminal record, not so much as a parking ticket. The festival is a tenuous link but Juliette Kimani signed a book for him so they must have met, even briefly."

"You don't think he bought a signed copy at the festival?"

Wild felt his eyes widening. "Are you kidding me? He lived on the other side of Lincoln. Wiltshire is a bloody long way to come to a literary festival, where Juliette happens to be appearing, only to pick up an autographed copy off a shelf. He could have telephoned and had one posted to him. Of course he wanted it signed there."

Ben thought for a minute. An actual minute. Wild counted in his head.

"There wasn't any personal dedication though."

"No, I'll give you that. Which is interesting."

Galloway looked really pleased with himself.

Wild threw a rope ladder across the silence. "What's the word on your transfer, Ben?" He never used first names if he could avoid it, but this felt like one of those teamy moments."

"Still waiting for confirmation, Skip — there's a possible opening at Gable Cross police station, so I wouldn't need to move out of home. Bugger, speaking of openings, I think we missed our turn-off." He looked over his shoulder. "Never mind, Skip, we'll catch the next one and loop round."

A few miles later, Wild wondered if the new team had any idea what they were letting themselves in for. Galloway was a good copper, give or take the odd misdemeanour. But by Christ he was off-hand about things that mattered. Like getting anywhere on time.

Thirty-four minutes later, according to the car clock, Wild's Ford Focus entered the respectable village of Kelhurst. Juliette's home lay at the top end, and the properties seemed grander the further up they travelled. He couldn't help but admire the house, although a bit Jane Austen for his tastes, complete with a circular drive that once would have conveyed carriages to the pillared door and then back out to the real world.

He switched off the ignition. "You know I always tell you to let me do the talking? Well, today is different. You know as much as I do."

"Which is very little."

"Exactly. So distract her all you want and I'll chip in as and when."

Ben nodded slowly, as if he'd been made party to a great secret.

The sound of classical music hit Wild on the doorstep. It felt contrived, given that they had arranged the time in advance. He rang the bell and the music stopped clawing its way through the door. Shoes clattered against tiles and then the door catch went.

"Good morning, gentlemen. Please come in."

Wild followed Galloway past a shelf of family photos, most of which showed a girl who looked precocious even in a hospital bed.

Juliette floated through to the lounge where a plate of small pastries awaited them. "Tea or coffee?"

Galloway turned briefly to Wild, who offered no clues. "Erm, coffee, no, tea."

Wild resisted the urge to swear.

"Make yourself comfortable, gentlemen. I won't be long."

Wild took a single seat. Galloway sat as close as possible to him on the adjoining sofa and leaned in. "I might try pressing her hard."

Wild chose a pastry; it was going to be quite a show.

Juliette placed a tray on the table with two teapots. She caught his gaze. "Earl Grey or Assam?"

He opted for the latter, deeming it the closest thing to normal tea. He coughed a little in Galloway's direction.

"I'll have the same, thank you. So, Mrs Kimani . . . or may I call you Juliette?"

She nibbled her pastry and perched on the edge of a chair at the other end of the table, as if undecided whether to stay. "By all means."

Wild smiled. If Galloway thought she was giving ground he had a lot to learn.

"Now, have you remembered meeting the man DS Wild asked you about yesterday?"

Wild took out the driving licence photo and unfolded it on the table.

She glanced at it for a handful of seconds and swallowed. "How did he . . . ?"

"Die?" Wild picked up a spoon. "A suspected overdose. We're awaiting the pathologist's report."

"Drugs," she said quietly, her tone flat and distant.

Galloway corralled her in. "The photograph."

She glanced down. "I've given this some thought and it is possible I met him earlier in the day. We do get people approaching us for signatures when we're walking around the festival. It's not really encouraged, but I try to be accommodating."

Wild shifted his cup and saucer. "It's the price of fame, I suppose."

She smiled coquettishly. "It's a small price to pay!"

A sullen voice called from upstairs. "Mum, have we got any biscuits?"

Juliette stiffened a little. "Of course darling, but I'm with people. Grown-up stuff."

Dull thuds on the stairs were followed by the appearance of a girl who seemed around sixteen, poking her head through the doorway. "Sorry, didn't realise you had guests."

Wild remembered seeing the upstairs curtain flicker when they got out of the car.

Juliette quickly folded the picture over. "This is my daughter, Izzie."

"Isabella," she corrected her. "Ooh, pastries. Mind if I grab a couple?" She prowled across the carpet and stretched towards Galloway, the blue tint in her jet-black hair catching the light. Her bare arms poked through a sleeveless T-shirt that bore the slogan 'Rebel Born'.

She could have been, Wild mused, anything from fifteen to twenty-five. Galloway's face was a study in scarlet. Wild noticed the way the girl's eyes flickered towards him, after she'd finished batting her lashes in Ben's direction. He reached across and snatched the page away.

Isabella turned sharply at the hips. "Don't mind me, I was just leaving." She sauntered towards the kitchen and threw a smile over her shoulder. Wild waited until her receding footsteps were rounded off with a percussive door slam upstairs.

Juliette touched a bone china cup to her lips. "Thank you for your discretion. I try to shield Isabella from the adult world. She's been through so much already in her young life."

Ben Galloway took out his notebook. "Is it usual to sign your books without a personal dedication?"

Wild nearly gave him a thumbs-up.

She faltered. "I . . . I don't follow you."

"Your signature was in the victim's copy of your book, but that's all."

"Right." She took another sip of tea, sat back and crossed her legs. "I suppose he may have been a book dealer?"

Wild reached for another miniature cake, paused, and tapped the folded up photo with his other hand. "A bit young for that, I would have thought. The victim was in his early to mid-twenties. We are looking into his background as part of the investigation, but early indications are that he travelled some distance to the festival."

Juliette glanced towards the kitchen doorway where her daughter had emerged, only for a second, but Wild clocked it and filed it in the mental space that all good coppers have, marked *curious*. She reached for one of her mini pastries and examined it before setting it down untouched on her plate.

She stood up suddenly. "Oh, I nearly forgot — I have something for you, Detective Sergeant. I shan't be a minute."

Wild waited for the sound of footsteps on the stairs, gestured to Galloway to button his lip, and tiptoed to the doorway. He heard muffled voices and, leaning further out, spied a carrier bag under the shelving by the front door, bearing a publisher's logo. The voices died down upstairs and a door opened.

"Just stay up there and I'll speak to you later. There's nothing to worry about, I promise."

Wild made it back to his chair and was sipping tea when Juliette returned, bag in hand. "Here we are — I said I'd sort out some of my other titles for you."

"Thanks for bringing the books down — that's very kind of you."

"I suppose you'll need to get your superior's permission, not that it's a bribe or anything!" She nibbled on a cake and then passed the bag of books to him.

"I'm sure it'll be fine," Wild smiled, making a mental note to check with Marsh when they returned to Mayberry police station.

Galloway looked at him imploringly. He'd either been struck dumb or run out of questions. Wild took his time, feeling the space between himself and Juliette like a physical presence, while he sipped his tea.

"One more thing and we'll leave you in peace."

Juliette seemed to sag a little in her chair.

"Was your, erm, partner at the festival as well? For some reason," he glanced at Galloway for effect, "there's nothing mentioned in our notes."

"My husband is a playwright and stage director. He's up in London at the moment, working on his new play."

He nodded. "That's fine then." As he was standing and trying to decide whether to pop a cake into his pocket for later, his foot touched the bag. He picked it up. "How does your daughter feel about your books? I remember you mentioned how you drew inspiration from the world around you."

"She doesn't really appreciate having an author for a mother."

"Kids, eh?" He made for the doorway and heard Galloway scrabbling out of his chair to follow him. "Thank you for seeing us, and for the cakes." By the time he reached the front door, which Juliette left him to open on his own, Galloway was only a step behind him.

The DC called up the stairs, "Bye, Isabella." There was no answer.

Wild saved the killer look until the front door shut behind him.

"What, Skip? I was just being polite."

"Sure you were. You do know she's fifteen?"

Galloway went beetroot.

"Always check the numbers, Ben. It makes all the difference."

As they walked to their car Wild gazed up and there was Isabella at the window, holding a picture of a pig to the glass. Wild saluted her with his index finger and saw her laugh.

Wild got in his car. "She's a smart kid."

"Well, why didn't we question her as well then?"

Wild didn't have an answer, other than Isabella wasn't seen at the literary festival. Plus, he always found teenagers tricky. Actually, make that lippy. Still, Galloway had a point so he added her to his reserve list.

Ben wore his thinking face on their journey back to Mayberry nick. Wild knew to let him simmer, like a casserole. Galloway's thought processes had tenderised by the time they reached Mayberry.

"If you don't mind me saying so, Skip, there's no reasonable grounds to suspect Juliette or her daughter had anything to do with . . ." he thought for a moment. ". . . Lee Rickard's death."

Wild kept his eyes on the road. "That we know of."

"But surely someone would have noticed a famous author wandering about and sharing coffee with a stranger."

Wild felt Lady Providence brushing his shoulder.

"Now, there you have a point, Ben. I want you to go back through the case notes of anyone we've spoken to at the festival. Get them to turn their attention to Juliette — and her daughter too — in case we've missed something. That alright with you?"

"Course, Skip. I'll get on it as soon as I'm at my desk."

"Good lad."

* * *

Marsh was busy haranguing DC Harris when they got back to Mayberry.

"If I task you to do something I expect it to be done. Otherwise, what's the point of you?"

Wild felt the furniture shudder and straightened his shirt. Marsh by name and harsh by nature. "Ma'am, do you have a minute?"

Galloway headed for his desk the long way round.

"Why not." She released her prey and prowled over to her office, while Harris stood there like a scratching post.

Wild shut the door behind him. "Problem?"

"No, just a difference of opinion on the definition of the word 'timely'. How did you get on with your author? I thought about leaving team discipline to you but you weren't here."

He held up the bag of books by way of a reply. DI Marsh took the bag, emptied the spoils, and immediately made busy with a desktop calculator. After she'd given him a total and reminded him to log the books in, she invited him to sit down.

"You've spoken with Juliette Kimani twice now. Level with me, Craig — what's your angle?" She raised both index fingers. "I'm not insinuating anything, but I want to make sure there's a clear rationale in case her solicitor ever comes back to us screaming harassment. And I need hardly remind you of the potential for misunderstanding on the grounds of race."

Wild flinched in his chair. "No way. Juliette's first interview happened because a signed copy of her book was found with the victim. That's a straight line of inquiry to a potential witness to see whether they met. Today's interview was merely a follow-up and *any* suggestion to the contrary is bullshit. Plus," he pointed to her desk, "giving me novels is hardly suggestive of a hostile experience."

"Duly noted. However, if you do need to speak to her again, I'd like a solicitor present — for all our sakes. I take it she is still on your radar?"

He assumed the question was rhetorical and sidestepped it completely. "Okay, my being here . . . I'd like to visit Lee Rickard's home in Lincolnshire rather than pass it over to the local force. I'll do it on the cheap." He knew that would hit home. "He died on our patch and I think that's significant."

Marsh pressed her fingertips together and tapped the index fingers like an insect's antenna. "I thought you might say that. Okay, agreed, as long as other lines of inquiry are set in motion and you're back the next day. This isn't a jolly. Best get packed."

"Already in the boot."

She arched an eyebrow, refilled the book bag and held it up. "I'll need to refer this upstairs for approval — you understand. Oh yes, regarding your trip — there's one small and non-negotiable condition . . ."

CHAPTER 4

Wild waited in the police station car park, feeling frustrated not to be able to get going. A deal was a deal though and Marsh hadn't really asked for much. He flicked idly through recent notebook pages to a short list of questions:

1. Why did the victim come to Mayberry from Lincolnshire?
2. Why would Juliette Kimani not admit to seeing the victim at the festival — if she had?
3. What else did the victim do with his life?

The sound of a motorbike brought a sense of relief. He pictured every window blind twitching behind him. Marnie Olsen parked in the designated bike area, got off and locked up her bike helmet. He watched her crossing the tarmac, a rucksack over one shoulder. She got in and he started the car, backing out in a wide arc to see who was watching their departure.

Marnie opened a bag of sweets and held them within reach. "Thanks again, Craig. I really appreciate you taking me along for the ride, so to speak."

He fumbled in the bag and extracted a wine gum. "Seems only fair — you were first on the scene." No point telling her she'd been forced on him. And besides, he'd had worse people riding shotgun.

"Well anyway, cheers." She sighed. Three hours on the road was a lot of time to fill. Wild was a decent bloke, but he could also be hard work. "Tell me about the victim again."

He relaxed a little. "Lee Rickard lived on the east coast, in a place called Miami Beach. Yeah," he caught the glimmer of a smile, "I know. Local police had no involvement with him whatsoever, clean as a whistle. And no one has reported him missing."

"Or dead."

"Yep, that too." He held out a hand for another wine gum.

"Listen, Craig, do you mind if I crash out for a while? Nothing personal but I had a bit of a late night."

He tried not to look surprised at the idea of her having a social life, turned on the radio and lowered the volume.

* * *

Wild tended to ruminate on long journeys. Steph, the former Mrs Wild — although she'd kept her own surname when they married, which he now considered a sign — had often accused him of lacking imagination. He shook his head at the memory. Not guilty as charged. He just preferred to keep his innermost thoughts to himself. He imagined poor Lee Rickard driving four bloody hours from home, only to meet his maker at the final destination. What must he have thought, Wild wondered, in his dying moments, when reality had bitten him on the arse. "Nah," he said to himself. Rickard wouldn't have known anything about it, not if he'd taken drugs. He'd heard that from addicts who'd been brought back from the brink. After they'd tipped over the precipice there was emptiness. Maybe it was the closest thing to peace.

His mind skipped from that moment of consolation to the coppers he'd known who had retired. Some of them, at the inevitable gold watch presentation and obligatory piss-up afterwards had looked like frightened rabbits staring into the abyss. A lifetime of service to the community and then they didn't know what to do with the rest of their time above ground. He reached across to the wine gums and grabbed three of them. Scary stuff.

He remembered Steph's pep talks.

'You know your other trouble, Craig? You have no ambition.'

"Not true. I made it to DS and that was the extent of my ambition. Unlike some."

The ghost of Steph past stopped speaking.

Marnie opened her eyes and yawned. "Did I just hear you talking to someone?"

"Nah, you must have been dreaming." He caught her looking around. "We're on the A46. Lincoln is next up. You've been spark out for a good couple of hours." He stopped short of asking about her private life. Relationships were a definite no-go area. She was as closed-up as a super-glued clam. Gay, straight, other? He had no idea. In point of fact, he didn't judge. He was curious though.

She stretched her arms and he leaned away.

"I don't think these seats are designed for sleeping. I could do with stretching my legs."

"Okay, how about we stop in Lincoln, or on the outskirts? Then there's about another hour to Miami Beach."

She rolled her tongue around her mouth. "Have you any water?"

"Sorry, drank it while you were asleep. Keep your eye out for a service station." He waited a minute or so and then glanced sideways. "What was it then, heavy date last night?"

The silence while she concocted a reply made him wish he'd never started.

"No such luck. Someone I knew from uni, down for a few days."

"What, you've left them to go investigating?"

She sighed. "Let's just say it wasn't a planned visit — I couldn't exactly turn him away."

Mercifully, Wild saw a sign for a petrol station and seized upon it. "This will do nicely."

CHAPTER 5

Having travelled the A157 in virtual silence, apart from agreeing that, yes, Lincolnshire *was* very green, Wild breathed easier as he pulled up outside a small block of flats.

He parked in Lee Rickard's space, partly to see if anyone came out to challenge him. There were no takers. He stared at the building, a ground floor and first floor, modernish build. Back when this was someone's idea of modern.

Marnie shifted in her seat. "It's sad to think that no one will mourn him."

Wild hadn't expected sentiment from her. "Well, we don't know yet. Come on, let's get detecting."

He took a set of keys from a clear plastic bag and selected the door key. Once they were outside he popped the boot and laid the keys on a plastic evidence box. It felt close, and a heat haze shimmered on the tarmac as they walked over to the stairs.

Marnie laughed as she led the way up. "Still not made your peace with lifts then?"

A faint smell of lemon and disinfectant permeated the stairway. Not, Wild realised, a typical council response to piss and litter. No, judging by the stain-free walls and lack of broken glass, this was the subtle scent of care. Even the door handles gleamed and the graffiti seemed almost decorative — some sort of horned creature with 'IMPS FOREVER' written underneath in red pen. Wild had it figured as a gang name until Marnie called down, "It's Lincoln City footie team."

"Oh, right." He lumbered up the stairs with the box in his arms, while she held the door open. He couldn't help thinking that Marnie was a smart one, although apparently not smart enough to ditch an unwanted guest.

As they stood by the front door Wild glanced along the landing in both directions. No curtains stirring, no one easing their door open for a squint at the strangers. Neighbourhood Watch must be on tea break, for this neighbour anyway.

The main door key didn't fit the lock. Wild stood there in mute embarrassment.

Marnie nudged him. Why don't you try it again?

He stared at her for a moment and then held out the keys. "Why don't you try?"

She huffed, shooed him to one side and made two unsuccessful attempts to force the key. "I don't understand. You said that they were the only house keys on him and the SOCO didn't find any others in the car."

He ignored the hint of accusation and peered through the window. Unsurprisingly, it looked like no one was home. Wild knew he had two choices, and he already knew which of those he favoured. Ring up the local force and they'd need to do some explaining. Whereas . . . "Wait here." He nipped back down to his car, took out an industrial-sized screwdriver, and slipped it under his coat.

Back on the landing, Marnie was examining the lock. She turned to face him as he revealed the screwdriver.

"It looks like a new lock," she said, stepping aside for the inevitable crash.

Wild made three valiant attempts to get the blade in the gap and lever the strike plate, before he dropped it on the last effort and swore like a trooper.

The door gave way on the fourth shove, hammering backwards to rattle against the passage wall. Only now, as they were about to effect an entry, did one of the neighbours put in an appearance. She looked to be in her seventies, a bag of shopping in each hand and a handbag over the shoulder of her tweed coat.

"Has it happened again?"

Marnie practised her community policing. "I'm sorry, madam?"

"The door. Someone from housing was here yesterday. I happened to notice he had a key with him but it didn't work. Some sort of trouble with the lock so he had to fit a new one."

"Right," Marnie nodded and smiled. "And, erm, out of interest what did he look like?"

"Look like?" She put down her shopping and scratched her head. "I don't know. Blue jeans, toolbox. What else would he look like? Don't you people keep records?"

Wild moved closer to her. "We do, madam. Now, if you'll excuse us."

As the woman ferried her shopping along the balcony he muttered to Marnie, "Keep an eye on which flat she goes into." Then he turned his attention back to the gaping doorway. No need to call out. The flat seemed emptier than a drunken promise. A local newspaper from a couple of days ago lay scrunched behind the door, probably delivered on the day the victim went off in search of culture. Wild was still examining an electricity bill envelope when Marnie crossed the threshold behind him.

She leaned over his shoulder in a way that irritated him. "The name and address matches the victim's driving licence."

"Yeah," he handed her the envelope for bagging up. "But that doesn't explain the lock change." He started walking into the flat. "We'll have to speak to the council unless it's a private rental."

She called after him. "Where do you want to start, Craig?"

"We'll walk the rooms together, just to be on the safe side, and then you can have the upper rooms to yourself."

They performed a perfunctory check — his word, not hers, and then he left her alone upstairs. What struck her most was the tidiness. Almost too neat, which suggested two possibilities — either he'd been in the armed services or he'd served time in prison. Except . . . there'd been no record of either.

The bathroom gleamed, even under the mat. Not so much as a grease mark. The only thing of interest in the spare room was a battered suitcase on top of an empty wardrobe, bearing a France sticker. Inside the case, floating around on its lonesome, she found a strip of paper from a Chinese takeaway menu. She recognised the 0117 dialling code for Bristol. A partial name remained, the rest was torn away Pat, Patricia or Patrice? She bagged it up.

Next door, the main bedroom — master bedroom would be overselling it — looked like a psychologist's dream. Two dumb-bells rested against the skirting board in the furthest corner of the room. A mattress on the floor served as a bed, with a lads' mag beside it, along with a book: *Nightmare Movies: A Critical Guide to Contemporary Horror*. The wardrobe held few surprises — sportswear, two pairs of casual trousers, two pairs of shoes, some good quality jeans, and five shirts. Clearly, this was a person determined not to stand out. In contrast, a shoebox at the back of the wardrobe revealed a treasure trove of bills and other paperwork, which she removed for Wild to dissect.

A charity-shop bedside cabinet (the label still on the back) housed an old watch (not working), some loose change, mobile phone charger, a couple of small pills (probably recreational), a leaflet for some sort of church network, two condoms, and a business card bearing the name Petra and a mobile number. She took the lot. A final examination of the carpet edges around the bedroom and then she was done. She wondered if Wild would double-check everywhere himself, like Ben Galloway had said once, and decided she wouldn't take offence. She'd been thorough and had plenty to show for her efforts.

Wild heard her coming down the stairs and paused his attack on the freezer. A zippable bag of peas and a choc ice lay on the kitchen table behind him.

"Snack attack?"

He looked up and shared the joke. "Hardly. Just a typical hiding place for a stash." He noticed the shoebox in her arms and the evidence bags that hung from her left hand. "Someone's been busy." He resumed his icy examination and then pulled back his hand with a grin worthy of little Jack Horner, waving a bag in front of her.

"Two pills from his bedside cabinet suggest he was a drug user?" She made it sound like a question, mostly to provoke him.

"A couple of pills does not a druggie make," he corrected her. "However," he held up the freezer bag so they could both see it better and rubbed away some of the frost. "While this lot isn't the find of the century, it does look like he was dealing."

"Unless he was stocking up for Christmas."

Wild smiled. Marnie's sense of humour had been something of a revelation. He knew her to be diligent from the first case they worked together, and she was keen. But this new banter thing between them, he liked to think, was all down to his influence. Well, DI Marsh had said to take her under his wing. "A shame to put a choc ice back but maybe one of the flat clearance team will appreciate it." He waved goodbye to the frozen foods and shut the fridge-freezer door. "We'll search the front room together and then see what treasures you've unearthed."

The room was sparsely furnished, and in haste by the look of it. A matching armchair and two-seater sofa backed against the walls left little space for anything else. A wall unit held five books on one shelf and a couple of cans of lager on another. On a middle shelf a painting of the sea, most probably a print, suggested an attempt at cosiness. The small baseball bat down the side of the armchair quashed that idea.

"He might want protection if he's dealing, or if people thought he kept a supply here?"

Marnie thought it best to state the obvious, so that Wild understood her thought process and could, at some point, report back on her brilliance to DI Marsh. If DC Ben Galloway was really leaving, she'd do everything in her power to try and convince DI Marsh — subtly — that she deserved a secondment. Besides, she didn't think she could face another parking dispute.

"Maybe." Wild didn't sound convinced.

Marnie frowned. The dealer angle had been his and he seemed to have abandoned it very quickly. Why the reticence? She smiled at the word in her head. It had been a relief to work with someone who hadn't been put off by her vocabulary. She hadn't let her background hold her back. Work hard, study hard, and no cutting corners. That philosophy had stood her in good stead in college and at uni, and she wasn't about to let a chance like this slip by without a fight.

"Craig?"

"Sorry, something just occurred to me. We don't know if the victim planned to stay overnight for the literary festival."

"True. It's a long way to travel for the day. Someone ought to check the B&Bs near the festival."

He smiled and opened a hand, as if to offer an imaginary tray of 'bloody obvious'. "One for Harris then. Rickard was, what, early twenties . . . ?"

"Just turned twenty-three."

"Not much to show for a life, is it? Come on, let's see what you found."

He picked up an old newspaper beneath the glass coffee table, checked it first in case anything was marked, and then spread the pages over the pristine top.

She talked Wild through the items in her bags, even though he could see them. "I found a slip of paper stuck in the inside of the suitcase." She passed it over to him as if expecting a magic trick — make something meaningful out of this!

"Well, it's a Bristol prefix. So either the victim or his suitcase have been over to the West Country at some point in time."

Next was the business card with just the name and number written on one side. He shrugged and took out his phone. He dialled methodically, Marnie observed, in a similar way that some of the older police officers typed with no more than four fingers, jabbing at the keys. Wild invited her to move closer so they could both hear, and she stood awkwardly beside him.

The call went straight through to message. "*Hi, you have reached Petra Michelson, please leave a message and I will return your call.*"

Wild huffed. Nothing to lose and everything to gain. "This is Detective Sergeant Craig Wild, can you please return my call at the earliest opportunity." He recited his number. "Alternatively you can ring the front desk at Mayberry police station . . ." he stalled and looked to Marnie. She leaned closer still and delivered the number down the phone.

"Think she'll ring back today?"

"What, to a stranger leaving his number and claiming to be a police officer? If she has any sense she'll be straight on the internet to double-check the front desk number before she calls. Hopefully she'll pick the message up and do all that before we head west to civilisation."

"What about the church leaflet? I looked it up on my phone and it's not that far away. We could check it out before we go to our digs."

"Let me have a browse first." He scanned both sides of the A5 page and felt his face hardening. His statue impression hadn't gone unnoticed.

"You don't approve?"

"Let's just say my mum was religious and a fat lot of good it did her. Dad still pissed off and I don't remember any of those worthy Christians she knew coming round with tea and sympathy."

"Not churchgoers then?"

He laughed, a spontaneous eruption of sarcasm and memory. "Oh, she went, fairly regularly. And my little brother toddled along, mostly to appease her. But wild horses or the wrath of God himself could not have persuaded me to give up my Sunday football game in exchange for a sermon and a singsong."

She looked at him expectantly.

"Okay, Marnie, if we're going there — and I haven't decided yet — you can do the talking."

He took more paperwork from the shoebox and went through it on the table. There were bills going back two years, a pristine birth certificate — probably a replacement for one that had been lost, a well-thumbed piece of paper with a dozen initials and mobile numbers, a history of Lincolnshire, a Street Guide to Lincoln, and an old bank statement. Wild suddenly remembered something, got up and went back to the kitchen. He returned with a small paper shredder. There were a few indecipherable ribbons in the bin.

The second batch from the shoebox only served to evoke a sense of pity from Wild. "How can someone have shuffled off his mortal coil leaving so little behind?" He considered his own words. Of course, there could be a kiddie somewhere in the background and hopefully some family to mourn him. All the same it seemed like a shitty ending.

The pills did not look the same as the powder. Wild figured there was coke in the bags and something a little less dramatic from the bedroom. He placed everything in the shoebox, including the coke, and replaced the lid, fastening it on both sides with elastic bands from his pocket. He ignored Marnie's smirking.

"One day, an elastic band could make all the difference. Mind if I double-check upstairs?"

She tried not to appear affronted. "Be my guest. Mind if I tag along? I might learn something."

He started in the bathroom and she trailed behind, pleased to see him follow her routine and come up with nothing, not even when he additionally searched the toilet cistern. In the spare room he wrenched the wardrobe forward, to no avail, and in the main bedroom he checked the weights for a concealment. Other than that he had no new tricks on offer. They were heading towards the door when he turned suddenly.

"Presume you checked the drawers thoroughly?"

She was already primed and recited her script. "T-shirts in the top drawer, jeans in the middle, and underwear and socks below that."

He started on the top drawer anyway, running his hand slowly through the clothes. He spoke without turning round. "I'm not testing you, Marnie, just satisfying my own curiosity."

She loitered by his shoulder, Wild not seeming to notice. At the third drawer he drew her attention to the underwear.

"What do you notice?" He gave her a couple of seconds. "No? Try again."

She took him at his word and moved her hand around amongst the deceased's boxers. Two pairs down she felt a different kind of material — lacy, good quality, women's underwear.

It seemed like a good time to state the obvious. Wild was an obvious sort of bloke. "Someone's been here with him, Marnie."

She nodded. "More than that, I'd say. You don't keep these in a drawer unless someone's coming back for them." She took her own cue and bagged up the knickers.

"Well, not unless it's a trophy. So . . ." He waited for her to say something and grew tired of waiting. "There's someone in his life — or there used to be."

She nodded, unclear how that helped. "I doubt we'll get any DNA from them."

He looked up and she smiled, in case he didn't get the joke. He returned the favour by letting her take everything back downstairs while he carried the burden of thinking. One thing was clear. They couldn't very well drive around with evidence stashed in the back of the car for the night, or worse, store illegal drugs in their overnight accommodation. And the victim's front door needed fixing. Time to call back to base.

DI Marsh listened with interest as he talked her through their discoveries. Her mood seemed to dip a little when it came to the part about storage of evidence and door repairs. This, Wild knew, would entail a phone call to the local chain of command and a temporary handover of the evidence.

Marsh mentioned inter-force politics and how the situation called for tact and diplomacy, so he wished her well with it and hoped for the best.

He lowered the phone. "She said she'll ring us back in a couple of minutes."

Two minutes became ten. Wild was tempted to make a cuppa, using the powdered milk in the cupboard — assuming it was milk — but that wasn't really the protocol he wanted Marnie Olsen to learn. When he announced he needed the loo for a slash, the look on her face reminded him of his mum the first time he'd said he wasn't going to church anymore — a mixture of outrage and incredulity.

He figured Marsh must have used up her entire charm quota for the month because she rang back with good news: the local police would be over to await a door repair and an inspector would take temporary charge of their evidence at a nearby police station. As they were packing up, Wild took out the business card, the slip of paper and the church leaflet from the box, before sealing it back up like a miniature crypt.

"No sense in both of us waiting. Do you want to flip for who gets to sit in my car?"

"That's okay, Wild. You go ahead. I'll stay by the door just in case."

CHAPTER 6

Wild got out to greet the patrol car and offer apologies, then watched as the PC reached the landing and had a changing of the guard with Marnie. She was smiling as she got back in the car, and he knew why.

"I saw you from down here, nipping along the balcony."

"I, er, thought it might be worth another chat with the neighbour — on my own. I never let the door out of my sight."

He put his seatbelt on. "Relax, Marnie. You don't have anything to prove as far as I'm concerned. What did she say?"

"You really mean 'what did I ask'?"

He clapped a couple of times.

"She confirmed that she had seen Isabella, or somebody like her, on at least one other occasion. She was pretty sketchy about how many times."

"Well, good work anyway." He nearly absentmindedly patted her leg and then freaked himself out so badly that he jolted his hand away. "Okay," he said too loudly, "can you direct us to . . ."

She picked up the piece of paper. "Alford police station. Let me get some directions on my phone."

* * *

Marnie stayed in the car while Wild dropped off the evidence. Her mobile rang. It was DI Marsh.

"Where's Wild? He's not picking up."

"He's been driving, ma'am, so he's probably on silent. He's in Alford police station with the DI at the moment. I'll ask him to call you back."

"No need. You'll do. Someone called Petra Michelson rang and the front desk verified Wild's credentials. What's it for?"

Marnie told her what she knew, which was very little apart from where the card had been found.

"Interesting. Keep me posted." Marsh rang off.

Marnie was still smiling when Wild got back in the car.

"Well, that was torturous. Hard to believe we're all on the same side." He tuned back in. "You look pleased with yourself."

"Er, yeah. DI Marsh rang. Said that Petra had called. She'll be ringing you back."

"Right, I'd better turn my phone up. Do you want to drive to God's house?"

Twenty minutes later, Marnie's mobile assured them they'd reached their destination. Wild had expected a modern church. Probably one of the happy clappy ones, as he told Marnie on the drive. St Cuthbert's was old though, the name being a clue for a start. Not a large church by any means, and surrounded by a graveyard boundaried by ancient iron railings. Because, as Wild couldn't resist pointing out, sometimes even God needed a hand with security.

"Remember, this is your shout," he insisted, which didn't sound as promising as Marnie had imagined.

She led the way up the path, clutching the leaflet. The main door of the church was closed and locked — earning scathing laughter from Wild. They entered through a side door and called out to announce themselves.

A woman approached, wiping her hands on an apron. Marnie took in a breath to speak and Wild forgot himself.

"Is the vicar around?"

Marnie winced. Not even a please. What an oaf. She smiled unrepentantly at the word and the woman smiled back.

"We're police officers. Are you Reverend J Houghton?"

"Jane is fine. How can I help you?"

"I'm PC Marnie Olsen and this is DS Craig Wild, from Wiltshire Police. Is there somewhere private we could go for a chat?"

"Of course, come across to the house."

Marnie waited for tea before she delivered the bad news.

Reverend Houghton nodded slowly. She didn't seem surprised. "I know he'd had *difficulties* — a troubled background, and he'd grown up in care. So sad, I really thought he had turned a corner in his life. How did it happen?"

Wild stared implacably.

"Was he religious?" Marnie forced herself not to glance in Wild's direction, turning a little so he was beyond her peripheral vision.

"Hmm, not in any conventional sense. I think he tried to be a good person." She stirred her tea. "Although he didn't take part in anything . . ."

Wild couldn't resist. "Godly?"

Marnie shot him a poisonous look.

The reverend smiled faintly. "Yes, you could say that. He never attended a service — not one — but he used to do little jobs for me. I think he was trying to make amends. It was a policeman who introduced us, actually. Do you know DI Stanton?"

Not yet, Wild thought, adding him to his list.

Marnie spoke again. "What can you tell us about Lee? We know next to nothing about his life."

"I'm sorry to disappoint you — it's the same for me. He never shared details of his past and I didn't pry. As to his recent life, well, let me dig out his post."

"You have some of his post here?"

She blinked at them. "For the hospital treatment."

Marnie could see Wild getting interested. "He was ill?"

"No, far from it. He was helping someone else. That's what I mean. Not a churchgoer but in every other sense a Christian."

Wild slurped his tea to get her attention. "Sorry, I don't follow you."

"Wait a moment. It'll be easier to explain with the letters."

* * *

Marnie noticed a print on the wall. "Is that a Poussin print?"

Jane turned to admire it. "Yes, it's the *Death of Germanicus*. Always a pleasure to meet another art lover."

Wild bristled. "And why were Lee Rickard's letters sent here?"

"He valued his privacy. And when you think about the publicity he could have gained . . ." She passed over a small bundle of letters.

"A cell donor?" Wild said it out loud because it didn't fit his impression of the victim.

"Not only that! He received some money through it and made a donation to the church group — we do a lot of outreach work that isn't specifically faith-based."

Marnie chipped in. "Do you have a statement for any funds you received?"

"I think so. I'll make you a photocopy."

Wild interrupted. "We'd prefer the originals, if you don't mind." He thought for a moment. "Hang on, aren't those cell donations made without payment, and anonymously?"

The reverend slid her hands together. "Why don't I make us another pot and start from the beginning?"

* * *

By the time Wild drove away from the church his brain was spinning. It was as if the victim were two different people. On the one hand, a humble pillar of the community — which

Wild didn't buy for a second — and on the other the sort of bloke who kept drugs in his freezer and kept a baseball bat for company.

"Marnie, seeing as you're sitting there with nothing to do, why don't you ring Marsh with the bank details so they can start chasing the money. This could all be about proceeds of crime and everything else is bollocks."

"What, faked hospital letters?"

"A private hospital? Yeah, why not. Okay, let's get over to our digs, a wash and brush up, and then, what, out for a curry?"

Marnie crinkled her nose. "It's the high life in CID, isn't it?"

CHAPTER 7

Wild had chosen a low-price, almost-hotel for the overnight accommodation. As he said in the car, "The sort that offers free shampoo like they're doing you a favour. And then you find out it's the same stuff in the soap dispenser. But they don't put on too many airs and graces, and you know exactly what you're getting."

They both used driving licences as ID, on the basis that few people had ever seen a warrant card if they'd led a decent life. He asked for two rooms on the same floor, adding that they could be as far apart as the receptionist liked, so she didn't get any funny ideas.

"Right, after you," he opened the door to the stairwell. "And what shall we say — twenty minutes?"

Marnie coughed quietly. "Can we make it forty-five? I want to squeeze in some yoga and a quick personal call."

"Sure. I'll come and collect you. You're kidding, right, about the yoga?"

She gave her best sardonic smile. "You'll never know." And followed it up with a *namaste* bow towards him, hands pressed together at her chest.

Forty minutes later, after a shower, a miniature cup of tea and half a TV programme about antiques, Wild ventured along the corridor. He knocked quietly and then took a step back.

"Who is it?"

He could feel the sarcasm through the door.

"Your mentor."

Marnie pulled the handle back. "I think you'll find DI Marsh is back in Wiltshire."

"Touché, Ms Olsen."

Wild accepted Marnie's pitch for the restaurant downstairs. Like she said, quick and easy. He got the impression she still had a call to make, but he knew when to stay his side of the line. It was called a private life for a good reason. She had been the only one to welcome him at Mayberry police station — Ben Galloway was more a case of follow-my-leader and DI Marsh wouldn't have known a welcome if it parked in her drive. She'd also inveigled him onto one of the police darts teams, which had to count for something.

He quickly bypassed the generic curry on offer — sacrilege — and chose salmon en croute. Marnie, in contrast, took her time choosing, while he did his best impression of patience, which wasn't a very good one. So much for quick and easy.

Finally, she put him out of his misery with the magic words, "I'll have the sole please."

The lass serving them scurried away, so Wild tried making small talk.

"Funny to think of a discount hotel having a chef's special." Then he shattered the awkward silence that followed with, "I wonder what's keeping Petra Michelson."

She mulled it over. "If she has already verified who you are, maybe she's been ringing around to try and ascertain what it's about. Or maybe she has something to hide and is busy working on her interview responses."

He raised his lager to her. "With cynicism like that, your future in CID will be a promising one."

"I'll drink to that! Incidentally, I meant to ask you, when do you think we'll be called to give evidence in London?"

He nodded. Armed robber Tony Weston, now in custody, and his stooge or accomplice, Jackie, probably out on bail and awaiting court. And Marnie mostly to thank for it not turning into as big a fiasco as the original police operation that sent Weston on the run. The op that put the final nail into Wild's Met Police career.

He paused for a couple of seconds, so she thought he was giving her question due consideration, even though he'd rung London a few days earlier.

"It'll be months yet. And I think you're more useful on the stand than I am — I'm what they call a PR disaster."

"You mean because of your previous . . . situation."

"It's fine, Marnie. You can call it a breakdown. Yeah, in case I do another Patsy."

She sipped cider and tilted her head, as if that might help her understand.

"Patsy Cline was a singer in the fifties. She sang a popular song: *I go to Pieces*."

"Right." She knew for a fact the song was called *I Fall to Pieces* but no sense in doing what she had often been accused of, using her intellect like a weapon. As DI Marsh said, 'Sometimes being part of a team is more important than being right.'

"Okay," Wild took a notepad from his pocket, glanced around to make sure there were no diners nearby, and assumed what he hoped was an authoritative gaze. "What do we know?"

Marnie took a breath and dived in. "Twenty-three-year-old victim, died in suspicious circumstances. OD'd most likely. His driving licence and car registration tie him to . . ."

"Miami Beach," Wild said drolly. Still funny, even now. "Evidence?"

"What appears to be two types of illegal drug — one for personal recreational use and the other probably," she conceded with a tilt of her glass, "for supply. Although there didn't seem much there."

"Everyone has to start somewhere! And I think we can rule out any county lines drug deliveries — I don't think he fits the profile."

She responded by sipping cider and not speaking for a few seconds. "A scrap of paper links him to Bristol, sort of . . ." She floundered for her next stepping-stone. ". . . And although he wasn't a churchgoer he helped out Reverend Houghton, in what she suggested was an attempt to turn his life around."

"From what, I wonder." Wild glanced at his phone, which had lit up a second before it trilled into life. He hit the button and waited.

"Hello, is that Sergeant Wild?"

"Yes. And you are?"

"Sorry, it's Petra Michelson, returning your call. I'm on my personal mobile rather than the business one where you left a message."

"And what exactly is your business?" In the three seconds of silence that followed, he imagined a couple of choice explanations.

"I'm a voice coach." The way she said it suggested she was used to dealing with philistines, which made him feel right at home.

"A voice coach?" He repeated, for Marnie's benefit.

She grabbed his notepad and committed the cardinal sin of writing on it. WHY DID LEE NEED HER?

He raised his eyes. Thanks for the tip, Sherlock. "And what was your connection with Lee?" He winced. Past tense . . . too soon.

Petra picked up on it right away, her voice rising like an airship. "What's happened?"

He went into default 'no comment' mode. "I'm sorry to have to tell you that Mr Rickard has died. All I can say at the moment is that it's an ongoing investigation. Would it be possible to meet with you?"

"I'm in Spain at the moment. Could we do it over the phone?"

He strained to hear the sound of sangria being poured, and was disappointed. He snatched back the pen and wrote SPAIN and then pointed to it with the biro.

"Yes, we can talk on the phone and arrange an interview at a later date, if required. What was the nature of your relationship with Mr Rickard?"

"I don't know if I can say."

He felt his hackles peaking. "May I remind you that . . ."

"I think you'd better speak to Detective Inspector Stanton first and then get back to me." She cut the call and, unsurprisingly, his call back went straight to message.

Marnie's meal arrived and with a little cajoling she started without him. There was only one thing to do. Desperate times . . . He made himself scarce in the lobby.

DI Marsh sounded harassed. "This had better be good, Craig. I'm just at the till. Hold on . . . ." He heard a couple of bleeps and then the DI saying thank you — a rarity he committed to memory — before her work voice resumed. "Okay, I'm fully loaded (he figured she meant the trolley). Now, what is it?"

He spilled the beans and tried to imagine the wheels turning in her head. "Okay, let me make a couple of calls and then I'll ring you straight back."

Half an hour later, well past the world's smallest ice cream scoops, Marsh rang again.

"Okay," she stretched the word out like a death rattle, "we're gonna need to tread very sensitively here. There's a reason why Lee's record is squeaky clean, despite the drugs and baseball bat in his flat — he's flagged with a Regional Organised Crime Unit under the UK Protected Persons Service. Basically, he's been provided with a new identity. When you retrieve the evidence tomorrow, DI Stanton has agreed to spare a few minutes of his valuable time. Give him the respect he deserves, and don't make an arse of yourself. Call me tomorrow once you've seen him. And maybe let Marnie do some of the talking."

Marnie put down her own phone as he returned. "Everything okay?"

"Not exactly. I'll settle up here and then we'll talk outside." He didn't trust the soundproofing in the rooms upstairs, especially after hearing his next-door neighbours getting acquainted.

* * *

"So who is Lee Rickard? Was, I mean. Before he became Lee?"

He knew what she meant the first time. "No name given yet. This is going to be tricky. If he was a witness for the Organised Crime mob," he caught her grin and ignored it, "they will be all over us like a rash. Mark my words, they'll want to know the ins and outs of a duck's arse."

"Charming. That explains the voice coach — help him blend in."

"Which means . . ." he left the floor open for her.

She beamed. "He didn't come from around here! And our only lead to his former identity is a scrap of paper, possibly."

"Well, unless DI Stanton decides to take us into his confidence tomorrow. And the chances of that are . . . ?"

She knew the line by heart. "Bob Hope, Cape Hope and no hope."

CHAPTER 8

Wild wished he'd brought a tie with him, chiefly because Marsh had asked him to earlier in a text. He decided not to buy one for the occasion and instead made do with freshly pressed trousers and a shirt. Marnie, keen as mustard, managed to outshine him in black, looking every inch the professional. If DI Stanton didn't know better, he could very easily think Wild her junior and Marnie a fast-tracked rising star. Wild suspected that's how she'd prefer to be seen.

The front desk rang through and a PCSO poked his head round the door. He looked cheery to the point of nausea.

"Hello there, welcome to Alford. I'm Sammy, if you'd like to follow me."

Sammy's conversation skills were somewhat lacking, so Wild tried to put a lid on the chatter. *Yes, they'd had a pleasant drive up from, where was it, oh yes, Wiltshire. Unusual to see West Country folk in their part of the world unless they were towing a caravan!* Hilarious.

They waited outside while Sammy knocked on the office door, entered when bidden, and then returned to usher them in. DI Stanton had the shoebox on his desk, his palm resting on top protectively. Wild stared at it for a moment before he realised that the long elastic band was now crossing over the shorter one, unlike the way he'd left it the day before. So, Stanton must have peeked inside.

They took the waiting seats and exchanged a glance. Marnie thanked the inspector for seeing them and stated the obvious, that they were aware of the sensitivity involved. That seemed to thaw the room a little and the DI's hand moved off the box.

"There are good reasons for thinking this death may be linked to an organised crime group, so until we rule out any connection to OCG activity I will be taking a keen interest in your investigation. DI Marsh agrees it would be good practice to pool our resources."

Wild got with the programme. "We spoke briefly with Lee's voice coach, Petra Michelson. She's currently in Spain, due back in a fortnight."

DI Stanton stated the obvious. "Yes, she rang me last night. She worked on his accent and dialect. Easier to blend in when you sound like a local — fewer questions."

Marnie took her turn. "And what about the church group?"

"Reverend Houghton has a good track record with released prisoners. I believe she worked in the prison service before she found her calling."

Wild choked a little. "Sorry, you said *prison*?"

DI Stanton's eyebrows raised. "I thought you knew? Lee served most of a three-year sentence and received a new identity on his release."

Marnie gabbled her deduction, "Because of his witness testimony — from time spent in Bristol?" Then she put a hand to her mouth as Wild's foot forcibly nudged hers.

"And how could you know that?"

Wild held his nerve under the DI's stony gaze. "We found a scrap of paper at the flat. Looked like part of a takeaway menu with a Bristol phone number." He reached into his pocket and offered it over.

The inspector barely glanced at it. "Shall we start again . . . ?"

* * *

Wild considered the pluses, as they were escorted back downstairs by Sammy. They had the box of evidence from Lee's new life, the inspector had let them go without a bollocking, and they now had good reason to speak to Reverend Houghton again. If nothing else, it was nice to hear a London accent.

In the minus column, they'd pissed Stanton off — nice work, Marnie — and he would probably speak to DI Marsh before they made it to the car. Despite that prospect, Wild tried to be magnanimous and kept his opinions to himself.

Marnie waited until they were safely ensconced in his Ford Focus. "Sorry, Craig, I dropped us in it."

He heard the text come in, glanced at it and smiled. "Hey, it happens to the best of us — even you. Read this." He showed her Jane Houghton's message: *Sorry, Lee's other letters were stuck in a drawer. Can you come back for them?* "Great minds think alike. We were heading there anyway."

"How come you didn't mention that Reverend Houghton had been receiving Lee's post?"

"Maybe it slipped my mind."

"Or maybe you have a problem with authority."

"Now you sound like my ex-wife."

She laughed, but only because she'd met DCI Stephanie Hutcheson once before.

CHAPTER 9

Privately, Marnie thought Wild was skating on very thin ice. She was also intrigued as to how he planned to bypass DI Stanton about the new evidence without one of the DIs using the word 'disciplinary'. Still, it wasn't her place, what with her being a humble PC.

Reverend Houghton welcomed them back to her study. Wild noticed a few history books clustered on one of the shelves. "You're a fan of Hannibal?" He turned briefly to Marnie. "The general, not the cannibal."

The reverend's eyebrows lifted. "I wouldn't have taken you for a history buff."

"And I wouldn't have taken you for a vicar, without the collar I mean."

Marnie watched, agog. Was Wild really flirting with religion?

"I'm particularly interested in the Roman era — what about you . . . ?"

"Craig." He paused. "Yeah, military history generally. Decisive campaigns, battles that changed the course of history. That sort of thing."

Marnie cleared her throat and then sipped some tea self-consciously. No one else seemed to notice.

The reverend went to an ornate desk, unlocked a drawer and produced a wad of papers in a clear plastic wallet. "Lee told me he was worried that some of his post had gone missing, and asked if he could use this address. He was pretty cagey but there wasn't much of it, so I didn't mind." She passed the letters to Marnie, who held open a plastic bag. "I don't know if they're of any relevance — I've never looked at them."

Wild found that hard to believe. "Never even been tempted?"

"Resisting temptation is my stock in trade!"

Marnie watched Wild out the corner of her eye. Clearly, he was loving this. They were on a schedule though, as DI Marsh was expecting them.

"Can I ask what sort of person Lee was — in your opinion? We know very little about his past." She said it in a way she hoped implied they knew more than they were letting on. "It's important to build as complete a picture of the victim's life as we can."

The reverend directed her comments back to Marnie. "I expect you mean his *criminal* life? I know he served his time and wanted to make a fresh start. That was good enough for me. And I think he really tried, although he wasn't perfect. But if what you're really asking is whether I knew what he'd left behind in his old life, I have to disappoint you." She leaned forward earnestly. "He didn't go in for cosy chats or confessionals — and that's not part of my remit. He could be contrary, belligerent sometimes. He helped out with general maintenance here and at the church — painting, a little carpentry, that sort of thing."

Wild added to the conversation, "Skills he probably picked up on prison training courses."

The reverend pretended not to hear him and carried on talking.

"Sometimes he'd arrange to come here and then not turn up. I didn't judge him for it. That must be difficult to understand in your line of work."

Wild crossed the line with a bulldozer. "Did you know he used drugs?"

The reverend laughed. "You expect me to be shocked, living here in my ivory tower? I can tell you from past experience that prison is a very hard place. No surprise that people find whatever ways they can to cope. And in case you were wondering, no — I have no idea what he was inside for, or for how long. It's none of my business. Anyway, I hope those letters are helpful in finding out whoever . . ." she fell silent.

Wild backed up a little. "Did you like him?"

She thought for a moment. "He was a bit of a closed book. But yes, I liked him — perhaps more for his potential than the reality. If his, erm, family want to contact me I'm happy for you to pass on my details. He was very cagey about exactly where he came from. I got the impression he was born in Lincolnshire and had lived away for a time. You could tell when he spoke, when he was animated, sometimes he'd lapse into . . . well, I don't know what accent exactly. Probably on your side of the country!"

Wild finished his tea. "We won't keep you any further. Thank you for your time, Jane, and for the letters."

"Any time."

She stood up to shake his hand and he felt a little squeeze.

"Thanks. If we need to contact you again . . ."

"I'm always either here or out in the community doing my bit. In which case, leave a message!"

CHAPTER 10

Marnie had her nitrile gloves on before Wild could say *queen's evidence*. He did the driving and listened to her running commentary.

"There's not a great deal of post here. Let me just see now . . ." She flicked through the envelopes in her lap. "There are some handwritten ones stuck in the middle. They span—" she paused to read the postmarks. "—a period of about four months. Do you want me to read them out loud, or just give you the gist?"

"Some facts would be good. Where were they sent from?"

She stared at the envelopes. "Hmm, it's a Wiltshire postmark. I'll check the dates on the front and start at the beginning."

Wild drove impatiently. He wondered if he'd been wrong about feeling a spark between himself and Jane. Maybe it was just a London thing, even though she'd come from south of the Thames. He huffed. Whatever Marnie was reading must be pretty absorbing — she hadn't spoken for over a minute. He decided to wait it out.

Marnie felt her mouth go dry. "Okay, Wild, things are about to get a little weird. This first letter is from Juliette

Kimani." She paused to let that sink in. "It's a follow-on letter — I'll check the envelopes afterwards to see whether there's a prior letter there."

He thumped the dashboard. "I bloody knew it. I said from the start she was holding back. Maybe Lee was a fan after all. That could explain his appearance at the festival, unless he was dealing there?"

"Be quiet for a sec, let me read on." Marnie cleared her throat. "*Thank you for the opportunity to write to you personally. You cannot imagine the difference your selfless act of generosity will make to my daughter and to our family's life.*" She stopped speaking and stared through the windscreen. "Lee Rickard donated cells for Isabella's cancer treatment."

Wild muttered, "Wow," almost inaudibly. He definitely hadn't seen that one coming.

"Here's something interesting . . . *I appreciate your desire for anonymity but if it were possible to meet I would like to express my gratitude.*" Marnie turned the page. "She promises no photographs or press, and it's pretty clear that she wants to offer some financial compensation." Marnie folded the pages back into the envelope.

"I bet Lee jumped at the chance of free money."

Marnie ignored him and opened the next letter. "No, he didn't bite. Juliette is explaining that she would like to help change *his* life in return."

"Poor sod," Wild changed his tune. "What a dilemma. On the one hand, hiding away in a new life with a new identity. A bit of a shit life if we are honest about it. And now he's being tempted out of the shadows."

Marnie read on at a pace. "The rest of this one is more of the same. Hold on, she really is a piece of work. She has started telling him a little about her daughter. Wait a sec . . . next letter. Right, here we are. *I can't wait to meet you. We will do it exactly as you wish. I will meet you at the coffee shop, at one o'clock. Thank you so much.*"

She paused again.

"It might be better to put them all into date order."

"Is that a question or a suggestion?" She curled her lip and spent a couple of minutes rechecking dates as she carefully rearranged the envelopes in sequence.

Wild begrudgingly gave her some time. "I could pull over if it helps?"

She didn't respond, opening the first typed letter instead and reviewing its contents. Without commenting, she moved on to the next one. "Okay, this is from a private hospital and sent to Lee at the reverend's address."

Wild connected some of the dots in his head. Lee was a private cell donor, but Juliette hadn't mentioned financial compensation until later in the correspondence trail. "So was he in Wiltshire to collect?" Before Marnie could answer he jumped ahead of himself. "Ring the police station and see if there's any progress with looking into his finances. And see if you can slot the reverend's financial statement into the dates of the letters."

Marnie made the call, covering the mouthpiece when she received an answer. "Craig," she hissed. "DI Marsh wants an update."

He took a breath. "Say that some letters have come to light and . . ." He raised a finger on his left hand. "Forget that. Tell her we're heading straight back with new evidence that ties Lee Rickard to Wiltshire."

She delivered the message and DI Marsh let her off the hook.

"You hungry after all that reading? I could murder a coffee and the reverend's tea has gone right through me."

She nodded and acted as pathfinder for the next roadside services.

Wild didn't waste time on chivalry when they got there. "Bagsy first for the loos. I'll bring us some drinks and snacks — any preference?"

"Milky coffee and a packet of shortbread, thanks." She sat still and watched until his head disappeared from view. Then she phoned the DI.

* * *

By the time Marnie had returned from the toilets, Wild had brightened considerably. She wondered if the second doughnut had done it.

"I meant to ask you, Marnie — how did you get Marsh to agree to your trip with me out east?"

For a tiny moment she considered admitting she'd been told to keep a psychological eye on him, but she knew Wild would never trust her again. So she went with a different version of the truth. "DI Marsh agreed to fund my costs and I'm using my own leave time as personal development time."

"Wow. I'm flattered."

She grinned. "Don't be. I didn't want to miss out on a suspicious death and a chance to impress the DI. All positive feedback to her greatly appreciated!"

Wild enjoyed his coffee as they sat together, watching the families and couples and lone drivers. It dawned on him how the victim had been deprived of a family — as far as they knew, anyway. He also realised that getting back to Mayberry police station inevitably meant a team briefing. On the plus side, they now had plenty to tell.

Marnie scrunched her shortbread wrapper into her empty cup, ready for the bin. "Wild," she looked straight ahead, "can I ask you something — without you blowing your top?"

He felt his hackles rising. "Sure." His tone conveyed nothing of the kind.

"Why didn't we share the additional evidence with DI Stanton?" She used *we* to soften the blow. One glance at his face told her it hadn't worked.

"With him being in the National Crime Agency and all that?"

"Uh huh." She took a deep breath and waited for his defence.

He swallowed hot coffee. "I don't like the bloke. He gave us next to nothing when we met him, so why would I do him any favours?"

"Well, he is a DI and he'll want to get involved in the investigation. He said as much."

"Not until we've had first crack at the letters and spoken to Juliette Kimani more formally."

"And how will we explain the material we've concealed from the NCA?"

He didn't bat an eyelid. "Already thought of that. I'll tell them the vicar posted the material to me and make sure I book it in much later." He could see she wasn't impressed. "Fine. I'll book it in tomorrow then."

She grimaced.

"Okay, Marnie, you want the truth? When the *situation* happened in London, before my exile to Wiltshire, the independent investigator came from the NCA. So you can see why I'm not exactly a fan."

He left it there and so did she.

CHAPTER 11

Wild drove straight to Mayberry police station with a nagging thought at the back of his head. It had been Marsh's idea for Marnie to accompany him and Marsh would have known his personnel file intimately. Maybe she knew about Lee's past identity all along and Marnie was there to keep him in check in case they encountered the National Crime Agency? He chewed on the idea for miles, only dismissing it as paranoia when they reached base.

Marnie deliberated about whether to go with him as she was still technically on leave. Hard to square that one with her uniformed colleagues, although Sergeant Galloway had given her his blessing to grab some extra training.

Wild read her uncertainty. That was one of the things he liked about her: smart, but not pushy. "Are you joining me?" He could see she hadn't made her mind up. "Come on Marnie, you don't want me taking the credit for your detective work. You found the Bristol connection after all."

She smiled, at least until he added, "Tentative as that is."

She carried the shoebox, while Wild held on to the evidence that Reverend Houghton had provided that morning. She wondered again how he planned to get it past the DI.

Wild directed her to book in her evidence and said he would meet her in the briefing room. Despite his own wayward inclinations he knew the best course of action — take DI Marsh into his confidence, ask her advice, and then leave her to decide whether she preferred honesty or complicity.

Marsh was in her office. He knocked sharply and put his head around the door. "Is this a good time, ma'am?"

Before she could answer, he had closed the door behind him.

"A good trip, then. Take a seat why don't you!"

He followed her lead, keeping hold of the paperwork on his lap.

Her next words surprised him. "How did Marnie make out?"

He blinked a couple of times, weighing up how to keep Marnie out of the firing line. "Yeah, she did really well. There was one complication though. We ended up going back to see the vicar and it turned out . . ." He paused to check the lie of the land. "The thing is, boss, the vicar handed me letters that the victim had left with her for safekeeping. It seems he'd been using her address as a mailbox. And we wanted to get back as quickly as possible . . ."

"Let me guess, so there was no time to inform DI Stanton in person or to take a detour to Lincolnshire Police HQ."

"Got it in one."

"And you'd like me to cover for you if he telephones today for an update?"

He didn't answer her directly, but flew the flag for team-building — their team. "I figured that it started out as *our* investigation and it wouldn't hurt for us to take a closer look at this unanticipated development."

"And I think a second hand car dealership is missing its salesman. But seeing as you're here," she opened her hand to receive the post, "I will buy it — for now. You can shut the door behind you. But mark me, Wild, if I feel DI Stanton needs to know about this today, you'll have to explain yourself."

"Understood." He eased himself out of the chair. "Thanks, ma'am."

She shook her head wearily. "Just go. And whatever happens, Marnie knew nothing about this."

Wild's mobile pinged as he sat at his desk, staring intently at DI Marsh — or what he could see of her through her office blinds. He lifted his phone for the text: *Evidence booked in — how did it go?*

He was on the verge of replying with *I'll let you know when I find out,* when he thought better of it and phoned her. "We can talk, you know."

"I didn't want to interrupt you if you were still with the DI."

"I'm not but the second lot of evidence is." He broke off for a moment, noticing that Marsh had picked up her desk phone. "I may as well wait with you in the briefing room."

"In that case make mine with milk and one sugar, thanks."

The briefing room had already been adorned with the victim's photograph from his driving licence and an earlier image from his prison record. Wild stared at them as he entered the room, a beverage in each hand.

Marnie sat there, alone. "I haven't added anything." Her voice sounded insistent, as if he might have doubted her.

He put the drinks down, picked up a marker pen from the whiteboard tray and walked it over to her purposefully. "On ye go then." His Scots accent was a passable impression of the DI, if she'd never been to Glasgow.

As she stood up he spotted the pile of A4 pages on another table — photocopies and blow-ups of evidence found in the flat. These she fixed to the whiteboard and wrote salient points beside them — *Bristol* next to Pat, and Petra's name and job role beside her number. "Hey, maybe Pat was actually Petra misspelt or misheard?"

"Could be. I wonder if other protected witnesses get a voice coach before they up sticks and move to another part of the country?" She didn't reply so he changed tack and speculated in another direction. ". . . And who's to say Juliette Kimani even wanted publicity? Perhaps Lee was blackmailing her with a threat to go public?" He frowned. That didn't make sense if Lee needed anonymity now.

As he looked to his right he saw DI Marsh at the door, her team behind her like a bridal train. She came in and the others dispersed into the room behind her.

"DS Wild, don't let me interrupt you — you were saying?"

It was just her way, he knew that now. She never played favourites — she liked to put everyone under the heat, like a kid with a magnifying glass by an ants' nest.

"Just thinking aloud, ma'am. Do you want me to bring everyone up to speed?" He really wanted to know. No sense in covering the news from Lincolnshire if most of them were still back at the festival, metaphorically.

Marsh sat down and waved a slow hand in his direction, like a conductor who couldn't be bothered. He took to the podium.

"Lee Rickard, twenty-three, suspicious death at the literary festival."

"He'd reached the final paragraph," Ben Galloway chipped in unhelpfully. At least it got a laugh.

Wild persisted. "Cause of death?" He scanned the room to see who'd picked up liaison with the medics in his absence.

Marsh's face broke into a rare smile. "Heart failure, attributed to ingestion of ketamine—" she glanced down at the piece of paper in her hand, "and possible side-effects of anti-anxiety meds — a Serotonin-Norepinephrine Reuptake Inhibitor." She sounded the words out carefully. "Not a happy mix. Ketamine residue in his coffee too so unless he was suicidal — and I don't think literary festivals are *that* dull — it's a murder investigation."

Wild's own heart skipped a beat. He opened his notebook for effect. "Also found in the car was a copy of *Junction Street* signed by a relatively local author, Juliette Kimani — a big hitter on the literary scene. PC Olsen and I interviewed her at the festival. She initially denied seeing the victim, and then changed that to 'she may have seen him but it didn't strike her as significant'. We'll come back to that little gem."

He flicked through a few pages.

"The victim's address, pulled from his driving licence, took us to Miami Beach, Lincolnshire. Evidence retrieved from a search of the flat—" he turned towards Marnie and she handed out photocopies. He waited until the room had settled again. "Marnie found a strip of paper potentially linking our victim to Bristol. We also recovered a business card for Petra . . ."

"Prostitute," DC Harris called out, as if he were making a request.

"A voice coach actually," Marnie snapped and then immediately regretted it. "Wild spoke with her and she's still away in Spain."

Harris took a second bite. "How do we know?"

DI Marsh silenced him with a stare. "We know because like any *good* police officer I corroborated the information. Just as you would have, no doubt."

Harris seemed lost for words.

Wild filled the silent moment. "And no one is wondering why Lee Rickard wanted a voice coach?"

Community Support Officer Lisa Wishaw's voice rose up like a freed bird. "Did he want to be an actor?"

Marsh raised a finger to quell the laughter. "In a sense, yes. Wild?"

"Lee Rickard had been granted a new identity for services rendered to the Crown Prosecution Service. In his former life, as Jordan Hughes, he gave evidence that helped put drug dealer Paul Maguire and several of his organised crime group behind bars. In point of fact that was already a done deal, but every little helps. Maguire and his second in command, Cody Faulkner, are doing a ten-stretch. Lee served around two years."

Harris chased the riddle. "But he cut a deal as a prosecution witness?"

Wild nodded. Well spotted. "Although Lee did his civic duty he'd also unwittingly passed on some bad drugs to someone who died, so prison was inevitable. And speaking of drugs, we found some Class A in the freezer at his flat. Not a hoard, but in small bags so it's likely he was dealing again."

Marsh tutted. "Old habits . . . Okay, now for the weird stuff." She read from her own notes. "Lee wanted to repent for his former life of crime — dealing on the side notwithstanding. He helped out at a local church and he signed up to be a cell donor. The recipient being one Isabella Kimani, daughter of our celebrity author, Juliette Kimani. Letters in my possession . . ."

Wild smiled on the inside. Smooth as sandpaper.

". . . show that said author wrote to the donor, care of the donor service and they passed the letters on."

Ben Galloway pushed in. "Is that ethical?"

Marsh didn't hesitate. "Well, Lee wasn't obliged to reply and this wasn't one of the established charities. Seems to be some sort of private scheme that advertised in a whole bunch of places, including a national church network. Juliette's daughter got better so it was only natural that she'd want to thank the donor."

Ben continued pulling at the thread. "And what would possess him to come out of the woodwork?"

Marsh seemed to go easy on Galloway this time. "The two things most important to Lee: an assurance of anonymity and financial reward. Speaking of which, Harris, what's the latest with Lee's bank, given that we know money went into it?"

Harris coughed quietly. "The bank isn't playing ball. I have escalated it and we should hear back later today."

"Could you get on to them now please?" Her tone left no one in any doubt that this wasn't a request.

Harris slipped out of the room, head bowed, without reacting to Marsh calling, "Thank you," after him.

Marsh continued once the door closed itself. "We have no witnesses for Lee's movements at the festival — no one even remembers seeing him buying a coffee."

Wild made eye contact with her. "Who's to say he bought his own coffee?"

"So he must have known his poisoner," Marnie cut in. "I mean, you don't normally accept drinks from a stranger."

"Quite so." Marsh tapped the air with a pen. "Background checks will be needed on all the staff at the refreshments tent — we'll share them out." She scanned the room for signs of dissent. "Craig — I'm sensing resistance."

"No, ma'am," he said distractedly. "I just think Juliette is the priority. She's already lied to us about knowing Lee. We should bring her in ASAP."

"Agreed. I have something else in mind for you though. I want you to dig deep into Lee's past — put a plan together and talk me through it later. Family and former associates, including the ones he helped put in prison." She drew a breath. "Not forgetting the family of the lad who died because of Lee's drugs. Like they say, revenge is best served cold, and we're talking three years here."

He accepted his assignment without comment, but he would rather have had another crack at Juliette. Top of his list of cardinal sins was lying to the police.

CHAPTER 12

Wild did everything by the book. He parked where he'd been told, signed the register and went through a succession of secure doors with only a warrant card, a couple of pens and a notebook for company. He would never claim to be a prison reformist — *nick 'em and bin 'em* had been his work mantra for as long as he could remember. Even so, he wondered how many long-term prisoners ever came out with any sense of hope for the future? He laughed at his inner voice. Craig Wild, the thinking man's Elizabeth Fry!

He had two interviews scheduled, both hard-core dealers serving a long prison sentence, helped to their cells by the late Lee Rickard, aka Jordan Hughes.

The first interviewee had insisted on a solicitor being present, while the second had waived the right. Wild wasn't sure which interview he was looking forward to most.

He'd read up on Paul 'Chalky' Maguire. A litany of robbery, threats with violence, theft, and receiving stolen goods, before Maguire graduated to adulthood and drug dealing, did not make for happy reading. Amphetamines were how he'd made his mark, hence the nickname Chalky. He'd made his mark on a few people as well. According to some, Chalky was quite handy with a soldering iron.

Maguire's solicitor had the look of a condemned man. In his sixties, the brown suit, scuffed shoes and diagonally striped tie did nothing for him. They shook hands and Wild felt the sweat caress his palm. And now the waiting game. Wild gathered his thoughts in silence, punctuated only by the solicitor clearing his throat and shuffling pieces of paper. The solicitor, Donald Jacobson, flinched as the door clunked open and Paul Maguire entered the room.

Maguire's eyes flicked around the room, as if he were estimating the dimensions for an escape attempt. The two prison officers with him — Wild thought ex-army — rendered that possibility unlikely. Despite his imposing presence Maguire said nothing, merely took a seat beside his solicitor and they shook hands. According to the records, Maguire had been a model prisoner for the past eighteen months.

Maguire spoke first. "You asked to see me?" His eyes narrowed, as if trying to understand something.

Wild gave him something to think about. "I did. Do you remember a man called Jordan Hughes?"

Maguire's face set like concrete. "Are you being funny? That piece of shit helped put me here. What I'd give for five minutes alone with him in a cell." He chuckled and stopped talking. "Just a figure of speech, you understand. So what is he saying now?"

Wild wrote it all down and replied, "He's not saying anything. What would *you* say if I told you he was dead?"

Maguire's face broadened into a wide grin and then the penny dropped. "Nah, you're not pinning that on me. I hated him but I didn't kill him."

"Maybe not personally . . ."

Maguire roared, "No way." Then he looked to his brief for guidance, or comfort or a plan.

The solicitor stirred into action. "Are you accusing my client? If so we would like to see your evidence."

Wild scratched his nose. "Mr Maguire is not under caution — this is just a friendly chat. Information gathering, you might say. And when did you last . . ."

Maguire cut him off. "I heard he got out some time ago. Rumour was that he'd gone abroad — Spain or Portugal, maybe. I might have asked someone to put a few feelers out, purely out of curiosity. And we're talking, what, a year ago?"

Wild didn't try to answer the question. "When you say ask, do you mean forcefully?"

Maguire smiled again. A tiger's smile. "I'm not responsible for other people's social skills."

"We will of course be checking your visitors in the last two years."

"Be my guest."

"And what about Cody Faulkner? Do you think he might have taken an interest?"

"You'll have to ask him yourself." Maguire's tongue tasted the air.

Wild was busy contemplating his next move when someone rapped on the door. He glanced over his shoulder to see DI Stanton, fresh in from Lincolnshire presumably, standing there like an unwanted guest.

He nodded curtly. "DS Wild . . . mind if I join you?"

Maguire shifted in his chair, sensing the change in the room. "Need a responsible adult to accompany you, Sergeant?"

DI Stanton took a seat. "No, this is purely for my benefit. I am Detective Inspector Stanton and I will be sitting in. Unless you have any objections?"

Wild wasn't sure who was being asked. All of them, probably. No one spoke — it was a done deal.

The DI made himself comfortable. No notebook, not even a pen, as if his presence had been an afterthought. Except, Wild knew, nobody drove from Lincolnshire to Bristol just to observe.

DI Stanton wasted no time. "Mr Maguire, before coming here today I had the opportunity to look at the court transcripts of your trial. As you know, our victim provided evidence that contributed to your conviction. Perhaps you remember one of your many outbursts in court? Let me quote you: '*I will kill you, Jordan. Wherever you go I will hunt you down. You are a fucking dead man.*'"

Wild chipped in. "And now he is."

Maguire's jaw lowered, exposing his teeth. He looked like a man wrestling with thoughts he could not afford to express. He nudged his solicitor and nearly sent him sprawling. The solicitor managed to steady himself against the radiator and regain some composure if not his dignity. No one else had lifted a finger.

"If this line of questioning continues, I suggest we put the interview on a more formal footing. In which case we will need to reschedule this meeting so that I have sufficient time to consult with my client."

Maguire patted his brief's shoulder and then sat back with his arms crossed.

The solicitor looked to the ceiling, found the rest of his courage somewhere in the lighting, and faced the police. "I think we'll take a comfort break while I talk to my client in private. Unless that's a problem for you?"

Wild let the DI do the talking and went to the door. The two of them waited in the corridor. Wild couldn't place the scent — somewhere between emulsion paint and floor cleaner.

Stanton opened the bidding. "I hope you've no objections to my being here?"

Wild blinked slowly. "Of course not, sir. Glad to have you here." His face suggested otherwise.

He offered Wild some chewing gum. "Sarcastic bastard, aren't you?"

Wild took it, peace offering or not. "I don't like surprises. DI Marsh could have informed me — not your fault."

The DI's face scrunched up. "It sort of is actually. I asked her not to. Didn't want to create conflict before I got here."

No, Wild thought, better to do it in person.

"So what's your plan, Craig?"

"See if we can provoke a reaction in Maguire, or his solicitor, or Cody Faulkner. Plus the usual — check visitor logs and any numbers called."

"And what about illegal mobiles?"

Wild flashed a grin. "I doubt we'll find grounds to search his cell for a burner phone. And by the time we get the paperwork completed, any phone will be long gone."

Stanton showed his ability to multitask by chewing and thinking aloud. "I think we're barking up the wrong tree here. They would be stupid to kill off Jordan Hughes. Incidentally, have you mentioned his new identity?"

"No — I wanted to see if he or his solicitor did. And as for stupidity, Paul Maguire and Cody Faulkner are in prison — hardly a calling card for intelligence."

"So why is Jordan Hughes dead now, a year on from prison?"

Wild countered the question with another one. "And why wait until *Hughes* was in Wiltshire?" He heard a noise along the corridor as a prison guard unlocked the door, and nudged the DI. "Round two, Guv."

Everything was the same in the room, but the balance of power had shifted. The solicitor asked questions and they were obliged to give answers if they wanted the informal interview to continue. In practice that meant sharing the date of death, where the victim met his maker and enough information to keep the solicitor sweet without overplaying their hand.

Maguire said far less and paid more attention, switching his gaze from copper to copper as if he was trying to figure out a sleight of hand con trick. Wild was doing something similar with Maguire and his brief.

DI Stanton had the last word. "One more thing, Mr Maguire, what do you think your associate, Cody Faulkner, will say when we tell him about Jordan Hughes's death?"

The solicitor seemed to rise a little in his chair. "You cannot possibly expect my client to speculate on Mr Faulkner's reactions or what someone else may or may not know. I would like to state on record that my client, Paul Maguire, has participated fully in the rehabilitation process and continues to do so. The prison will confirm that he has been a model prisoner for the past year and a half."

Wild was tempted to ask about the time prior to that, but he was more interested in the solicitor's *my client* statement. The implication was that Cody Faulkner was not his client, which was interesting because a single legal team had represented them both at the trial. And even more clearly, the solicitor wanted to move the searchlight over to Maguire's former subordinate.

Maguire and his brief left the room. Wild and Stanton remained there for a quick tea break, during which the DI said nothing of any value, and then it was time for Cody.

CHAPTER 13

One look at suspect number two and it was easy to see why Jacobson wasn't offering a package deal. Cody was a different animal, his face lean and his eyes hungry. Even if you discounted the tattoos — many of which looked homemade — this was an apex predator. Cody's solicitor wore a sharp suit. Her large glasses suggested exuberance but the face behind them showed all the warmth of a cliff face. She offered curt handshakes and handed over a business card the same way other people give out written warnings.

"Caroline Myers."

Wild checked the name on the card. Myers and King, a formidable legal powerhouse in the West Country, whose reputation extended even to Wiltshire. He denied Faulkner the satisfaction of explaining why he'd decided to have legal representation after all. If Stanton was surprised he hid it extremely well.

Cody's solicitor skimmed over a sheet of paper. "My client is prepared to answer preliminary questions about the victim on the clear understanding that he had nothing to do with the incident and can shed no light on any persons who may have been responsible, or their motivations for committing what must surely have been a dreadful crime."

The DI sighed heavily and nudged Wild under the table. Wild understood. He'd be the litmus paper.

"Ms Myers . . ." he said it with a straight face. "Can I start by asking how your client knew about the purpose of our visit?"

Wild clocked Cody gazing beyond him before looking back down at the table. That told him all he needed to know. He held no malice towards the prison officers who had been given strict instructions not to prep the prisoner on his way to the interview; they were only human. He saw Stanton folding his arms in his peripheral vision. Time for the second verse.

"We are very keen to understand if your client was aware of any threat to Jordan Hughes or can think of any reason why someone might have targeted him."

Caroline Myers didn't bother to look at her client, who in any case was staring into space, presumably counting the minutes until he could return to his cell, or the gym, or wherever he passed the time during the day.

"My client has no knowledge about this terrible crime and nothing further of value to add to your investigation. Should any information come to him by . . . unbidden means . . . he would, of course, be willing to meet with you again to discuss that."

Wild got the message. Cody would have his listening ears on but any information would come at a price. Somehow, he didn't think the DI would be buying.

"Now, gentlemen, is there anything else?"

Cody decided this was the time to try out his stand-up routine. "Don't you want to ask me where I've been for the past couple of weeks?"

Wild could almost feel the DI's teeth grinding.

"That won't be necessary, Cody. We know exactly where you were. Of course, if you can tell us where your friends on the outside were that would help us enormously."

Cody smiled. "Like Ms Myers said, I can make enquiries. And then perhaps we can talk again." He waggled his hand like a puppeteer mime act. "Maybe see if we can meet in the middle. That way, everyone gets something they want."

Wild wasn't aware that they had a deal, but it was a better offer than the one Maguire's solicitor had come up with so far.

The solicitor didn't stay long after Cody was returned to his cell. Never mind, Wild thought, more rich tea biscuits for him. The prison officers let them have the room for a little longer, giving them space to chat.

The DI got up and walked to the opposite corner of the room. It was a small room and a short walk. "What do you think? Be frank with me."

"Honestly? This is probably a waste of my time and definitely a waste of yours. We have nothing to link either one of them to the victim's death. I imagine they will go back to their respective cells and celebrate. It's a great message to put out on the streets. If you cross us we will always find you. Except, of course, they might not have." He realised he was out of biscuits. "Are you going to level with me about why you are really here?"

The colour drained from Stanton's face. "When someone under the UK Protected Persons Service is the victim of a serious crime, which is basically never, there is a root and branch investigation into every aspect of their case. Could they have talked? Could someone close to them have talked? Was there a failure in our processes or the manner in which they were carried out?"

Wild nodded to himself. So basically, the DI was there to cover his own arse. "I take it your next stop will be Wiltshire?"

"Yes, I think it may be beneficial to spend time with the investigation team and lend my support. I can act as liaison for the witness relocation team and for the local force in Lincolnshire. Plus, you could probably use the extra manpower. Don't worry," he smiled weakly, "I'm not going to rock the boat. My objectives are the same as yours, Sergeant — get to the truth and hold those responsible accountable."

"Do you want to follow me down to Mayberry?"

"No, that's okay, I have satnav. No need to wait around for me."

In that case, Wild figured he'd make a little detour once he left the prison. Having already decided to visit Maguire's solicitor — on the off-chance — it occurred to Wild that the DI might be thinking the same thing. But he figured DI Stanton would probably go for the decidedly more upmarket Caroline Myers. Birds of a feather and all that.

Wild was first out of the car park, mobile phone primed for voice commands. The app directed him across Bristol, taking in St Mary Redcliffe church and Temple Meads railway station before he landed at his destination. Thankfully, the DI wasn't waiting for him.

Wild's warrant card secured him the cooperation of a receptionist, who checked if Donald Jacobson was in and whether he was free. On this occasion, fortune favoured the brave.

"He's just returned from a meeting. I'll buzz you through — go up to the second floor."

The building screamed late 70s with a thin veneer of refurbishment. As Wild climbed the stairs he heard a lift door slowly closing nearby. Random boxes of A4 paper lined the snaking corridor, like a Health & Safety nightmare.

The upper half of Jacobson's office door was corrugated glass. Wild could still make out a blurred mass of brown suit. The door was open slightly. He went in.

". . . And let me know the moment he calls, even if I'm in a meeting." Donald killed his conversation when Wild appeared. "Detective Sergeant, this is an unexpected surprise."

An underling backed away to the door.

"Well, I was on my way back to Wiltshire so . . . you know."

"Would you like some tea?"

"Thanks — one sugar please."

The solicitor led the way to an inner sanctum. "Come through. I must say I never expected to see you again so soon, and not like this."

"Well, I thought we could both talk more easily without our respective masters."

The solicitor laughed, which told Wild he was on the right track.

Jacobson called out through the still open door. "Henry — can you fetch the biscuit tin as well."

Wild cast a glance around the office. Judging by the sprawl of paperwork and the state of the furniture, few meetings were held in-house. More likely, in prisons or police stations or remand centres. With all the box files piled on the desk and on filing cabinets, business was either booming or the place had gone to seed.

Henry knocked on the doorframe and edged his way in with a little tray. The look on his face suggested that the knock had been sarcasm rather than professionalism. He placed the tray on the clearest surface available — the carpet — and then receded like a butler, pulling the door to behind him.

Donald reached into the biscuit tin, pulled out a chocolate finger and dipped it in his tea before sucking it to oblivion. He smiled at Wild and eased back in his creaking wooden desk chair.

"What are you after, Mr Wild? You know I'll need to report this meeting to my client. Maybe it would be best to record any discussion."

Wild rummaged around in the biscuit tin, found something in a wrapper and peeled the foil back carefully. "Yeah, that's one option. Just as I might get suspicious about why the convicted head of an organised crime group, who is doing a ten-stretch, would choose a small-time solicitor — no offence — when he'd peddled enough coke and amphetamines to the good people of Bristol and beyond to have bought himself a better class of legal representation."

He saw Donald's eyes flare and headed him off at the pass.

"A cynic might think that Maguire feels more comfortable having someone like you to run messages to what's left of his organisation, especially if he's known you a long time." He blew on his tea and then sipped. "DI Stanton, my new friend from the National Crime Agency, could conclude that it's worth a detailed look at how you earn your money and what you do with it. I'm sure he has friends in Revenue & Customs who'd be only too happy to join him."

Now he slurped his tea triumphantly.

"As for me, my priority is investigating a suspicious death. The way I see it, if Paul Maguire learned where the victim lived he might have sent someone to do the job there. Makes no sense to wait until the victim was in Wiltshire, apart from a cheaper train fare. Unless someone else in the organisation — by which I mean *drug gang* — discovered the victim's travel plans and decided to resolve matters in Wiltshire, for reasons as yet unknown. Are you following me?"

The solicitor nodded slowly. "I have represented Paul Maguire since he went to prison. I, er, knew of him prior to that — our paths crossed once or twice after we were introduced by a mutual acquaintance, and that's all I'm prepared to say."

Wild's eyes ranged over the debris in the room. "If he's responsible for that boy's death and you are in any way implicated you can say goodbye to your . . . thriving legal practice."

Donald smiled over his tea. "I won't be because he isn't."

"I hope that you're right, for your sake. And, I have to say—" Wild tapped his own unadorned ring finger on his right hand and then pointed to Jacobson. "—I'm surprised to find a worshipful brother working for a scumbag like Maguire."

Jacobson shifted a little in his chair and rubbed at the Masonic band, as if it could make someone disappear. "Unless you're 'on the square', Detective, best not speak about something you do not understand."

"I may not be Lodge material but I do know about duty. I have actually been approached a few times over the years, only . . . well, I lack the dedication. Much like you now, I imagine." He could see that Jacobson was pained by his comment and he was sorry for it. "Look, I'm guessing all that stuff means something to you or you wouldn't still wear the ring."

"Forty years," Jacobson turned the ring slowly. "Man and boy! Engraved with my first Lodge meeting, much like me! And for the record, I might represent Mr Maguire but I have never knowingly assisted him in committing any criminal enterprise — I don't know if his accountant can say the same!"

Wild shared the joke but the word *knowingly* hung in the air like a bad smell.

CHAPTER 14

Wild took his time driving back to Mayberry, which made it even less of a surprise to see Stanton's silver Mazda in the car park. He met him in the gents, interrupting his mobile phone call. He heard the words, "I'm looking into it now, sir," before the call abruptly ended. Wild didn't react — he had that effect on real conversations as well.

Stanton headed out. "You made it back then. See you in the briefing room."

"Yeah," Wild muttered under his breath on his way to the urinal, "not if I see you first."

After the traditional two shakes and a careful zip-up he washed his hands and splashed water on his face.

Ignoring Stanton's invitation, he avoided the briefing room and went straight to Marsh's office. His luck was in, to a degree. Marsh was in a meeting with Marnie. He figured it was only some mentoring thing, knocked and went straight in.

She threw him a laconic smile. "Pull up a chair. We were just talking about you."

Marnie blushed.

"Your investigation, of course. DI Stanton is in the briefing room, looking over the boards."

Wild nodded. "I saw his car."

"Go on then, how did you make out in prison?"

Wild glanced to Marnie and then regretted it.

"Don't be shy, Craig. Marnie has to learn the ropes any way she can, even with the crudest of tools."

Nice. He went through the interviews like an ABC of irrelevance. "Maguire's solicitor seems a bit downmarket to me." He left out the part about his private tea party. "Cody Faulkner also sprang a brief on us. She seems a cut above Donald Jacobson. Maybe we could work on driving a wedge between them. There's little to link either of the scumbags to Lee Rickard's death right now."

She sighed. "Another great loss to prison reform. DI Stanton bumped into Caroline Myers, quite by chance, in a café in Bristol."

Wild's face dropped under the weight of coincidence. Did he bollocks. "Right," he said, mostly to his own assumption about Stanton.

Marsh continued. "Yes, she was eager to move our attention over to Maguire. Said she would speak to Cody Faulkner again and ensure his cooperation."

"In return for . . . ?"

"Never you mind about that. Maybe he wants a nicer cell — what do you care?"

He sucked at a tooth. In point of fact he minded a lot. Dealers were the scourge of society as far as he was concerned. And as for all the 'no one forces people to take drugs' bullshit, try telling that to an addict, or the child of an addict, or the poor sod who has to identify the body when they pull them out of a river. Or, on one occasion, a skip.

"Right, well, ma'am," he nodded, "I'd better go and keep DI Stanton company."

"Aye, you do that. And get chummy because you are his liaison with the team. Maybe you can take him out for a curry tonight and *bond*?"

"Only if we can find somewhere that sells pheasant jalfrezi."

"You know what, DS Wild, you are an inverted snob."

"Not really." He took a shot to see where it landed. "I don't like people who flaunt their authority or turn up unexpectedly in the middle of one of my interviews. One boss is enough for me."

"Glad to hear it. Off you scoot now and play nicely."

* * *

Wild peered through a crack in the door. DI Stanton was facing one of the boards and his marker pen was moving. Wild coughed as he pushed the door.

The DI glanced behind him. "Did you get lost on the way?" He returned to his notes.

A space on the board had been left clear and the DI had used that for his working hypothesis. Namely, that one of the organised crime group had somehow located the victim and killed him when he came to Wiltshire.

"Hmm . . ." Wild critiqued it from a safe distance. "A bit of a stretch."

Stanton thrust the pen towards him like a blade. "You have a better idea?"

Wild sidestepped the pen and moseyed over to one of the chairs. He sat down and folded his arms. "Suppose one of Maguire's people did find the victim. Why not see to him in Lincolnshire?"

"Perhaps someone saw him in Wiltshire by accident?"

"I can't see Maguire's lieutenants being the literary type, can you? And going on the tox results—" he pointed to the toxicology summary pinned to the board, "—the victim ingested a significant amount of ketamine, which points to premeditation. So again that makes no sense. Why not the simplicity of a bullet?"

"It would draw too much attention."

"Then muscle him into a car, or force him to drive, and once he's away no one can see him. Job done."

"They said you were funny."

Wild smarted. *They* being DI Marsh. "How did you get on with Cody Faulkner's fancy solicitor?"

The DI smiled faintly, as if recalling a happy memory. "We shared a pleasant coffee."

"I'm sure you did."

"It transpires that we know the same people — friends in high places!"

Having exhausted their initial salvos, the two of them reviewed the board in silence. Wild played the waiting game and sure enough Stanton caved first.

"Shall we make a pact, Craig, seeing as we'll be working closely?" He didn't wait for an answer. "We'll focus on the investigation, stop re-enacting the class war, turn this situation around and then go our separate ways. Agreed?"

Wild didn't bother reminding him that the victim's situation would never be turned around. Instead, he proffered a hand and shook on it, like two best friends making up after a fight. He withdrew his hand when he heard voices approaching in the corridor.

In they came, Mayberry's finest — a smorgasbord of CID and uniformed officers with Marnie among them, sticking closely to DI Marsh. Wild inwardly shrugged. You do what you have to.

DI Marsh made the obligatory introductions and then let DI Stanton have the floor, so he could reminisce about the original organised crime case and the victim's witness testimony before he went inside.

"Questions?"

Wild got in first. "How many people knew Lee Rickard's whereabouts after his relocation?"

Stanton went a whiter shade of pale. "I'm not able to comment on operational matters relating to the UK Protected Persons Service."

Marsh traded glances with Wild. He got the message. Toe the party line and don't make waves. He nodded — no further questions, your honour — and took a back seat for the rest of the show.

CHAPTER 15

After the meeting, Wild found himself in an awkward triangle with Marsh and Stanton at her desk. She didn't say anything at first. She didn't have to. The bag of books on the desk plus her stony countenance beamed a clue like a lighthouse.

"The senior view is that it would be inappropriate for you to accept these books." She patted the bag, as if it were an ailing pet. "Sorry." She sounded as far from the word as was possible without writing it backwards. She gave the bag a little shove towards him, which caused him to lurch forward. "You knew that anyway."

He watched her smile reflecting his own.

"And you think that gives you an excuse to return them."

He tried to feign ignorance. It had never been his strongest suit.

"For your information, Craig, Juliette Kimani is coming in for a formal interview."

He tried to mask his enthusiasm, and failed.

"DI Stanton and I will take this one." She looked straight at Wild as if daring him to cross her in front of an audience.

He knew it would not be a happy outcome. But bronze was still a medal. "I can do some background checks on the family. We know the husband is away and it's a pound to a penny that the daughter attends a private school."

Marsh's nose twitched. "Ben Galloway can do that. I want you to go and see the family of . . ." She checked her notes. ". . . Conor Hoyle, who died because of the drugs Lee Rickard gave him or sold him. Lisa Wishaw can get you the address. One of the local officers in Bristol will go with you. I'd be very surprised if the family aren't already aware about Lee Rickard's demise and I doubt they're in mourning."

* * *

According to the notes, DC Grazia Kelley had been the family liaison officer throughout Rickard's trial — back when he had been Jordan Hughes. She was waiting for him at the roadside café, which doubled as a briefing room.

"Family is pretty close. Their son who died was a bit of a lost cause. Usual story — in trouble at school, possibly dyslexic — according to Mum, although never formally diagnosed, left school early. Drifted. Some sort of garage apprenticeship, thanks to Dad, and seemed to be making headway until—"

"Until Jordan came along."

"Exactly. They were old friends, apparently. Only now Jordan was a runner for Maguire's organisation. Looks like he tried to branch out on his own."

"Skimming off the top?"

Kelley didn't reply. He took that as a yes. A dangerous way to make money. The rest, in essence he knew. A bad batch of drugs — cut with something else to bulk it up or deliberately contaminated, or not diluted enough. Whatever the cause Conor wound up paying the price.

"Come on, finish your coffee and I'll introduce you to the family."

"Have you told them that the man responsible for their son's death is dead?

"I thought it would be best sharing that sort of news in person."

Fifteen minutes later, Wild surveyed the scene. A typical terraced street. Nice front gardens, neatly trimmed hedges. A working-class neighbourhood and all the better for it. He felt at home as he parked up. Kelley was a few spaces along the street and he watched as she crossed the road to wait for him by the gate.

He wondered if their news would bring the family some sort of closure — an eye for an eye and all that. How many times had he heard that speech before: you make sure they pay! Too much television. Real life wasn't a series of checks and balances. You did the best you could and tried to make good choices. Not so for Conor Hoyle, or Lee Rickard come to that. Both had been marked from their earliest days by the sound of it. Two people who fell through the cracks.

Kelley waved him over with all the subtlety of a hand grenade. He caught up to her.

"They're waiting for us."

He could see a silhouette behind the glass. Kelley rang the doorbell. Wild held back until someone invited him across the threshold. These things mattered.

He followed Kelley into the living room. The mother sat in the middle of the sofa, perched on the edge, hands clasped between her knees. Her partner's hand was on her shoulder. No wedding ring, Wild noted without judgement. A young woman sat at the other end of the sofa, her face expressionless. Wild had seen that blank facade before — always in the victims or the families of victims, where circumstance had raised the drawbridge against life.

The mother wiped away tears and sniffed. "You said on the phone that you wanted to talk to us again."

DC Kelley moved to the middle of the room. "This is DS Wild from Wiltshire Police and he is investigating . . ."

The father blinked a couple of times. "He's done it again, hasn't he?" The bitterness in his voice made him catch his breath.

"No," Wild said calmly. "That's not why we're here. We wanted to tell you in person that Jordan Hughes is dead."

Robert Hoyle looked back at him, cold and unyielding. "Well, you've told us now, so you can go."

Kelley crouched down, meeting him at eye level. "We need to have a bit of a chat first, Rob."

The daughter turned to face the police officers. "How did he die?"

Her voice jarred Wild and as he turned towards her he noticed the family picture on the wall above the sofa — a family of five, which meant someone was missing.

He kept it brief. "We are investigating a suspicious death."

Rob's face seemed to brighten a little. As far as Wild was concerned it was not a good look.

"So someone's finally done him, or has he taken the coward's way out?"

"We are still making enquiries, sir."

There was no reaction from the mother.

DC Kelley stood up again. "The thing is, Rob, Kath, we . . . well we need to know everyone's whereabouts on the day in question. It's just a formality." She opened her pocketbook. "Is Stuart around as well?"

Wild heard rapid footsteps on the stairs and lunged for the door handle. As he wrenched it open and made a dash for the space, a body blurred past, sending him flying. By the time Kelley responded to the commotion Stuart Hoyle was out the door and Wild was on his arse.

"Craig, are you okay?"

"Never mind me," Wild snarled, nursing a fat lip. "Get backup and detain the boy."

He dragged himself to standing with the help of the stairs and returned to the living room, one arm tight against his chest. No one said a word as he occupied an empty seat.

"While we wait for my colleague to return—" he paused, sarcasm dripping from every syllable. "This might be a good time to confirm everyone's movements on the day in question." He made notes and, when pressed, explained where the victim died.

The daughter put him on the spot. "What was he doing at a book fair?"

"That's what we're trying to find out. I understand how this must seem, like we are hassling you more than two years since your son died."

Kath Hoyle put him straight. "It's more than three."

Wild felt ambushed with only himself to blame. He should have read the file more carefully. No point reminding them he was from another police force. He fell back on the time-honoured tradition of asking more questions.

"Any idea why Stuart would have taken off like that?"

The sister saw red. "No offence, but we're not exactly friends of the police."

"None taken." He turned to the father. "Any chance of a cup of tea, Rob?"

As Wild anticipated, as soon as Rob was out of the room the tension diminished and Kath and her daughter opened up a little. He got the information he needed, and more besides, jotting it down for future consumption. Jordan Hughes and Conor Hoyle had met at an educational facility. Not borstal exactly, more of an alternative provision for young people at risk of missing an education. According to Kath, the two lads had become close friends and then Jordan had changed foster parents.

"Not his fault," Kath pointed out, with what Wild saw as unexpected generosity.

He carried on taking notes and she carried on talking.

"The couple had split up so he was moved on. By the time Jordan was back in the area, Conor had secured an apprenticeship at his dad's work."

The daughter had just started another story about her brother when the door handle turned. Both women retreated behind their grief. Rob looked around the room as if he half-expected to see someone else there. Tea was dished out in silence.

Wild addressed the room. "Can I ask, what was your son like?"

The two women looked to Rob and waited. Wild had seen that before. How women dealt with their emotions openly while men locked them away, or else they drowned them in booze.

Rob stared into the distance. "He was mad keen on motorbikes. Do you remember, Kath, how he painted a number on his bicycle after we took him to speedway racing for the first time?" There was pride in his voice.

Kath smiled sadly and then she glanced to the window. The bell rang and the daughter, who Wild realised he didn't know the name of, got up to answer it. A uniformed police officer followed her back into the room.

"DS Wild?" He faltered. "I've been asked to take you to Keynsham police station where Stuart Hoyle has been detained for questioning."

Rob lurched to his feet. "No one's talking to my boy without me present."

The uniformed officer swallowed. "I'm sorry, sir. Your son is eighteen and specifically said he did not want his family to attend. He is entitled to a duty solicitor, if he so desires."

Wild thought the copper must have practised that last line on his way over. He took a gulp of tea. "I'll see if I can straighten things out, Kath — give me your number. It wasn't intentional."

He saw Kath mouth the words 'thank you' on his way out.

CHAPTER 16

As soon as they reached the police station Wild located DC Kelley so she could fill him in.

Her colleague, DC Megan Tench, never gave her the chance. "Stuart Hoyle was apprehended at the end of his road, caught single-handedly by Kelley's sprint and rugby tackle." She grinned. "A search revealed a small amount of weed in his jeans."

Kelley gave her verdict, almost apologetically. "I think we just spooked him."

Tench, senior in age and probably experience, set out her vision of the interview. "You can sit in, Sergeant, but I don't want you interrupting me. We have him for assaulting a police officer and possession."

Wild broke the bad news early. "I won't support an assault charge. It was accidental — we ran into one another and I came off worse." He saw a flicker of a smile cross Kelley's face.

Tench glowered. The frown on her forehead looked like a fault line. "Are you sure about that?"

"Yep. And if he doesn't have any previous for the cannabis and it's only for personal use, we'd be best off giving him a warning."

Tench shook her head in disgust. "Another bloody social worker with a warrant card. Then why are we bothering to hold him?"

Wild played his last card. "Because I need to know where he was when my victim was murdered."

Stuart Hoyle was brought into the interview room. He looked like an oversized child — wide-eyed and out of his depth. He sat down and sipped some water. Wild noticed one of Stuart's legs vibrating.

Once the tape was rolling Tench confirmed that Stuart Hoyle had waived his right to a solicitor and did not want anyone else contacted, especially his parents. Wild had seen it so many times before — suspects stripping everything back in a misguided belief it would speed up the process.

Tench put her stamp on proceedings. "Now, Stuart, Detective Sergeant Wild has decided it is not in the public interest that we charge you with assault . . ."

Wild threw her a leaden glance, but he wasn't about to contradict her on tape.

". . . And as this is your first offence we will stick with a caution for the cannabis."

Stuart's body unwound like a cat before a roaring fire. "Does that mean I can go?"

Wild spoke up from his observer's seat. "Not quite. I still need to know where you were on . . ." he flicked his notebook open and read out the date.

"I was in a pub in Bristol."

"Which one?"

Stuart paled. "Can't remember."

Wild's bullshit detector went into overdrive. "Anyone with you in this Bristol pub you can't remember?"

The lad froze. "No."

Kelley and Tench turned towards Wild, waiting for a response. He was waiting too. Stuart's leg started twitching again. He was getting off with a caution and yet he was still scared of something, unless he had taken something — or needed to. Nah, Wild dismissed that possibility based on years of experience. That left one conclusion: young Stuart had been in the wrong place or in the wrong company on the day in question. Wild wished Marnie was there with some psychological insight. In the absence of any of his own, he decided to go with his gut.

He leaned forward across the table. "DS Wild is requesting a short pause to this interview so he can consult with DC Tench." They adjourned to the far end of the corridor.

"Sorry Craig, It looks like none of us are winners with this one."

"Certainly seems that way. Tell you what, once you have released him I can run him home on my way back to Wiltshire. Save you the bother." He smiled then, implying that no one else would have bothered.

She smiled back. "Fine by me. Better your petrol than ours."

Twenty minutes later, a chastened — and cautioned — Stuart exited the police station. Wild was waiting out front. "Come on, Stuart, I'll drive you back."

There was a moment's pause while Stuart considered the alternative option of ringing his parents, before he followed Wild to his Ford Focus. He got in the passenger side, buckled up, and sat with his hands on his knees.

"Probably not the *Subaru Impreza* you were hoping for, like on the telly!" Wild pulled into traffic and headed east. He made his pitch once they were on the move. "How about we play a game of yes and no? And to make it interesting, if you play along and tell me what I want to know I'll do something for you."

Stuart shared his best adolescent sneer. "And what if I don't?"

"Come on, Stuart, you're smarter than that. It's your choice though. This is an off-the-record conversation so you are not obliged to say anything and even if you do there's no proof. You could tell me to piss off or worse! Help yourself to a wine gum."

Stuart smiled.

"Here's what I'm offering. You get twenty-four hours to remove anything incriminating from the family home. The alternative is that I drive there now and look myself."

Stuart didn't answer, which Wild took as a good sign.

"Right, here we go then. Question one: do you want to get out of whatever shit you're mixed up in?"

A subdued "Yes," was the reply.

"Were you dealing drugs in a pub in Bristol?"

Stuart croaked, "No."

Wild knew he was in the right ballpark. "One more question and then we're done. Have you ever heard of either Paul Maguire or Cody Faulkner?"

Stuart almost hyperventilated.

"The thing is, Stuart, their names weren't mentioned in the trial for your brother's death because there was a wider organised crime investigation going on at the time." He slowed down as they approached traffic lights. "You'll need to direct me from here. Geography's not my strong point."

Stuart looked like a caged animal with no hope of escape. "I'm scared for my family."

"You get rid of any drugs at home and then leave the rest to me."

"When Conor died, we had a visit. Big fella in a suit. Offered condolences, like a lot of people did, but he also said a local businessman had done some fundraising to contribute to funeral expenses. Mum and Dad weren't going to turn it down. They didn't have that sort of money and they wanted to do right by Conor."

Wild already knew how this story ended. "How much money?"

"Three grand."

Wild paused for a moment so that Stuart didn't feel quite such a sucker. "And then they came calling." It wasn't a question because he already knew the answer.

"Yeah," Stuart tilted his head, as if burdened by remembering. "It happened two or three months later. Someone came up to me in a Bristol pub, obviously knew all about my family and me. Invited me to a drink in another pub a few days later. By the time we finished our conversation I was press-ganged."

Wild smiled a little at the historical reference.

"I don't deal drugs. Honest. I ferry stuff around and sometimes keep it safe at home. I never ask what it is but I'm not stupid." He ran a hand over his face. "Mum and Dad would kill me if they knew."

"Then make sure they don't." Wild handed him his card as they reached the top of the street. "Call whoever you need to and tell them what happened — that the police came round to talk to the family about Jordan, and your brother, and drugs. You panicked, tried to leg it and ended up getting cautioned for a small amount of weed." It felt like a script, but only because he'd seen this film far too many times. "And for fuck's sake, don't get caught moving the gear. Once it's done, stay out of trouble."

Stuart met him at eye level. "You're alright for a copper."

"Yeah, I know. Don't let it get around."

Wild waited until he got home to ring Keynsham police station and left a message for DC Tench to call him. DC Kelley would have been a better option, based on the day's performance, but he could hardly expect a family liaison officer to front a search of the deceased's family home. With any luck, Tench wouldn't get back to him until midday, giving Stuart a little more time if he needed it. Either way, Wild's conscience was clear. Stuart would be seen by Maguire's criminal organisation as a liability and they'd drop him like a stone. Stuart might even have worked off the debt by now.

He celebrated a good day's police work with fish and chips, and a can of lager in front of the telly. When his work phone rang, he took it for granted that Marnie was ringing with news. Wrong caller.

"Is that DS Wild?"

It never ceased to surprise him how often people rang his mobile and still checked who it was. "Speaking."

"It's Stuart. I've done it — what we talked about."

Wild nearly choked. "Don't say any more — not a word. Spend some time at home with your family tomorrow."

"I wanted to tell you something else, but you mustn't tell anyone."

"I can't promise that until I know what it is."

"Look, it doesn't make any difference now. I just need to tell someone because it's gnawing away at me."

Wild knew when to keep his mouth shut. "I'm listening."

Stuart sighed, like he was expelling bad air. "Okay, when my brother died, he and Jordan were setting up in business together. Equal partners. That's what the bloke in the pub told me." He dropped the call.

CHAPTER 17

Next morning, Wild found a post-it note stuck on his computer screen: *Meet me in the canteen*. DI Marsh had helpfully added her name and rank at the bottom. He found her by a window table, staring out at the world. From the way the other officers were seated it looked as if there was a half-mile exclusion zone around her. Knowing a free coffee would be too much to hope for, Wild bought his own drink and joined her at the loneliest table in Christendom.

"Morning, ma'am. I got your note."

"Evidently."

He wondered if she'd always had that knack of making people feel small, or whether it came with the training when you made it to DI. Another of life's mysteries to be denied to him.

"So, Craig, how did you fare in Bristol?"

He gave her the bare bones, those he wanted to share anyway. And while he'd considered telling her about the family's unfortunate connection with Paul Maguire, experience told him that Stuart would never be a reliable source. And besides, hadn't the family already suffered enough?

Marsh listened with a critical ear and asked a few uncomfortable questions, mainly about why Wild had spent so much of the day there. He weaved and he wavered, and somehow managed to evade the full weight of her scrutiny. Fortunately, her focus seemed to be elsewhere.

"Craig, I'd like your opinion about a mutual colleague. I know how much Marnie Olsen wants to cross the floor and join CID. However," she paused, "there is a world of difference between a few astute observations and the mindset of a detective. I know you two are pals." She said it without the usual innuendo that hung around them at the police station. "So I value your professional and objective opinion."

He forced a five second pause, even though it was killing him. "I think she's ready. No, I'm sure of it. Sure, she lacks experience but we all have to start somewhere."

Marsh nodded slowly. "Okay, well, I'll give it some further thought and take your views into consideration. With Ben Galloway getting a transfer, maybe it's an ideal opportunity. Not a word to her, mind." She sat a little straighter in her chair. "Right, on you go and update your notes." She glanced at the time on her phone. "I'll be down in fifteen, when I've made some of our colleagues over there squirm a little, and then we can rally the troops for a briefing."

Wild met Marnie on the stairs, heading in opposite directions. Before she could open her mouth, he gave her a thumbs-up and suggested not sitting anywhere near Marsh. "I'll fill you in later."

To which DC Harris called up the stairs, "I bet you will."

* * *

Wild hadn't noticed a silver Mazda when he'd arrived, so Stanton's presence in the briefing room was an unexpected displeasure. Stanton stood at the front of the room, like an eager conductor, while the rest of the team tuned up. Marsh appeared last and took her usual seat, which had been left empty like the *Siege Perilous*.

Stanton spoke first. "Good morning, everyone. DI Marsh and I formally interviewed Juliette Kimani yesterday.

We have now established that Lee Rickard was not only known to the family but had also received payments from her in gratitude for cell donation to Juliette's daughter, Isabella. In that interview, Juliette confirmed that Lee visited the family home on two occasions and also that he first met Isabella when she was recovering in a private hospital."

He looked to Marsh, who waved a bunch of papers in the air to let the circus continue.

Ben Galloway raised a hand. "Does that put her in the clear or make her more of a suspect?"

Marsh drew in a breath. "That's a very good question, which brings us to financial checks." She pointed to DC Harris like an avenging angel.

He flustered a little and sought sanctuary in his notes. "A series of five payments into his account over four months, totalling £18,000."

Wild decided to satisfy his curiosity openly. "Were they all bank transfers?"

"No, two were cash deposits." Harris read aloud from the paperwork. "For £1,000 and £3,000 respectively."

Wild continued his cross-examination. "What was the sequence of the payments?"

"Erm," Harris blushed, like a man unfamiliar with his own research. "First was a £1,000 bank transfer." He called out a date and Wild directed Ben Galloway to the whiteboard.

Galloway stared at the timeline that covered Lee's known interactions with the family.

"That's three days before the operation."

Marsh's voice sailed across the room. "Thanks Ben. That'll be expenses then."

Harris glanced up and took a cue from Wild. "Three grand a week or so later."

Wild speculated. "Lee, back home and recovering?"

Galloway looked over his shoulder with a glint in his eye. "That fits the timeline, Skip."

Harris reeled off two more dates for transfers, each to the tune of £2,000.

Wild did the maths. It wasn't difficult. "So the last payment was ten grand?"

Harris smiled, as though he had done some actual detecting. "Within the last month."

Wild shook his head and tutted.

Marsh turned towards him. "Are you thinking what I'm thinking, DS Wild?"

He hoped so or he was about to look bloody foolish. "It reeks of a payoff."

"Aye, so why the need to pay him off if he's on the other side of the country?"

Galloway got in on the act. "Maybe he was blackmailing her, ma'am."

"In which case," Wild leaned back in his chair, "that puts her firmly back in the identity parade."

Marsh seemed lost in thought. Wild knew from experience not to interrupt her, in the same way that Vatican priests probably left the Pope to his own devices when his door was closed.

"I think I'll discuss this with the DCI," Marsh said, in a rare moment of uncertainty.

Wild didn't hold it against her. As she herself had said, a smart lawyer with an axe to grind could easily make this look like harassment. All the same, Juliette was hiding something and he would make it his mission to find out exactly what that was. He looked across at the clock, noticed it was broken and checked his phone instead. An icon alerted him to a missed call.

Marsh turned her gaze on him. "Are we keeping you from something?"

He took the punch and tried not to fall. "No, I promised to ring someone."

"You may as well do it now."

So what if he looked like he'd been sent out of class. He could live with that. He went outside, keeping close to the building and away from prying eyes.

DC Tench picked up on the first ring. Her surprise gave way to interest as soon as he mentioned the magic words,

"Can anyone else hear this conversation?" He cut to the chase. "I have been thinking about Stuart Hoyle. Maybe he does have more grass at home . . . yes, I'd say there are reasonable grounds after yesterday. Even if he doesn't, it's a good deterrent for the future. Maybe don't involve DC Kelley though, as she was family liaison officer. And perhaps we could keep this call to ourselves? Great. Glad we're on the same page. Good luck with it, Megan."

CHAPTER 18

Wild took an incoming call as he went back to his desk. Marnie sounded flustered.

"Everything okay?"

"Not exactly, Wild — we have a bit of a situation. Juliette Kimani left a message at the station and asked me to call her."

Wild pressed the phone to his ear as he changed direction and headed back down for the main door. Somewhere in the distance he heard Marsh's voice like a spectre. "Okay Marnie, go ahead. I'm just finding somewhere I can talk privately." A stray thought came to him. "How come she rang and asked for you? No offence."

"It's complicated. She remembered me from the literary festival and it was me who ferried her in and out when she had a formal interview with the two DIs."

"So why are you ringing me?" It came out worse than it had sounded in his head.

"Calm your ego, Wild. She wants to see both of us, right now. Can you pick me up without troubling my sergeant?"

Twenty minutes later Wild collected a very shifty looking Marnie from a pub car park. As soon as she got into the car he gave her the bad news.

"I have to let DI Marsh know where we're going. I can tell her that Juliette requested our presence together."

She didn't look thrilled. "Then maybe I should drive. Juliette sounded keen to have us over there ASAP and refused to go into any details over the phone."

Wild reluctantly got out the car and walked around to the passenger door while Marnie scooted across. He tried not to show his indignation as she set about adjusting the seat and the mirrors.

As he expected, Marsh did not react. He figured she would assume — correctly — that he was calling on hands-free, and would not want to let her guard down with Marnie around. But the few words she did share, of cautions to document everything and follow procedure to the letter, left him in no doubt that she was not happy. And if he'd learned nothing else since transferring from London to Wiltshire, it was that nobody did unhappiness like a Glaswegian in authority.

"Understood, ma'am. I'll get back to you as soon as we are clear."

"Aye, you do that."

Juliette was standing in the drive. Judging by the grooves in the gravel she'd been pacing back and forth. She led them inside and didn't speak until the door was firmly closed.

Wild and Marnie had agreed on the way over that she should take the lead. After all, Juliette had asked for her specifically and Marnie had the advantage of her psychology degree. Also, he still felt that Juliette looked down on him.

Juliette Kimani stood in the middle of the room, arms clasped around her waist as if to stem a wound. "Isabella is missing."

Marnie sat down to take notes and Juliette mirrored her. "We had *words*."

It wasn't the comment Wild needed; he would have rather heard something like: 'My daughter is vulnerable or in danger.'

He spoke on autopilot. "You've checked with her friends?"

"Well, of course I have," she snapped. "She said she was going to stay with her father for a couple of days. He has a flat in London — for the play. She hasn't arrived and she never called him. It's been hours."

Wild made a last ditch attempt at 'good cop'. "What was the argument about?"

Marnie spoke when Juliette didn't. "May I ask, how did Isabella react when you told her that Lee — her cell donor — had died?"

Wild nodded gently. Good question.

Juliette lowered her face. Wild wondered if there were tears somewhere beneath that facade.

After a moment to compose herself she said, "That's just it. I haven't told her yet. I know it's going to come out but I was waiting for the right moment. Look, shouldn't you be tracking her mobile phone or something — I can give you the number."

Wild straightened his jacket. "It's a little more complicated than that." He spared her the intricacies of a Missing Persons Risk Assessment. "Would it be possible to take a look around the house and see her room?"

When she agreed he looked to Marnie and flicked a finger to the ceiling. "You go, Marnie. I'll stay here and talk with Mrs Kimani."

Marnie left them to it, torn between Wild's confidence in her and irritation at the thought of missing out. She climbed the stairs, still listening to Wild's London accent as it cut across vowels and landed glottal stops like punches.

Upstairs, she changed focus and checked all the other rooms and walk-in wardrobes, before making her way to Isabella's bedroom, pausing briefly to admire the butterfly design on the door.

Inside, wall-to-wall purple was the order of the day. Not quite gothic though a rebellious hue compared to the rest of the house. Despite the edgy colour scheme, the room was pristine. A laptop was perfectly aligned with the edge of the desk, posters neat on the walls.

She almost heard Wild in her head — *start with the obvious places and work the room methodically*. Nothing under the mattress and the only thing of note in the bedside cabinet was a copy of Madame Bovary. The wardrobe revealed a designer label box containing some black leather boots Marnie's younger self would have died for, and inside the boots she found four ten pound notes. No obliging diary came to light, but a search of the underwear drawer revealed a familiar label. She bagged an item and felt an adrenaline rush worthy of a treasure hunter. As she turned about the room for a final sweep she noticed the lace curtain and reflected on how the window to the world was so different to what lay behind it. She smiled. Wasn't that symbolic of every teenage girl since the dawn of time?

It took all her self-control not to run down the stairs in triumph. Instead, she went down slowly and quietly so she'd hear the conversation without interrupting them. Wild's voice was still as clear as a cracked bell.

"Why was your last payment to Lee Rickard much greater than any others? More than the previous four put together in fact."

Juliette sounded defeated. "It was a final show of gratitude."

Marnie lingered by the lower stairs. Final seemed an interesting choice of word.

"May I be frank, Mrs Kimani?" Wild paused and then decided for her. "I think giving ten grand to a twenty-three-year-old, especially after already funding him to the tune of eight thousand pounds, sounds highly suspect."

"Shouldn't you be out there looking for Isabella?"

He didn't bother quoting statistics to her on the number of teenage mispers who miraculously appear at a friend's house once everyone has calmed down. Instead, he went for the jugular.

"You've given no indication that Isabella is at risk. I think you're wasting our time and that maybe something else is going on."

Marnie realised the conversation had tipped into an interrogation. Time to intervene. "Excuse me, Sergeant Wild, I need to speak with you."

He didn't bother looking round. "I'm nearly done. So what was it, Juliette? A payoff? Blackmail? I can always ask your husband."

Judging by the look of indignation on her face: bull's-eye.

"Alright," she rubbed her cheek. "I found out about Lee's past and although we greatly appreciated what he did for Isabella, we didn't think he was a good influence. I offered him the money and he accepted it — to get out of our lives for good."

"Well, he certainly did that."

Marnie gulped. "Mrs Kimani, was your daughter in a relationship with Lee Rickard? It's really important we understand all the dynamics."

Wild's jaw slackened and Juliette's face tightened, like a muscular exchange programme.

"Lee was twenty-three for God's sake. Isabella is still a child."

Marnie adopted a conciliatory tone. "With respect, she's hardly that. And you had your suspicions? Mothers usually have a sense of these things."

"I thought she was becoming too attached to him — to the idea of him. We worried things might become *physical*. Isabella has been through so much already and I didn't want that for her yet, and not with him. So yes, if you want to see it that way, I bought him off."

There was nothing left to be said. "We should be going, Wild."

He took the hint after a pointed stare. "Sure. I just need the loo."

And maybe, he thought to himself as he headed off to pee, the two ladies could have a heart-to-heart. Marnie was so much better at that stuff anyway. Like every good copper, he went through the bathroom cabinet. On the top shelf, he found a bottle of pills. He moved the label into view and took a picture of the label on his phone, then gave the bottle a rattle and pocketed a couple of tablets to compare with the toxicology report.

He returned downstairs, collected Marnie and was out the door without another word. He did his talking in the car. "I don't like being interrupted when I am questioning a potential suspect." He felt his lips pursing.

"From where I was standing, it sounded like you were haranguing the mother of a missing teenager."

He sighed. "So what did you need to say so urgently?"

She held the evidence bag down in her lap, just in case Juliette was watching from the window. "Isabella's designer underwear — same brand and size as we found in Lee's flat." She looked at him earnestly. "In Lincolnshire . . ."

He nodded slowly. "Okay, we can update DI Marsh on the way. But I need to make a detour first — to see a man about a pathology report."

She didn't get the joke.

* * *

Wild escorted Marnie inside.

"Have you met Dr Bell, our pathologist at large?"

The good doctor extended his hand and she noticed the immaculate fingernails.

"A pleasure . . . er . . ."

"Marnie. Marnie Olsen."

"So, DS Wild, you said you were coming bearing gifts?"

Wild handed him a bag containing two tablets. "There's more," he showed him his phone. "Where do you want me to send it — email or mobile? I can write it out as well, to be going on with."

Dr Bell peered at the screen and then took the bag. "I'll need to check the tablets of course — one can't simply go by the label. And then we'll compare them with the post-mortem. Ah, Belinda, you remember DS Wild. And this is . . ."

Belinda beat him to it. "Hello, Marnie." The pathology technician's face froze.

Marnie had the advantage of being prepared. "Hi, Belinda. How are you?"

"I'm fine." Never did the term sound less accurate.

Wild clapped his hands to break the tension. "Right, well, we'd best get on. Thanks for your time, Doc. I'll await your call."

"And where did you get them?"

He sidestepped the question. "The label will tell you everything you need to know. I've sent it to you. Call it serendipity."

"Ah, yes, the unsung hero of police work. And I take it you photographed it in situ?"

He nodded and turned on his heels, a half-wave to Belinda as he and Marnie walked back to the car. He was itching to ask her about Belinda, but this required the gentle touch. As did another matter.

Once he'd put enough distance between them and Mayberry, Wild made some calls. First, to the team, to pass on Isabella's mobile number and the details of the meds she had taken with her.

Then he called DI Marsh.

"It'd be best to have a female officer present and Marnie is already with me so . . ."

Marsh's initial response, "You've got to be kidding me," gave way to a grudging acceptance of Wild's logic. "Where are you now, Craig?"

He glanced at a road sign. "On the A429, not far from the Loxley turn-off."

Marsh actually laughed. "I'll say this for you Craig, You've got some brass neck. For your sake I hope you get a result."

CHAPTER 19

The journey east had a terrible sense of déjà vu, only this time with the added burden of delivering some very bad news. He pictured the sight of a distraught fifteen-year-old and put his foot down.

Marnie hadn't said much in the last half hour. She wondered whether Marsh's previous instruction to keep an eye on Wild remained a condition of her promotion prospects. Now seemed a good time to put Wild in the picture, at least partially.

"You remember when we met on the stairs at the police station?" She saw the bewildered look on his face and jogged his memory. "I was on my way to see the DI and you gave me the thumbs-up. How much did you know?"

He smiled broadly. "Ah, right. Well, I doubt I was any great influence on her decision, but she did ask me if I thought you were ready to move across to CID."

She stared at him for signs of irony. "Are you being funny?"

His blank expression told her otherwise.

"I've been given a project — a sort of initiative test. The DI wants me to look into a spate of shed burglaries." She watched the corners of his mouth rise up. "It's not funny,

Wild. I went in there thinking . . . well, you know exactly what I was thinking: This is it, I thought — what I've been pushing for. Only to sit there and pretend that investigating shed break-ins is the opportunity of a lifetime."

"We all start somewhere, Marnie. And you never know where it might lead." He timed the pause to perfection. "Next time it could be a summerhouse."

She laughed. "You are such a dick. Actually there's a summerhouse on the list."

"You see? You're already expanding your repertoire! Listen, seeing as we're talking freely, what's with you and Belinda? The atmosphere back there was colder than a body storage unit."

She mulled it over for a few seconds. "We were friends, sort of. Only we ended up seeing the same person — with an unintentional overlap. Her partner became my partner, and when I found out it became someone else's problem. All water under the bridge as far as I'm concerned."

The word *partner* flashed out at him from the sidelines of their friendship. Did she mean a man or a woman? And was she waiting for him to ask? He was never one to gamble so he let it drop and wished away the next four hours of his life.

* * *

Wild stopped the car outside the flats and gazed up at the first-floor landing. It was hard to see clearly in the shadows. "You know I'm, err, not very good with kids. Especially girls."

She patted his arm. "No problem. I can deal with the emotional stuff." She turned towards him, the doubt as readable on her face as newsprint. "We're really out on a limb here, aren't we?"

He laughed and pulled the key out of the ignition. "That's probably what Marsh thinks as well. But Isabella is still a missing person and no one had a better idea." As he bleeped the car lock, reality dawned. "Oh, bollocks."

She stopped when she reached the foot of the stairwell. "Excuse me?"

"Sorry, thinking aloud. The front door lock's been changed — twice. If Isabella had a key it wouldn't fit now." He thought for a moment. "We'll split up. You take the far staircase so both exits are covered, in case she's sat outside the flat and tries to do a runner." He watched Marnie sprinting off into the distance, started counting to two hundred, got bored at one hundred and climbed the stairs. He saw Marnie at the end of an empty balcony and they converged on Lee Rickard's door.

"Marnie have you got a nail file?"

She threw him a look of disgust and then handed one over anyway. He gripped the very tip of the rounded end and slid the file under the door. As he applied pressure and pulled it out carefully the corner of a note came with it. He extracted the piece of paper with a fingernail.

"Lucky guess," he said, holding it up so they could read it together.

Where are you? You don't answer your phone. I couldn't open the door? If you get this, you'll know where to find me.

Marnie stated the obvious. "Maybe we should have alerted the local force."

Wild headed along the balcony and she trailed in his wake. He knocked on the neighbour's door and dug out his warrant card. A curtain flickered and then the woman they'd spoken with previously appeared at the window. He pressed the wallet to the glass and waited while she stared at it for too long then opened her door.

"You're back again then. I thought you looked a bit casual for housing."

He skipped the social patter. "We're looking for a missing girl. Teenager, probably with a bag. She is black, five foot four and has a bluish streak in her hair."

"Oh, her. She came here, asked if I'd seen *him*! I said to her, the housing came round a couple of times and forced their way in. That's what happens when you get behind with the rent."

Wild felt himself losing patience. "What time was she here?"

"I don't know. Earlier. It was daytime."

He looked out at the growing dusk. "Thanks, you've been a big help."

Marnie stepped forward. "Anything you can remember would really assist us. Her mother is worried sick."

"I heard her on the phone after I shut the door. I wasn't listening on purpose — I'm not one to pry into other people's lives."

Marnie nodded in encouragement.

"The woman she spoke to was called Jane. Well, I suppose it was a woman. You can't always tell these days."

Wild started back along the balcony and rang Marsh with an update. ". . . Yes, ma'am. We're heading over to see the vicar right now. I know . . . at the very least she's been less than honest with us, but no real harm done. I'll call you again when we have the misper in the car." He waited at the top of the stairs for Marnie. "Oh, did he?" He spoke louder for her benefit. "And what did Dr Bell discover? Right, so it seems to be the same compound as in the victim. Yes, I understand. Speak soon."

He jabbed his phone to cut the call and fist pumped the air. "I bloody well knew she was off, from the first moment I clapped eyes on her." He faced Marnie's ignorance. "Juliette. Her meds in his stomach."

Marnie swerved around him and went down the stairs, her voice trailing behind her. "That doesn't mean she put them there."

Wild conjured several scenarios on the drive to the church. He imagined Juliette angry that Lee had seduced her daughter, meeting him at the literary festival — maybe promising another payoff — and slipping something into his coffee. "Nah," he said aloud. That didn't ring true. How would Juliette get hold of ketamine?

Maybe Lee had to come to Wiltshire to make peace with Juliette? His next thought hit him like a bullet. "Shit, what if he was really serious about Isabella and wanted Juliette's blessing?" He glanced left. "Marnie, are you listening?"

"Sorry, I was thinking about your call with the DI at the flats. Could Lee Rickard have been prescribed that medication?" She played with her mobile phone. "Used for treating anxiety and depression. It's not that long since he left prison and changed his identity."

He felt his mouth widening. "That's brilliant. We can check that with DI Stanton tomorrow. Come on, Marnie, you're the psychology expert. Why was Lee in Wiltshire?"

"What if he wasn't meeting Juliette at all?"

"Who then? No one mentioned seeing Isabella there." He rapped the steering wheel three times. "It doesn't make sense. It's the ketamine . . . Anyway, now we know Isabella and Lee were on, erm, intimate terms, she'll need to be interviewed."

"Hmm, Juliette will want to be there. Her husband is probably travelling back from London. Or maybe Isabella will opt for a responsible adult instead."

Wild stopped talking. The low skyline out to the sea was glowing a misty orange. By the time he had line of sight he saw the complete set of blue flashing lights — fire engine, ambulance and a patrol car crowding the street outside the church. He and Marnie shared a look of silent recognition. It could only mean one thing. Wild tried to muscle his way through and pull rank on the PCs, but they held their ground. Only the emergence of a fellow sergeant clued him in on the situation.

"Two females inside. Suspected arson. Fire officer identified where it started — front and back doors. They're looking for evidence of an accelerant."

Marnie asked, "How are the two people?"

"They were lucky, just smoke inhalation."

Wild felt panic congealing in his veins. "The girl has previously had treatment for cancer. Her immune system may be weakened. She should have medication with her."

The sergeant took it all in his stride. "We'll need her full name and her doctor's details if you have them."

Wild left Marnie to take care of it. With the local coppers' permission, he ventured nearer the building. The air reeked of charcoal and a dull heat emanated from the house. He figured that the presence of the ambulances meant that Jane and Isabella were still being stabilised, which was probably a positive. Probably. He stared at the scene in disbelief. No two ways about it, this was an almighty fuck-up.

A firefighter zeroed in on him. "Excuse me, sir, you can't go any closer."

"I'm a copper," he said, as if that made any difference.

The man opposite him stared hard. "Until the fire investigation officer has given the all clear, *no one* goes in, understand?"

He veered off towards one of the ambulances, trailing his guilt behind him. Of course, he'd been stupid not to think Isabella might be in danger. As soon as they'd confirmed a relationship with the deceased, that implied risk. He rapped on the rear door of an ambulance.

The medic who answered looked far from impressed. Wild showed his credentials and kept his inquiries brief — a quick update and which hospital they'd be taken to. He also managed to confirm Isabella's medication regime.

And now for the really hard part, ringing DI Marsh. He went to find a quiet spot, the same way a wild animal crawls off to die in private.

Marsh spoke in the slow, deliberate manner that told him she was trying to keep a lid on things. In a way, that made it worse. A bollocking would have released some of the tension.

"DI Stanton will be with you in the morning for a full report. In the meantime I expect you to contain the situation, as far as our investigation is concerned. Understand this, Craig, I can't protect you from any repercussions — even if I wanted to. Now, if you'll excuse me, I have to go and ring the parents."

He was still swearing at shadows when Marnie reappeared.

"How are you doing?"

"Not great. Ambulances are heading to Lincoln County Hospital. We should go too. Listen, Marnie, do you think we should have . . ."

"Wild, there was no way of anticipating this."

She was right but it wasn't good enough. Still, if the shit really hit the fan, he'd make sure it didn't affect her prospects.

* * *

Wild had done overnight hospital stints before — a three-ring circus of hyper-vigilance, insomnia and vending machine caffeine. And if you were really lucky you got an hour's sleep at a time in a chair that doubled as an instrument of torture.

The medics kept them at arm's length when they arrived but fortunately the reverend managed a few words about wanting them close by. He let Marnie sleep, seeing as she could. No point in both of them suffering.

DI Stanton arrived around two in the morning, surprisingly subdued. Wild made more sense of it when they had a chat together beside the coffee machine.

"If Maguire's organisation is still active they might suspect Lee Rickard told Isabella something that could be used against them. Tonight's arson attack could have been a warning — to keep her quiet — or we may have a bigger problem. We'll know more when she is able to talk with us."

Wild tried to pick it apart. "Why wait until she's with the vicar? That means they must either have followed her to Lincolnshire or else they've been watching Lee's flat. So they didn't know?" He massaged one of his temples. "But that would mean they didn't kill him? Nothing adds up."

He imagined Marsh railing at the sight of an overtime budget to keep Isabella safe.

"By the way," Stanton opened his case. "I thought you should see this. Your DI read her team the riot act about it yesterday."

Wild took the local newspaper and unfolded it. The front page, bold as brass and just as cold, read: *EXCLUSIVE!*

Suspicious death at local literary festival. Victim believed to have come from outside the county. Police investigating overdose.

And just when Wild thought the day couldn't get any worse.

CHAPTER 20

Wild awoke from dreaming he'd been lying on a raft, rocked by gentle waves. Turned out it was Marnie bringing him back to the real world.

"Time to get up. Reverend Houghton wants to speak with you."

He yawned and stretched against the wall, feeling a patch of sweat press into the small of his back. "What time is it?" He rubbed his face. "Couldn't you deal with it?"

"It's seven thirty in the morning and no, it's a command performance for you. I've been up since before seven — thanks for asking."

He accepted the scold and peeled himself away from the chair. His mouth felt like cardboard. "Got any mints?"

She passed him a couple and he crunched them up before swilling them around his mouth and swallowing them. He asked at the nursing station and despite a look of disdain someone took him along to the room. He checked through the glass panel and then knocked. An arm slid out from the bedsheet and waved.

Reverend Houghton removed the oxygen mask from her face and gestured towards a chair beside the bed. As he sat down she struggled to pull herself up the pillow. Wild offered to help but she declined.

She smiled weakly. "I have my reputation to think of."

"What happened? Tell me what you remember."

She coughed and made a feeble reach for the water jug. This time he intervened and helped her with the glass. She took a couple of slow gulps.

"Thanks. That's better. First, I need to apologise for keeping you in the dark about Lee and Isabella. I felt it wasn't my place to reveal a confidence like that."

"Did you know she was underage?"

She looked startled. "No. Lee told me she was sixteen and I had no reason to doubt his word. I never read *any* of Lee's letters. If he chose to share something then that was down to him." She flinched suddenly. "How's my church?"

"It's fine. Only the vicarage was attacked. Can you talk me through it?" He took out his notebook.

She closed her eyes in memory. "It was an awful night. Isabella arrived in a state, desperate to see Lee. I couldn't leave her like that so I broke the news about his death — I hope that doesn't put anyone in a difficult position."

"Only her mother, probably. How did Isabella respond?"

Jane Houghton took a couple of breaths from the oxygen mask. "Strange question. As you'd expect, she was devastated . . . a little hysterical. At one point she mumbled something about receiving a text from him. I sat with her and she pretty much cried herself to sleep, exhausted. I fetched a blanket and sat with her, praying for them both. When I woke up I didn't know where I was — thick smoke curling around the edges of the carpet. The electrics were out and the windows and doors had jammed. Must have been the heat, I suppose."

He did her a kindness by not suggesting they'd been fixed that way.

"I wasn't thinking straight — I broke a window and that made things a whole lot worse. Thank God for good neighbours. Someone must have seen the flames and dialled 999. I got us to the middle of the house, under a blanket, and I soaked some towels from a water jug to put over our faces. I didn't know if that would do any good but I've seen it on the telly."

Wild heard a noise outside and saw a nurse peering at him through the glass: time was up. He was on his way out the door when she called after him.

"Craig, what was Lee mixed up in?"

"I don't know for sure. But I promise I'll find out. Where are you going to stay when you leave the hospital?"

"They're keeping me in for a couple of days and then the church will make arrangements. Look after Isabella, she's been through so much — especially this past twenty-four hours."

A quick chat with one of the nurses told him that Isabella was going back to Wiltshire later that morning — by private ambulance. It made sense. Better to be close to her parents. And besides, money talked.

Around eight thirty, DI Stanton returned with a Support Officer. "Vernon's here to keep an eye on things while I take you two to grab some breakfast."

Wild went with a full English, ignoring Marnie's 'artery clogger' opinion. "I'd like Marnie to travel in the ambulance with Isabella — can you fix that, sir?"

Stanton looked a little surprised. "I'll arrange it. We've not had a statement from her yet. She's in better shape than the reverend so she might be talkative on the way back. I'll be overseeing things here but I also want to be kept up to speed when you get back to Wiltshire. What's your next move, Craig?"

"Speak to the local paper. Find out where their leader piece came from — there's no attribution."

DI Stanton nodded.

"I noticed that too." Marnie thought she'd remind them she was still there. "Might be worth keeping an eye on the nationals as well."

Wild smiled. Good point. "Marnie, I'll catch up with you at Mayberry. If there's nothing else, I'll get on the road." He left them to chat and headed back down to Jane to say goodbye.

CHAPTER 21

DI Marsh had been a brick about it, meeting the parents once Isabella's father had returned in haste from London. That left Wild free to follow some leads. First order of the day though, back in Wiltshire, was a hot shower and a toothbrush. After that he searched the web for the newspaper offices. No great surprise that the local rag was run from Chippenham, twenty miles away. Local with a small 'l'.

The Chronicle's editor-in-chief, Norman Easton, said on the phone that he was happy to make time for the police. Well, maybe happy was overselling it. He'd given Wild a thirty-minute window with the suggestion that a solicitor might be present.

Wild arrived at the front desk and made friends with the receptionist, a pasty-faced lad of around twenty who looked as though he was waiting for something better to come along. Maybe he was a cub reporter filling in for the day. All Wild could say for certain was that he hadn't mastered the phone switchboard. On the third try, he managed to reach the correct extension and then told Wild someone would be down directly.

Norman Easton leaned over a glass balcony, called Wild by his rank and beckoned him up. He climbed the stairs while Easton held the door, its plaintive buzzing reminiscent of a fly under a glass.

"We're in here, Sergeant." Easton navigated through an open-plan office where no one gave Wild a second glance, the constant thrum of keyboards and distant telephones suggesting a hive of industry if not virtue.

Wild followed him into the glasshouse, where blinds hung at half-mast and obscured the interesting part of the view. A woman sat at the head of a rectangular glass table, crimson nails resting on a coffee cup. This, he surmised, was the boss, since even solicitors knew their place. He sat to her immediate right and Easton sat opposite him, rendering the rest of the table redundant.

Easton pushed his rolled-up shirtsleeves past the elbows. "Let's get one thing straight before we start, Sergeant — we ran a legitimate story of local interest."

"No one is suggesting otherwise, Mr Easton. However, there was information in the article that was not public knowledge, and as there was no byline we are understandably keen to speak to the *journalist* responsible." He stretched the word out for effect.

The woman turned to Easton. "Norman?"

"We, er, have a number of freelancers, you might call them, who supply us with stories on the basis of anonymity."

Norman's boss stared across at him without speaking; a look familiar to Wild from similar encounters with DI Marsh. It took maybe ten seconds to wear him down.

Easton sighed like a teenager who's been asked to clear up their own mess. "Okay, I'll look into it and get back to DS Wild."

Wild went for the kill. "The thing is Norman — can I call you Norman? You wouldn't run a story like that unless you trusted the source. So either a police officer has been speaking out of turn, or your mystery . . . journalist . . . is someone you can rely on. Someone well known to you. How about you go check your records, while I wait here with . . . ?"

The woman smiled, gently tapping a coffee cup like subtle applause. "Gretchen Lambert, owner and managing director." She proffered a hand.

Easton skulked away to lick his wounds. As the door closed behind him he found time to bellow at one of the underlings.

The newspaper proprietor rolled her eyes. "How are you finding Wiltshire, DS Wild?"

"Surprisingly lively. Please, call me Craig. And how is the newspaper business?"

Gretchen rubbed a lipstick mark on her cup with a napkin. "Fighting a continual rearguard action against the internet." She caught him staring at her cup. "Sorry, bad manners. Would you like some coffee?"

"That depends on how long I'm going to be here."

As if in reply she picked up the phone. "It's Gretchen. I'm in meeting room one. Could you be a dear and bring a coffee for my guest? And a couple of Danish pastries if you can find them. Thank you." She put the phone down.

Wild took a stab in the dark. "I take it you know my DI. I imagine you're one of her network's movers and shakers."

"Wow. You really need to work on your small talk, Craig. Yes, of course I know Morag — as you say, we move and shake together."

An underling appeared, bearing gifts. Wild received them with gratitude and made himself comfortable.

Gretchen took another sip. "We'd like to do a little feature on you actually — if you're willing. London Detective starts new chapter in Wiltshire."

"I'll pass, thanks. I'm not much of a story."

"Yes, that's what Morag said." She got up and checked through the blinds. "I imagine Norman is ringing his source."

Wild felt his lip curling. Hedging his bets, more like. At least the coffee was good.

When Easton came back, he did not appear a happy man. "My freelancer has agreed to let me share his phone number."

"I'll need more than that — name, address, landline and mobile."

Gretchen's gaze was implacable. "Do it, Norman."

"Okay," he took a piece of paper out of his pocket and handed it over like a guilty secret. "His name is Adam Napier."

Gretchen nearly popped a vein. "Why didn't you tell me that we're still sending money his way?"

"It's the editor's privilege to use the journalists and stories he chooses. You agreed to that a long time ago. Napier's work is still good, even if his reputation isn't."

Gretchen explained to Wild, "He used to be on the staff. In his heyday he was a good reporter, especially crime. Even had a criminal biography published. But we had to let him go. A bit arrogant and we caught him double-dipping — moonlighting for other outlets with the same stories while on my payroll."

"Any thoughts on where I'd find him at this time of day?"

Gretchen didn't miss a beat. "Try the Red Lion."

* * *

Ben Galloway was his usual enthusiastic self on the phone. "What's on, Skip?"

"I'm meeting a lead in a pub — thought you might like to join me in the Red Lion."

"Right, the thing is, I was going to take my break with my uncle."

"That's fine. Bring Sergeant Galloway along too."

Adam Napier would have been easy to spot even without Norman Easton's description. A tall man in his mid-50s, wearing a leather bomber jacket that looked as if it had actually been in a war. He sat alone, nursing a pint as though it were a grudge — always within reach and seldom ignored. On first impressions he was poring over a newspaper. Wild's guess would be a crossword or the racing pages, judging by the flickering pen. As he got closer Wild spotted the pen travelling to Napier's lap and a waiting notepad.

The two Galloways arrived and headed over to the bar. Napier sat a little straighter and sought sanctuary in his pint. Wild knew that Napier and Anthony Galloway were well acquainted.

He approached the journalist, a job that ranked high on his top ten of least respected professions. "It's Adam, isn't it? Can I buy you a pint? Or maybe a short?"

Napier licked his lips, any sense of caution outweighed by the prospect of a free drink. He looked Wild over, edged out a chair with his foot and lifted an empty whisky glass from the floor beside him. "A scotch would be lovely."

Wild returned with a whisky in one hand and a fruit juice in the other.

"Let me guess — you don't drink while you're on duty. Is that what they taught you in London?"

Wild sipped his orange juice and tried not to choke on it. "I want to talk about a recent story you supplied to the Chronicle."

Napier tried his whisky, nodded appreciatively and then sank a mouthful of lager. "I was thinking about a follow-up piece from a copper's perspective — perhaps one of the investigation team. Any chance of a quote?"

"Sure. 'Withholding information from the police is never a good idea and likely to bite you on the arse.' Now, your article."

"Look, officer," Napier mocked, spreading his hands wide as if pleading his innocence. I'm a journalist — I hear things and I write them down. That's not a crime."

"So you're saying someone gave you this information?"

"I'm not saying that — you're saying it."

Wild took another slug of orange juice and chose his next words carefully. "Did you receive information from a serving police officer about an ongoing investigation?"

Napier sat back for a moment. His face suggested he was enjoying every moment, and Wild badly wanted to rearrange that face. "No, Sergeant Wild. No one has *intentionally* fed me information. But police officers were asking questions of several people at the literary festival, on the day in question."

Wild glanced over his shoulder to the bar. "Thank you for your time, Mr Napier. We may need to speak with you again."

"I look forward to it."

As he got up, Wild noticed the tremor in Napier's hand. When Wild reached the bar Galloway Senior raised his glass a little, as if in commiseration.

"Adam Napier has always been a difficult bugger. Sometimes he's the policeman's friend on the Chronicle, other times a thorn in our side. Would you like me to have a word?" Galloway's tone suggested something more persuasive.

"No. You could do something else for me though. I need to know which of the uniforms spoke to Adam Napier after we found the body. He's suggesting someone said something inadvertently, within earshot. You two coming back to the police station?"

Galloway glanced at his nephew. "No, that's alright, Craig. We'll see you there."

CHAPTER 22

A tête-à-tête with DI Marsh was inevitable. Like Christmas or occasional diarrhoea. She wanted answers and Wild figured he had a lot to answer for. He didn't bother rehearsing his half of the conversation on the drive over. When it came to the DI it never paid to be too prepared.

DI Stanton was present at the debriefing. Only he seemed to be in the spotlight too. Wild couldn't help wondering, based on recent events, just how well Lee Rickard had been protected.

Marsh picked up a glass paperweight and pressed it between her palms. "So let me get this straight, we have no witnesses to the arson and threat to endanger life. And Juliette Kimani and her husband are considering legal action. If you have any good news this would be the time to share it."

Wild waited to see whether DI Stanton had anything to offer. Not a word. Fair enough, he'd give it a go himself.

"With respect, ma'am, we now know that Isabella Kimani and Lee Rickard were in a relationship, which explains why Juliette was willing to cough up a further ten grand to keep him out of her daughter's life. Juliette never mentioned any of this before."

Stanton joined the conversation. "Had she done so, we might have taken pre-emptive and additional steps to keep Isabella safe."

Marsh placed the paperweight on her desk with infinite care. "Spoken like a lawyer."

Wild stood behind Stanton's chair. "He's right though. We could only act on the information available. And let's remember that we weren't the ones who drove Isabella away from the family home."

"We'll need better than that, Craig. And what about this newspaper article?"

"Napier says . . . well, he *implies* that he overheard information from one of the uniformed team. Sergeant Galloway is looking into it. It's possible. I can't see any of ours speaking to a journalist voluntarily."

Marsh stared into the gap between Stanton and Wild. "I'll prep the DCI and see if we can head Juliette off at the pass."

Wild thought this a good moment to impress. "If you're meeting Juliette Kimani and her legal team, it might be worth mentioning that the pathologist identified traces of anti-anxiety medication in Lee Rickard's body. And then add that I saw anti-anxiety meds in her bathroom cabinet." He paused for a moment and then said what he surmised Marsh was thinking. "Similar to the ones I used to take."

Marsh ignored his last sentence. "Yes, Dr Bell advised me that you'd opened up another line of enquiry. I prefer my officers to keep me briefed."

Wild took umbrage. "Understood, but I was waiting for results and I sort of had my hands full."

Marsh slapped her hands down on the desk. "Okay, shall we stop treating this briefing like a sarcasm support group? If this goes against us, we are all in the shit. So let's coordinate and cooperate. I will deal with Juliette. DI Stanton," she spoke directly to Wild, "is liaising with the Lincolnshire Police and the National Crime Agency over the arson attack. And you, Craig—"

He sensed a put-down approaching. "Can I just say, there's a world of difference between poison and arson, but the crimes must be connected because the victims are. And if we were looking for a prime mover — albeit without any evidence at this point — Paul Maguire must be top of the list."

Marsh bobbed her head side to side. "There's a certain kind of logic to that. First revenge and then loose ends? For all we know, Rickard may have held back information from Maguire's trial as a sort of insurance policy."

Stanton ventured, "For all the good it did him."

Wild's head hurt. "So what are we saying here? That Rickard gave information to Isabella?"

Marsh drummed her fingers on the desk. "Or somebody thinks he did. Either way, we need to interview Paul Maguire again. And by *we*, I mean myself and DI Stanton." She paused, as if she'd suddenly made up her mind about something. "Craig, you'd best liaise with Bristol CID to check where the Hoyle family were."

"Okay. It might be a good idea to speak to Maguire's solicitor as well."

She stared at Wild while he did his best impression of inscrutable. "It's your call, literally. He'll want to know why we're re-interviewing his client in any case. That'll be all, Craig."

* * *

Wild knew one thing for certain: this called for strong coffee. He fuelled up on caffeine and doodled on some scrap paper.

"Yes, hello, I'd like to speak to Donald Jacobson. My name is Detective Sergeant Craig Wild. No, I'd rather not discuss this matter with anyone else."

He waited while the bureaucratic machine slipped into gear — painful muzak, two bursts of static as someone tried an extension, and then Donald came to the phone.

"Mr Wild, to what do I owe the pleasure?"

He wiped out Jacobson's telephone smile with one sentence. "I'm ringing to let you know what sort of man

Paul Maguire is. I spent last night in a Lincolnshire hospital while a woman and a teenage girl were fighting for their lives, following a targeted arson attack. Thankfully they're going to be fine. Curiously, the teenager was the girlfriend of Jordan Hughes, the prosecution witness who helped put Paul Maguire and Cody Faulkner away." He hammered the point home. "The one who died."

Silence.

"Are you still there, Donald?" He assumed so. "My DI is making arrangements to re-interview your client. I suggest you take a long hard look in the mirror and ask yourself whether he's worth it. If anything further happens to anyone connected with this case, there'll be nowhere to hide." He quickly flipped the piece of paper for the quote he'd lifted off a Masonic website. "Isn't justice one of your four cardinal virtues?"

Wild heard laboured breathing on the phone and then Donald swallowed.

"I'll speak to my client." It sounded like an admission of failure.

Wild added as an afterthought, "You seem like a reasonable bloke. Do yourself a favour and get out while you can."

Jacobson took his time replying. "And you think I ever had a choice? Thank you for your call, Detective Sergeant."

Wild had heard that tone before — from his father's lips, in a hospital consultant's office, when the test results confirmed a diagnosis. He took a walk to the canteen for more coffee and to get some distance from his thoughts. Marnie waved him over.

"Hi, Craig, I was hoping to run into you. Cheer up, Isabella is doing really well — she should be home tomorrow. How is your vicar friend?" She couldn't help smiling as she said it.

He stalled, realising he hadn't bothered to ring the hospital since returning to Wiltshire.

"Anyway, like I said I'm glad to catch you. What are you up to later? I could split a curry with you."

"Curry house or takeaway?"

She blushed. "I was, er, hoping for a takeaway. I've still got my houseguest so I was . . ."

"Hoping to make up numbers? Okay, It will be nice to see your place finally."

"No, not, uh . . . I was thinking of yours. Just for an hour." She shook her head. "Sorry, what was I thinking? You've got the darts match tonight." Her face fell in time with his.

"No, I . . . er . . . asked them to leave me on the reserve list. Didn't want to muscle in as an outsider and take a regular slot." He hadn't even convinced himself.

"Quite right too." She smiled gamely. "Give the others a chance." Her face grew serious again. "Seven o'clock okay then, or we could make it earlier?"

He thought she sounded desperate. "Any time from six onwards is fine by me."

"Great," she nearly lurched forward in relief. "Let's say six, and maybe you could order in advance?"

* * *

Wild got home not long after five. Marsh hadn't made it back from Bristol but as far as he was concerned he'd been on duty since the early hours. There wasn't much to tidy up but he gave the sink a scrub — and the toilet, changed a hand towel and put down a fresh tablecloth. The food arrived at five-fifty when he was wondering whether he could squeeze in a quick call to Jane Houghton. Not long after, the doorbell sounded.

Marnie stood there expectantly. "Thanks Wild, I really appreciate it. Wasn't it Oscar Wilde who said that guests and fish start to smell after three days?"

"Actually, some people say it was Ben Franklin." He stopped talking, aware that he sounded like a complete anorak. He stood aside and held the door open. As she eased past, motorbike helmet in hand, he noticed the rucksack on her back.

Marnie found talking easier with food.

"I don't mind helping people out if they are going through a rough patch, but contrary to popular belief psychologists are not therapists. And I'm not even a psychologist! He is driving me mad. He doesn't leave the flat. He doesn't clear up after himself. He just sits there and watches television, and not the good stuff either."

Wild ate some lamb bhuna in lieu of Dutch courage. "So what is he then, an ex-boyfriend?"

"No," she stabbed a piece of broccoli, "not quite. He's an old friend and yes, back in the day, maybe there was a possibility of something happening." She stalled. "We are talking years ago. But it's always been strictly mates and he's just had a difficult marriage breakup."

"Is there any other kind?"

She laughed. "Honestly, Wild, I don't know what to do with him. I was even wondering if, you being a bloke, maybe you could take him out for a pint and bond."

"No, no . . . you've got me all wrong. What you are looking for is a dog person — social, affable. I'm a cat person — antisocial, prefer my own company." He paused for a moment. "A bit like you really in that regard."

"I see your point. Thing is, I can't just send him back to his lonely flat in Chislehurst."

He wrinkled his brow.

"Just south of London. God, you really don't do geography at all. Well, not unless there's been a battle there."

He defended himself with a fork. "Never needed geography in London. As long as you can read a Tube map, or a railway map at a push, you have everything you need." As soon as he said the words he regretted it. He must have sounded like a sad sap. He changed the subject. "What's in the bag?"

She showed him by way of a reply. He appreciated the attention to detail, not only a map indicating the garden thefts but also colour coded and tabulated folder for items taken.

"Do you think it's over the top?"

He studied one of Marnie's lists. "It'll be a bloke and he probably needs money for drugs, statistically speaking."

"There is no chance of getting a forensic team out for a shed burglary — I did ask."

They shared the joke over the last two pakoras.

"If it was me," he dabbed the last splodge of curry from his plate. "I'd review everything I know. What you've done gives you a framework. Now you need to see the pattern. There's always one. Nothing is ever entirely random."

"The thefts are all easy access and mostly good quality garden tools."

"Mostly?"

"Yeah, some other things too. Vintage stuff — from the eighties. Some men have a shed as a hideaway so there's a radio taken, an old laptop and some vintage porn apparently — reported on condition that I don't mention it to his wife."

"Presume you're checking all the car boots and usual online trading spots." He said it as a statement.

"Not yet, but planning to. Any other thoughts?"

He turned the puzzle around in his head. "What about knocking on doors and encouraging people to mark their possessions with a UV pen? At least you'll be able to prove they were stolen if you find anything in the future."

"I like that." She stared at her watch, as blatant as a curry stain. "I had better be making tracks. Thanks, Wild."

"Any time. Good luck with your guest. How long is he staying?"

She sighed. "I don't know. Like I said, he was very good to me when things got difficult at uni. It's only fair I return the favour in his hour of need." She delivered the lines unconvincingly.

"If you want to give him my advice . . ." One look at her face told him she didn't, but he carried on talking. "Better he makes a clean break of it rather than prolong the pain. Rip it off quickly, like a plaster."

She blinked, incredulous. "A plaster? Thanks, I'll be sure to pass that nugget of wisdom on."

He shrugged. "I speak from experience."

Seven o'clock in the evening and the silence was deafening. He cleared the table and picked out a DVD at random from the box, one hand over his eyes to avoid cheating. *Father Ted* — a sure-fire comedy winner. Washing up first and then a cup of tea. He caught his reflection in the TV screen and remembered when he and Stephanie were all about vodka jellies and sushi. The absence of any bitterness now was almost tender. He tried to picture her, heavily pregnant up in London. Unless she'd had the sprog by now. Best not knowing. Different worlds.

His mobile jolted him back to the present.

"Craig, it's Anthony Galloway. Listen, mate, I know it's short notice but we're a man down on the team tonight. Glenn Ebury has cancelled last minute and we were wondering . . ."

He gazed around the living room where unpacked boxes of his stuff still hugged the walls. He stopped the DVD. Not tonight, Mrs Doyle. "Where are you playing? I'll get a cab and meet you there."

"No need, I'll send Ben over if you text him your address."

CHAPTER 23

Wild wasn't into socialising anymore, especially with people he didn't know well, but he had little else to do with his evening now and he was tiring of his own company.

Ben Galloway picked him up from home, having drawn the short straw as designated driver. He let Ben wait outside and he seemed quite happy there when Wild glanced out of an upstairs window. Galloway was still perky when he emerged five minutes later.

"Big game tonight, Craig. It'd be nice to wipe the floor with the Gable Cross team."

Wild buckled up, realising that Galloway was capable of saying his proper name if he chose to. For once, he decided, he'd try and let his hair down. The Mayberry nick wouldn't lose face against its nearest neighbour if he had anything to do with it.

* * *

Morning arrived like an unwanted guest. He remembered the night in flashback sequences; the flashes firing in his head. He'd started off lightly with a pint and a chaser. He had played like an artist, a Michelangelo of darts. And as if by osmosis, most of the team had made a good fist of it as well. Only Ben Galloway, the teetotaller for the night, had abstained.

Then things got hazy, a grey canvas of noise and revelry interspersed with magical dart throwing, a triumph of precision and physics. A one-forty, a one-three-eight, and even a ninety-six finish. He had held his own, and maintained his centre of gravity, managing to leave the pub upright and climb into Ben's car unaided. Safely deposited at home, he had shut and bolted the door, filled a pint glass with water and made a half-arsed attempt to clean his teeth. And then . . . nothing . . . the sleep of oblivion until seven a.m., when he woke with his head pounding like a disco.

He reached for the water and painkillers, raising a glass to himself for his foresight. One Olympically long piss later, he washed his hands and tightened the sink tap that had dripped all night before manoeuvring his way to the kitchen, nursing the mother of all headaches. He was still staring into space gone eight a.m. with a half-drunk cup of tea in his hand when his home phone erupted into life.

"Wild, it's Marsh. Why is your work phone switched off? You better get in here, soon as. The word on the wire is that Maguire's solicitor is dead. Apparently his office looks like an abattoir."

Wild felt his stomach spasm in sympathy.

"We'll be leaving for Bristol once you arrive. Incidentally, I heard about your exploits last night. You better bring some painkillers — it's going to be a long day."

Once he was off the phone with Marsh he turned on his work mobile, chugging back warm tea as he picked up a new message sent the previous night.

"Wild, it's Donald," the voice trailed off, replaced with a leaden groan. "After the interview . . . in prison . . . I told Maguire I was through . . . I won't be party to firebombing children. John Donner came here, attacked me — on Maguire's orders. Wild, it's bad . . ."

Wild heard frantic breathing and as it began to fade it he realised he was hearing the last seconds of a dying man. Then a strangled cry of agony cut through.

"Oh God, they're coming back." Jacobson swallowed hard and then said in a forced, guttural whisper, "Get them, Wild. Get them for me."

The next thing Wild heard was muffled voices, rooting through drawers and cabinets by the sound of it. And then one voice that he had to concentrate to hear.

"Are you sure he's dead, John?"

Another voice drew closer, more distinct. "Take a closer look if you want." And then laughter, as the same voice added casually, "This isn't my first time. Chalky wanted him to suffer first and wanted him to know why. No one walks away. You'd do well to remember that, junior. Right, have you found something suitable? Chalky loves his little trophies. Let me just take a picture to send to him."

After the footsteps receded and the door closed there was only a deathly silence.

* * *

Wild was at the front door in ten minutes. Donald Jacobson's phone call replayed in his head. Marsh would no doubt tell him that he couldn't have done anything, and maybe that was true. But he could do something now. He marvelled at Donald's courage, providing crucial testimony in his last moments that pointed the finger at Maguire. Wild wondered what *he* would do with his final minutes. And who the fuck was John Donner?

His head was still throbbing as he parked up. He had believed, when he first signed up with the Metropolitan Police, that their primary job was to keep the peace and protect the public — sometimes from itself. Since making detective he'd realised that his role was more about mopping up and holding others accountable for the mess. He marched straight into Marsh's office, phone in hand.

"About time! I was thinking of sending out a search party."

Wild shut the office door and Marsh sat back down again. "What's wrong?"

He cued up the message and let Jacobson speak for himself. Afterwards, they sat together in silence until Marsh spoke. She simply said, "Fuck."

Wild had nothing to add.

"I'll pass this on to the Bristol team." She caught the look on his face. "Give me a few minutes to make some calls — I'll need your phone. And you look like you need some coffee and toast."

"Ma'am," He closed her door behind him quietly, wondering when the painkillers would start to kick in.

By the time Marsh appeared in the canteen, Wild had puzzled out two thoughts. First, if John Donner was telling the truth — and why wouldn't he be? — Maguire was at the heart of all this. Maybe they could use that to leverage something else from Cody Faulkner. And second, could John Donner be involved in the death of Lee Rickard? If he were working for Maguire he'd probably have access to ketamine.

What Wild hadn't decided about was whether Donner still had a job to complete on Isabella Kimani.

Marsh took her time coming over to his table. "Are you fit?" It sounded more of a challenge than a question.

He tidied his notes away. "Never better."

"Good because you're driving."

CHAPTER 24

Wild figured they would call in at Keynsham first but Marsh had other ideas. She'd rung ahead and directed Wild — he knew she was good at that — to the crime scene. The presence of police tape and uniformed officers outside had attracted the great British public like wasps to a picnic. Wild parked where he was told and walked a step behind Marsh, using her as a human shield. They flashed their warrant cards and ducked under the tape, ignoring the arsewipe with a camera who seemed intent on earning a trip to the cells by boosting his social media profile.

They donned white boiler suits and facemasks at the doorway and followed instructions from one of the team, carefully picking their way along the corridor. A junior officer was bent forward, just outside the office door, breathing slowly into his knees. Wild prepared himself for the worst.

Dust hung in the stilted air and the quiet, delicate movements of the SOCO and her team lent the room an almost religious atmosphere. Only the body was absent, but the copious amount of blood sprayed around the room and soaked into the grey carpet created quite a horror show.

The SOCO got up from her crouched position and enunciated clearly through her mask. "You'll be the team from Wiltshire then? I'm Dr Shah." She pointed to a bloodied mobile phone in a clear plastic evidence bag. "It fell out of his sock when they moved the body." She looked at Wild. "Were you the one he called?"

He nodded, and wondered how long he could keep his unscripted visit to Donald Jacobson quiet. As he turned his head slowly to take in the panorama a dreadful thought lodged in his brain. He might have been the catalyst for this bloodbath.

After they'd seen the sights, Wild and Marsh went outside to wait for the local DI. An Audi — old enough to be a used car, but still beyond Wild's means — pulled into a space. Wild watched a friendly face emerge from the passenger seat — DC Grazia Kelley, family liaison officer to the Hoyle family.

They approached and Wild raised a welcoming hand.

Kelley cut him down to size. "You bastard! Tench told me everything."

He stood there and took it, partly because senior officers were present and partly because it was a small price to pay for getting Stuart Hoyle out of the shit. Besides, he had a bigger albatross around his neck.

Marsh barely looked at him. "Go and wait in the car."

He watched the three of them walking away, like a dog behind glass, and decided to make good use of his time. A quick internet search nabbed him an out-of-office mobile number for the late Donald's office.

Henry, the tea boy, spoke softly and slowly, as if each word had been wrung out of him. Wild cut him some slack. Trauma did that to a person.

"I was going to stay late, but he rang me after his prison visit and insisted I go home. Do you think he knew . . . ?"

"No, Henry, he was simply looking out for you." He waited for the inevitable question, the one that always tore a copper's guts out.

"They wouldn't let us inside the building. I stood outside for a while and I saw a police officer come out crying. Would it have been quick?"

Time for a well-practised lie. "I don't know. We are waiting for the pathologist's report." He tried distraction. "Did you know Donald well? We want to build up a picture of his life."

"Not really. I heard that his daughter died in a fire some years ago, when she was in her twenties I think. And his ex-wife emigrated to Australia." There was a leaden pause. "Are you attending the funeral? It will probably only be a few work people otherwise — one of the senior staff is organising everything."

Wild wriggled on the hook for a couple of seconds and then told himself he might get more information there. "Sure. Give me the organiser's number and I'll make sure I get the details."

Next on his to-do list was Sergeant Galloway, who confirmed that every officer at the literary festival had been questioned — tactfully, he emphasised — about what they might or might not have let slip to Joe and Joanna Public.

"Another thing, Craig, I got Napier's picture off the web — from a few years ago, mind. None of the team remembered speaking to him or seeing him there."

"Maybe he's good at blending into the background. I've never liked journalists — not even London ones."

"How's your head by the way? You were pretty hammered last night."

"I'll live." He cringed at his own words. "Gotta go. Thanks, Anthony."

He saved the best call until last.

Marnie wasted no time on small talk. "How are you, Wild? I heard about the Bristol solicitor — word gets around."

"Yeah, it does. Listen, I was thinking about your 'temporary' flatmate. Why don't you set him up on a night out with Belinda? She's pretty . . ."

"Oh, you noticed that, did you! And why would she do me a favour?"

"What if the four of us go for a meal and we leave them to it? Say a work thing has come up or something. I can ask Ben to ring me."

She hesitated. "We leave *together* . . . ?"

"Yeah, and then we go our separate ways. It'd save me cooking for a night — and washing up."

She sighed. "Well, it would get him out the flat, I suppose. But who's going to convince Belinda?" That was obviously a hint for Wild.

"Okay, leave that with me. I'll tell her it's a spur-of-the-moment thing, either tonight or tomorrow night."

"That's a bit sudden, don't you think?"

"Let's see what she says."

One awkward phone call later he was inviting Belinda to a pub meal for four. Once he explained — in confidence — about Marnie's close friend and his broken marriage, Belinda didn't need much convincing. He was still congratulating himself when Marsh appeared on the horizon heading his way. He watched her parting company with the Bristol CID duo, none of them looking in his direction.

"Cheers for that," he said to his reflection. "Invisible as a journalist."

He started the car as soon as Marsh got back inside.

She said one word, "Mayberry," and then stayed silent for the next fifteen minutes.

He figured she was pissed off because of DC Kelley's outburst. He was wrong.

"You see, Craig, I can't get my head around why Donald Jacobson telephoned you. I mean, you're a virtual stranger . . . why did he even have your work mobile number." She gave him her best Medusa impression. "You gonna tell me about it?"

It had already been a shit day, bar the prospect of a meal out, so what was there to lose? "I went to see Donald Jacobson after DI Stanton and I met Maguire in prison."

Her fingers interlocked. "Go on."

"That's about it really. We had a chat, I drank some tea and then I left. As you'll recall, DI Stanton did something similar with Cody Faulkner's solicitor."

"Yeah, but he told me about it."

"Sorry, boss. I didn't think it amounted to anything."

"That's for me to decide."

CHAPTER 25

Wild started getting ready at six o'clock. He enjoyed the ritual of an evening out — this part anyway — especially as there was nothing riding on it. No nerves this time, no agonising over what impression his shirt conveyed, or whether he was sporting nasal hair. Since his arrival in Wiltshire, a few months back, he'd had two social drinks and one nearly-date with a woman from the Labyrinth community café — the less said about that the better. This time he couldn't fail because he wasn't competing.

He glanced at his clock: six fifteen. If everything went to plan he'd be home and dry before nine, alone. Marnie texted him confirm the kick-off time and that Belinda was still coming. He answered in the affirmative, neglecting to mention that Belinda was meeting him a few minutes early. Marnie had been pretty cagey about the fourth seat at the table, this bloke from a failed marriage who'd been hanging around her flat. At least he'd have something in common with him.

To pass the time he switched on the TV, flicked through the channels and landed in the middle of a documentary on the Battle of Jutland. He wasn't that interested in Naval conflicts, but he stuck with it for the remaining half hour.

He timed it to perfection. Out the door before seven p.m. and approaching the pub at seven fifteen. The Plough Horse had great reviews and few pretensions, as its menu was casual enough to pass for pub food but a cut above chicken in a basket.

Belinda looked at least half a million dollars. She knew how to dress well without trying too hard. He admired that level of confidence. Steph had it too. Maybe it was a class thing, or money. He joined her at the table and thanked her again for making up a foursome at short notice. He didn't bother telling her she looked great. Hopefully Marnie's visitor would take care of that.

"To be honest, Belinda, I didn't know who else to ask. I really appreciate it."

She didn't seem to take offence, which he took as a good sign. Plus, she'd made the effort so maybe had a game plan to outshine Marnie and score points. He offered to get her a drink although she already had one. She declined. The silence seemed to expand around them. He tried not to check his watch and she saved him the bother by returning to her phone.

"We're a couple of minutes early," he explained, in case she thought Marnie and Leo had changed their minds. Unless of course, they had.

"How do you find working with Marnie?"

It sounded like an innocent question, except with the benefit of Marnie's private history lesson he knew it was nothing of the kind.

"Yeah, good. She's really going places." He felt himself blush, aware that Belinda was watching him intently. "How long have you two been . . ."

"Friends?" Her gaze turned inward for a moment. "Oh, we go back years." She lifted her wine glass and then put it down again. "You said Leo is a close friend from her uni days?"

He nodded a fraction and smiled. Clearly, Belinda had never heard of him. He played it like the poker games in the police station canteen, back in London. Those after-hours sessions had taught him more about psychology than any lecture Marnie might have attended. Slow and easy, small details that allowed Belinda to fill in her own blanks.

Leo and Marnie arrived a few minutes late. Marnie had neglected to paint a picture of Leo but now they were here she didn't have to. *Rugby player or maybe a rower at uni, good looking and knows it so probably a serial cheat.* And he had that whole smart-casual thing honed like a blade.

Marnie made the introductions and as soon as they sat down someone came over to take their drinks orders. Wild stuck with half a lager to start and let the others argue the toss about wine. It intrigued him to watch Marnie in a new environment, so different from takeaways at his place. She looked great too, not that he'd ever tell her that!

The conversation had all the excitement of a wake. He guessed that Leo had been told to steer clear of discussing work, so he launched in.

"What do you do for a living, Leo?"

Marnie narrowed her eyes.

"I'm a surveyor. People often misunderstand what we do."

Belinda seemed to suddenly find surveying the most fascinating subject on earth. After ten minutes of non-stop discussion about property horror stories and the ins and outs of why a chartered surveyor was the only one you could really trust, Wild was losing the will to live. Any more of this and he'd go and cook the food himself.

Leo finished a thrilling story about concrete and then returned the favour. "I know you two uphold the law," he laughed a little at his own wit, "but what about you, Belinda? How did you end up working with dead people?"

She was cagier than Wild had expected, spending more time talking about the minutiae of the job than how she got into it. He didn't mind — it was similar to his own job — and clearly neither did Leo, who seemed fascinated.

Part way through the food, Wild excused himself and managed to avoid using the word *piss*. He texted Ben

Galloway from a cubicle, setting a ten-minute gap before Ben should ring him at the table. Then he made sure the volume on his phone was set to maximum. It all went perfectly to plan. A sudden phone call, near the end of dinner and just after they'd discussed dessert. He took the call away from the table but stayed where they could see him. And when he returned, it only took a couple of sentences to excuse himself and Marnie.

Belinda asked, "Is this the *you-know-who* case?"

He nodded dolefully, full of apologies, and they both left money on the table. Marnie said she'd ring if there were any chance of getting back to them. One glance from the door told Wild all he needed to know. Outside, he gave Marnie some advice.

"I reckon you can lock the front door tonight."

"Don't judge other people by your own standards."

He took it on the chin. Maybe she was right. "I'll give you a lift home."

She shook her head as if dislodging a bug. "I can get a cab."

"Don't be silly."

She thought about it and relented. "Sorry, Wild. I'm a bit weirded out seeing Leo flirting — if you can call it that — with someone other than Faye. She's a friend of mine too, remember."

Wild was pretty sure *weirded* wasn't a proper word, but he let it go. He dropped Marnie off at an up-and-down house, long since split into two flats. She never invited him in and he certainly wasn't going to suggest it, so he made it home in double-quick time.

Part way through *Father Ted* Marnie's number flashed up on his mobile.

"Sorry about earlier. I might have been a bit harsh with you . . ."

He knew her well enough now not to interrupt.

". . . Only it felt like you were pimping Leo out."

He paused the DVD player. "I didn't see him complaining."

"No," she squeezed every ounce of disappointment into one tiny word. "The thing is, Faye rang tonight for Leo. Their breakup might not be as permanent as he thinks."

"Ah."

"I lied and said he was out with you. I hope you can live with the guilt, if anything happens tonight."

He hoped she was joking.

CHAPTER 26

Henry from the solicitors' office hadn't undersold it. There were so few people at the funeral that Wild had no chance of fading into the background. Four staff, one of whom had already asked Wild on the quiet what would happen to the business, and a couple of clients who'd decided at the last minute that they wanted to pay their respects. No flowers because Donald 'didn't believe in them'. Not much of a tally for a life and no local coppers present due to operational commitments, which Wild read as 'couldn't be arsed'. Jacobson must have sat opposite the police in many interview rooms *and* he'd worked for Maguire, which collectively covered a multitude of sins.

A perfunctory service played out like an amateur dramatics production. The padre who spoke in clichés and opened with the line, "I never knew Donald personally but I like to think . . ." The sobbing secretary who probably held a torch for the departed. A fleeting reference to Donald's late daughter (no mention of his ex-wife in Brisbane) and a turgid reading on the frailty of human life that Wild half-remembered his mother quoting in his youth. And after fifteen minutes the curtain came down to Frank Sinatra's *My Way*. You couldn't make it up.

Although drinks afterwards sounded like an excellent idea, he declined the invitation and went off to sit in the park by himself. The same thought reverberated in his head: had he unwittingly sent Donald Jacobson to his death? Unable to arrive at a definitive answer, he opted to phone-a-friend.

"Hi Jane, it's Craig. Craig Wild."

She coughed to clear her throat. "Hello, Craig. Lovely to hear from you . . . oh, of course, today's the funeral. How was it?"

He stared at a toddler chasing hungry pigeons while a doting mother watched her savage-in-training. "Oh, you know . . . You always feel for the family left behind, but in this case there isn't one and somehow that's worse."

"You want to talk about it?"

"Nah, there's nothing else to say." He changed the subject. "What's the latest on your house?"

"It should be as good as new in a month. The parishioners have rallied round. I'm very lucky." She paused. "Any leads in your investigation?"

"I can't really talk about it."

"Of course. Sorry, silly of me to ask."

"Right, well, I'll leave you to it. Best be getting back to Mayberry."

"Thanks for ringing. Give my best to Isabella if you speak to her. I'm here if you ever feel like a chat, and if you happen to be in my vicinity the biscuit tin is always filled . . ."

He laughed, and for a few fleeting seconds he warmed to the idea. Then a pigeon fluttered towards him in blind panic and the moment passed.

Jane seemed to sense his mood. "You're not to blame for any of this. Not Donald and not Isabella. There are bad people in the world."

He snorted. "The presence of evil?"

"If you want to look at it that way, yes. You're doing everything you can, Craig, and that has to be enough."

When he got off the phone he thought about doing more. That meant another private chat with his boss.

* * *

"I see how strongly you feel about this, Craig, but the budget is finite. Two days of police protection in hospital is one thing. We can't station officers at her home indefinitely."

"He's still out there. Look, I'll do it for free. I can take a week's leave."

"Don't be bloody stupid. We've offered Juliette a panic button." She looked him right in his eyes. "We have to be pragmatic, Craig."

He felt his heart rate shifting up a gear. "Okay, hear me out. Three days at the house, incognito. And armed police on alert to respond."

She adopted a conciliatory tone. "There's no guarantee he'll try again — and certainly not to order."

"Maybe we can force his hand . . ."

Marsh hadn't liked the plan, although she conceded it had possibilities. After what she later described as a tense discussion, the *bean counters* — his words not hers, although she didn't object — approved her request. Marnie was easier to convince because Isabella specifically asked for her.

Before they moved into the Kimani family home under cover of darkness, Wild had another journey — back to Chippenham.

Gretchen Lambert didn't need much persuading, especially as *Morag* had pre-approved a deal. Juliette would give the Chronicle an exclusive, complete with a taster of her next novel, which they were free to syndicate afterwards. All Wild asked for in return was another generic front-page story, along the lines of: *Local girl receiving medical treatment at home after mysterious arson attack when visiting a friend on the east coast. The unnamed teenager, who has already battled cancer, is slowly recovering and local police are anxious to interview her about her ordeal when she is well enough.*

Wild collected an early edition and sent it to Paul Maguire's new solicitor's office anonymously, marked for Maguire: *as requested*. Now it was a waiting game.

CHAPTER 27

Marnie double-checked the locks, like the previous night. If it had been up to her she would've spirited the family away. At least she had been able to spend time with Isabella and improve her opinion of the police. The fly in the ointment was Isabella's father, Philippe Kimani, the playwright. He'd made his views very clear, that the police — two police forces, no less — had already let the family down. She still found it strange that Juliette had convinced him to allow them in their home like this, although Wild had said he'd spoken to her privately.

She found Wild sitting in the kitchen on his own, an extendable baton by his side. "Where is everyone?"

He pointed skyward. "TV room, upstairs. Having a little family time."

"What makes you so sure he'll come here?"

He stifled a smile. Part of Marsh's deal was keeping Marnie at the margins. He could give her a little, though. "We think Paul Maguire gives John Donner his orders, and Donner's none too bright."

"What if he's armed?"

"Unlikely. When he killed Donald Jacobson he wanted to terrorise him first. A gun would have been cleaner." He could tell by her face that he hadn't reassured her.

She glanced at her taser. "Are you sure we are up to this?"

He wiped the moisture from his lip with this thumb. "D'you know the last thing Donald said in his phone message to me? He said 'get them for me'. That's what we're going to do."

She broke eye contact. "I'll make some tea. Do you want to check on the family upstairs?"

He nodded politely and then went on his way. They looked startled when he put his head around the door. "Sorry, should have announced myself. Marnie is putting the kettle on if you want anything."

There were no takers. Juliette pulled Isabella close. "What will happen if the person you're after doesn't come here?"

An easy question with an uneasy answer. "We'll move you somewhere safe."

Isabella looked up from her mother's embrace. "I don't know anything, honest. All Lee told me was that he used to run with a bad crowd and it landed him in prison. He said he changed his name when he came out, but I never asked."

Juliette's face told Wild she knew far more than her daughter.

"I'll say goodnight then. See you all in the morning."

He crept back downstairs and made the promised ten p.m. call to Marsh.

"Keep your wits about you, Craig. And don't take any chances."

He signed off without pointing out the incongruity. This was all about chance. If this gamble worked, John Donner would be off the streets.

"Well," Marnie picked up her tea. "G'night, Wild."

Neither of them said what he knew they were thinking, that this was the third night in situ — hard won by Marsh from the DCI. *Third time's a charm* never felt more sinister.

He reminded her of the drill, just for something to say. "Leave the bedroom light on for about an hour, and then wait it out again. Goodnight."

* * *

Marnie felt a change in air temperature, the lightest of breezes, and sensed a heavy black shape at the window. She fought her instincts and stifled a scream, watching in dread as the window slowly eased open. Where the hell was Wild?

She knew that Donner could still back out now if she screamed, but if she let him get inside the house they could get him for burglary and possibly witness intimidation. She shifted silently under the duvet and felt for her taser.

As Donner dropped into the room with a soft thud he whispered in a throaty voice, "Make a sound and you're dead." She sat up, still in the dark and pressed back against the headboard to free up her arm.

"I'm going to teach you a lesson so you know to keep your mouth shut."

She saw a glint in the half-light and heard a movement by the door. In one swift moment she pulled out her taser and fired into the abyss. As she heard the pins strike the wall the door burst in, casting a pale light across the room. Wild charged forward and when Donner turned to him he caught a faceful of powder. Marnie could smell the spice from the bed.

"For fuck's sake, taser him," Wild barked.

Donner grabbed at him but Wild managed to evade him. Marnie took careful aim and discharged the second cartridge, fixing her quarry with 50,000 volts. Donner juddered to the ground, convulsing on the carpet.

A light came on, further along the landing.

"It's all under control, stay where you are," Wild called behind him in his standard issue public order voice. No one ventured out. Wild had already started, "You are under arrest on suspicion of burglary and murder . . ." so Marnie rang DI Marsh and tried to steady her nerves so she could get her words out.

Support arrived within ten minutes, along with Armed Response. It felt like the longest ten minutes of Marnie's life. Wild seemed unnaturally in control, almost enjoying it as he handcuffed Donner, who alternated between issuing threats and pleading for water on his face.

Wild joked to Marnie on the way to the police station that hell hath no fury like a midnight debriefing. Except he wasn't joking. DI Marsh was waiting in the otherwise empty open-plan office. Wild and Marnie went in together, like co-defendants. As they passed through the swing doors, Marsh got up from the edge of Wild's desk and put her mobile phone away.

"John Donner needed medical attention to wash his eyes out. Whose bright idea was it to throw pepper in his face?"

Wild raised an index finger. "I improvised." He didn't bother explaining that it was actually chilli powder.

"And you happened to have it handy when you reached the bedroom to support your colleague?"

He tried not to smirk. "I was putting things away in the kitchen."

"Not smart, Craig. And then, when he was already incapacitated," she turned her ire on Marnie, "you went ahead and tasered him!"

Marnie glanced to Wild.

"I told her to."

"Where were your brains, man? A clever solicitor will call that a disproportionate use of force and probably put in a complaint."

Wild pushed his shoulders back, the way he'd always done in the witness box. "With respect, ma'am . . ." He stared across the room. "I assessed the situation in line with the National Decision Model and I considered John Donner to be high risk because he was already suspected of murdering Donald Jacobson and committing an act of arson against two people — one of whom lived in the house he tried to burgle." He rolled a closing thought around in his head and then set it free. "The bottom line is: we got the job done."

"That you did," Marsh conceded. "But we're still on shaky ground. There's been no DNA or other forensic evidence as yet, linking anyone to Jacobson's murder."

"We have Donald's own testimony — that has to count for something? And there was another voice in the recording."

Marsh shook her head slowly. "It's all circumstantial until proven otherwise."

Marnie joined in. "So where does that leave us exactly?"

Marsh sighed through her nose and it sounded like a snort of derision. "Apart from the burglary, where he was caught bang to rights, we have nothing substantial. Donner has no record either — people have a habit of withdrawing complaints against him or 'realising' there was a misunderstanding. We're holding Donner for now and we'll interview him in the morning. Don't get your hopes up."

Wild felt bile rising. "He did it though."

"The Crown Prosecution Service needs something more credible in court than your opinion. Anyway, Donner's solicitor will be coming in first thing so, as the arresting officer, make sure you're at your best. Good teamwork, Marnie — it'll not go unnoticed. And don't forget to complete the paperwork for the discharged taser."

Will was still awake at 1 a.m., sitting in his living room, staring at the wall and vaguely aware of Radio 4 struggling on in the kitchen. Too late for a lone game of darts now, being neighbourly and all that, and no escape from Donald Jacobson's beyond-the-grave punchline in his head: *get them for me.*

He went to bed, closed his eyes and tried not to think — a recipe for insomnia that has failed to work since the dawn of time. As soon as he opened his eyes again, at four forty-nine, according to the clock, Marsh's assessment of the situation rushed back to taunt him. She was right of course. Without irrefutable forensic evidence, there'd be no prosecution for Jacobson's murder, especially if Donner concocted a cast-iron alibi. Plus, Donner had no previous record, the cunning bastard, so the burglary would be a first offence and he'd claim he didn't know the family were home. The threats he'd made would be Marnie's word against his and there was nothing incriminating so far from the arson investigation. Donner would opt for a guilty plea and remorse, suitably rehearsed by a solicitor would probably get a year, tops, or even walk free with a suspended sentence. So much for justice.

As he lay there, making shapes out of shadows, an idea burrowed up into his skull. Maybe it was sleep deprivation, or plain and simple vengeance for Donald Jacobson, but it suddenly seemed obvious that there was one way to punish Donner — and only one man to do it. After that he drifted off and slept the sleep of the just. For a couple of hours, anyway.

CHAPTER 28

Wild rang his DI at seven thirty sharp. She was not impressed.

"This had better be good, Craig. I'm eating my toast."

"I was thinking that this would be an ideal time to speak to Maguire. He'll be on the back foot with a new solicitor and John Donner in custody . . ."

"He won't know about Donner."

"He will if I tell him. We won't get another opportunity like this, especially if — as you said — we end up releasing Donner."

"Right." She crunched down the line. "I need to know exactly what you plan to say."

He rang HMP Bristol at eight thirty and managed to organise an interview at eleven a.m. sharp. Maguire was only too happy to see Wild again, even at short notice, with a solicitor present.

Marsh guaranteed Donner would still be in custody, even if they had to hold him pending other enquiries. It would also give the Bristol forensics team more time to deliver a very early Christmas miracle by finding some evidence against him.

Buoyed up by the fortunate turn of events, Wild rang Marnie.

"Hi, what time did you get away this morning?"

"About half an hour after you, Wild. The DI waited while I completed my taser paperwork. And when I say waited, I mean she hovered over me. I came in early today to catch up with Sergeant Galloway and now I'm being pressured to make progress on the garden thefts. So much for resting on my laurels."

"If it's any consolation, despite all our efforts yesterday I'm still not flavour of the month in CID either."

"When are you on your lunch break — I could meet you?"

"Sorry, I'm heading back up to Bristol to see Paul Maguire."

She didn't respond and he found himself answering a question she hadn't asked.

"It's all legit."

"Some advice from a friend? Call it practical psychology if you must! Don't get drawn in and don't antagonise him. You know what Maguire is capable of now."

* * *

Wild parked up on the outskirts of Bristol convinced that a bacon roll and a plastic tea would set him up for the day. An hour ahead of schedule he rang the prison to confirm it was all systems go. He had hoped that Cody Faulkner's brief would step in but apparently someone rustled up a stand-in instead.

He remembered Marsh's three words of advice, as he followed the escort to the interview room: don't bait him. Maguire was already there and beside him was a man aged about thirty-five, good looks and a good suit to match.

Wild took his seat and opened with, "Shall we make a start?"

Maguire had his arms folded across his chest. He looked bemused, like a Doberman staring down a smaller dog that refused to move. Wild made like a Jack Russell.

"Before we start, Mr Maguire, I'd like to offer my condolences about Mr Jacobson."

Maguire hardly moved although his breathing slowed, as if he were waiting for a danger to pass. "Thanks. He'd been with me for years. You can't put a price on that kind of loyalty." Maguire raised a hand to the man on his left. "This is a new brief I'm trying out — Mr . . ."

"Kershaw. Stephen Kershaw."

Wild sensed this was all an act for his benefit. Imply that you don't really know your solicitor and give the opposition a false sense of security.

"Well, Mr Kershaw. Let me explain why I'm here. Mr Maguire's previous solicitor was brutally murdered in his office." Kershaw's change of pallor showed Wild this was new information. "In the course of our investigations we identified a person of interest we wanted to speak with, a John Donner, who was arrested last night in the act of burglary. I believe you know Mr Donner, Mr Maguire?"

Maguire looked like he was concentrating, probably on not implicating himself. He unfolded his arms and rested his hands on the table. "I do know a John Donner, as it happens. Not well, you understand. As a businessman I encounter a lot of people."

"Your *former* drugs business you mean?"

Maguire gave a small shrug. "I have other business interests as well. You'd be surprised. It's a small world and getting smaller every day. I might know people who have met your former missus in London." He leaned forward a little and tapped his fingers on the table.

Wild noticed the Masonic ring and a chill ran up his spine. He felt Maguire watching him, flaunting it, and realised he hadn't seen that ring at the last interview. No, but he had seen a ring just like it on Donald Jacobson's hand.

Now he made a point of noticing it. "I didn't realise you were on the square." He smiled at Maguire and nodded towards the G in the centre of the ring "Is that a Guildford Lodge?"

Maguire rubbed his hand as if to conjure a demon. "You, er, on the square yourself?"

"No," Wild forced a grin. "Maybe that's why I'm still a DS."

"And lucky to keep that after what happened in London."

Wild got the message. Maguire knew his life inside out. And how might that be, he wondered. He took a couple of seconds to compose himself.

"Anyway, like I said, John Donner is in custody — down at Mayberry police station in Wiltshire. From what I hear, he's been very cooperative. Talkative, you might say. So much so that they'll probably release him later today. I'm here to give you an opportunity to speak to me, in case any information arises that could implicate you."

Maguire's whole body grew rigid. As he opened his mouth to speak, Wild made a final push.

"What exactly is your relationship with John Donner?"

The solicitor turned slightly in his chair. "My client has already acknowledged that he knows an individual named John Donner."

Wild held up a printed image. "Is that him?"

Maguire appeared to study it. "You know what, Detective? I think it might be! Now that is a coincidence."

Wild put the picture away. "Here is another one for you. Your friend was found in the house of a girl whose boyfriend helped put you away. And even more coincidentally, he's dead now."

Maguire's right hand twitched and Wild jerked back in a reflex action. He stayed there to keep some space between them.

"Perhaps we'll see how good a friend this John Donner is, once his own neck is on the line."

"This is a fit-up," Maguire roared. "I thought you were here to talk about Conor Hoyle."

Wild eased his chair behind him. "Thank you both for your time."

He was still collecting his thoughts in the car park when Stephen Kershaw came into view. He lowered his window and called Kershaw over.

"DS Wild, I think your behaviour is deplorable. You deliberately goaded my client."

"Everything I said in there was the truth. Do yourself a favour, Stephen — get a new client. And don't let him give you any messages to deliver to his friends. That's what his last brief did, and look where it got him."

Kershaw seemed rattled. "I hope you're not insinuating anything."

"I'm telling you what I know. It wasn't pretty, when they found him."

After he sent Kershaw on his merry way he rang Marsh and traded interview updates with her. It did not make for a happy exchange.

"John Donner had no weapon on him — Marnie mistook a metal comb in the heat of the moment. We couldn't raise the topic of Jacobson's murder because the Bristol homicide team want more time to build their case. Donner is still making his mind up about a complaint against you. Personally, I think he's pissing in the wind."

At least that was something. "Thank you, ma'am."

"The Bristol team are happy for him to be released. He has a swanky apartment in Clifton so he shouldn't be difficult to keep an eye on."

"And what about Isabella and her family?"

"Aye, I know. A condition of bail is that he stays away from their property and does not make any attempt to contact them. It's enough for now."

"Yeah, well, it'll have to be. What time does he get out?"

"Bristol asked us to keep him here until they can get a surveillance team together. We can stretch his stay by checking against some other impulse burglaries. Marnie is going through the list as we speak. She'll come up with nothing but it gives us reasonable grounds to hold him a wee bit longer — still within his twenty-four hours. When he gets out of here Ben Galloway will keep tabs on him to make sure he's Bristol-bound and then a team up there will take over."

"Do you want me to inform the Kimanis?"

"Yes, you do that. Then get back here quick as you can — there's work to be done."

CHAPTER 29

Unsurprisingly, Juliette took the news badly.

"Isabella wants to move to London to be with her father. This has put an incredible strain on our family, on our marriage."

Wild had little comfort to offer, other than Donner's bail conditions. When that failed to help he picked at a familiar bone — what she knew about Lee Rickard that her daughter didn't.

"Alright, Mr Wild. I almost admire your tenacity. Fine. I could see Isabella was becoming fond of Lee. Too fond, if you take my meaning? It started with a personal letter. She denied it was him of course, but who writes letters these days? And she hid it away in her room."

Yeah, Wild thought to himself, and I bet that didn't stop you looking for it. "So what did you do, hire a private detective?"

"God, no. Nothing so dramatic. When I did a puff piece for a previous book, my publisher put me in touch with a local journalist. He was very good. Too good in fact."

Wild knew the sound of an approaching train wreck and he let her tell it her own way.

"Doubtless, you know all the details of Lee's criminal past. I could forgive that to a certain extent, especially when I discovered he had grown up in care. And then I learned about Conor Hoyle's death . . ."

He took a breath. She really had done her research, in a manner of speaking. "I need to know who dug into Lee's background on your behalf because they may have compromised his protected identity and contributed to his death."

The line went quiet. "I don't think I should say anything else without my solicitor present."

* * *

Wild turned it all over to his DI. Except his contempt for Juliette, which he retained. As far as he was concerned, the only decent thing she'd done since Lee Rickard's murder was sign one of her books so he could flog it. Objectively, he knew it wasn't all down to her. He wasn't big on objectivity right now, though. His instincts told him she had more to tell. Meanwhile, he felt hemmed in by half-truths and inconsistencies. If he could make sense of all the information floating around and put it into some kind of order he might see the bigger picture. He smiled at the fantasy.

As he approached Mayberry he experienced something unexpected — a sense of homecoming. For months he'd been based at Mayberry and living nearby. He'd even stopped dreaming about being in London and riding the Tube. If he wasn't mistaken, he was starting to settle in.

A car swung wide as he indicated for the police station — a BMW. Juliette seemed to recognise him, as did another pillar of the community beside her — the local solicitor, Clarence Hollings. Interesting.

Marsh's office was empty when he arrived upstairs, which could mean she was still cleaning blood off the walls. He pictured Mr Hollings solemnly advising his client to say as little as possible, while DI Marsh advanced like a terrier on a farm rat. He'd barely logged into his computer when a voice behind him pierced the white noise in his head.

"DS Wild. My office in five minutes. And bring me a coffee would you? I think I've earned it."

He caught a text from Marnie, suggesting they catch up after work. He fired one back, wishing her luck with the house-to-house and garden-to-garden enquiries.

When he opened Marsh's door she greeted him by holding up a hand for her coffee. "Thanks Craig, you are a lifesaver. Grab a seat." She took a gulp of hot coffee without batting an eyelid. "Ah, thank God for caffeine. Okay, I'll start with the good news. Juliette is now fully cooperating with our investigation and has apologised for inadvertently withholding information in her efforts to protect her daughter."

Wild felt one side of his mouth curving. "Prepared statement?"

"Naturally. And in return for her continued cooperation I have agreed that another officer will liaise with her, should we require further conversation."

"Meaning?"

"Anyone but you. You can hardly blame her, Craig. You took agin her from the start."

He smiled at the Glaswegian in her.

"Clearly there was some basis to your . . . bias, but we need her onside now."

Wild felt inspiration jab him between the eyes. "Adam Napier — that's her freelance journalist." He took a celebratory sip of tea. "He is local, he's freelance now and he's long in the tooth so I imagine he is well connected."

She beat him to the punchline.

"Take Ben Galloway and go pick Napier up for questioning. It's time we found out exactly what he knows."

CHAPTER 30

Wild watched the traffic through his windscreen, listening to the pitch of each vehicle as it approached and drove past. Marnie had told him that computers could be used to codify pretty much anything and a specimen could then be checked against it. Animals, chemicals, fingerprints — obviously, even soundwaves. It boggled the mind.

"Are we going in or what, Skip?"

He turned slowly to Ben Galloway with a half-smile. "Going in? We're not raiding a crack den. We're picking up a person of interest from his local."

Ben nodded, as if he'd received the wisdom of Solomon. "Shall I cover the back exit?"

"I think we'll manage fine from the main door. But if he squeezes through the window of the gents and tries to make a break for it, you have my permission to bring him down by any means necessary."

For once, Galloway seemed to get the joke.

Wild waited another minute, for no reason at all, and then stirred into action. "Come on then, Columbo, let's go get our man."

Napier clocked them straightaway. Wild saw him looking over as they entered the saloon bar. He steered Galloway to the barmaid, ordered half an alcohol-free lager for the boy and a lime and soda for himself, and then ferried the drinks over to Napier's table.

"Mind if we join you?"

"It's a free country, Detectives. Be my guests."

Wild lowered his voice even though there was no one at nearby tables. "Mr Napier, we'd like to interview you at Mayberry police station."

"Am I obliged to go with you?"

It felt like orphaning Bambi. "No, although if you decline I will arrest you and you can go there in the back of a police van. This way, you keep your dignity. Finish your drink first." He sank his lime and soda in three gulps. "DC Galloway can keep you company."

Two men at a distant table paused from their devotion to the sports channel to look across and then tuned out reality again.

Napier downed the last of his pint and lifted his jacket from an adjacent chair, tucking a notebook and sports paper under his arm. He stood up. "What's this all about?" Napier's naïveté carried all the conviction of a guilty politician, which as far as Wild was concerned was most of them.

Galloway took his cue from Wild. "It's better we discuss that in an interview room, sir, with your solicitor present." He took a sip of his lager-lite and left it on the table.

Napier said a fond farewell to the barmaid, who nodded indifferently. Outside, his bravado took flight and he got into the back seat with Galloway without a peep.

Wild said nothing and, mercifully, Galloway picked up on the vibe and kept schtum. Napier looked about as comfortable as an estate agent at a lie detector demonstration. Wild hoped he was sober enough to interview, not that he planned to test him beforehand. He took a leisurely drive back to the police station, serenading the silence with something on BBC Radio 3 that he thought might be Mozart. Someone who did sonatas, anyway.

CHAPTER 31

At the police station, Napier asked for a glass of water so he could take a tablet. Wild sat with him as he took it, confident it wasn't a cyanide pill. Napier kept his head down after that until his solicitor arrived. Wild wasn't overly surprised that Napier's brief was a senior partner from Santers, the solicitors out on the trading estate. He figured Napier had crossed paths with them professionally as a newspaperman.

Wild gave them twenty minutes to meet, greet and concoct, and then Marsh came down to work her witchcraft. Ben Galloway made himself scarce. He didn't seem bothered. Mostly, Wild, surmised, Galloway was counting down the days until he transferred to Gable Cross — where he had more chance of making a favourable impression before the rest of the team relocated there in a few months' time.

Out in the corridor, Marsh gave Wild a jagged pearl of wisdom. "Say nothing until I tell you."

He went in first, at peace with his role as observer. Marsh had a methodical, almost mechanistic approach to interviewing suspects. She set the scene, explaining that Juliette Kimani had told them she'd paid Napier to pick Lee Rickard's life apart. A tad dramatic, in Wild's opinion, but it was her show and Napier never contradicted her.

"And what did you discover, Mr Napier?"

Now Napier turned to Roger Santer, whose face contorted in disapproval.

"I, er, I did my job as an investigative journalist."

"Specifically, for the recording . . ."

Napier's solicitor's eyes narrowed, as if he were laying a difficult egg. "I have advised my client to respond proportionately."

Wild cleared his throat, hoping Marsh could take a hint. She waited. Napier was sweating now.

"Would you like a comfort break?"

Napier looked like he really wanted an open door. Wild felt a Scottish foot making contact under the table. Time to play her wild card, which was his nickname around the station apparently, after his unexpectedly impressive turn for the darts team.

"Mr Napier, how did you discover where Lee Rickard lives? I mean, *lived*, after Juliette put you on to him?"

Napier blinked a couple of times. "I followed him home."

"What, all the way to Lincolnshire?"

"It's what she paid for. Took me two trips an' all. Lost him the first time, but I had a little electronic help after that." He smiled in self-congratulation.

"When did you find out about Lee Rickard's past?" Wild assiduously avoided asking the real question: *how*. He was only half-listening to Napier's proportionate reply because something else was troubling him. How did Napier's private investigations tie in with Paul Maguire? Another tap against his foot brought him back to attention and ensured he re-applied the mute button.

Marsh rubbed her hands together slowly. "Given that Lee Rickard's death is suspicious, what you knew and when you knew it is central to our inquiries. Of course, as your solicitor has explained, you are not obliged to say anything. That may not play out well in court — in the witness box, you understand. Suffice it to say, we need to verify your communications with Juliette Kimani so we will take the appropriate steps."

Napier went very still, eyes staring at the wall behind them. If he had glimpsed his future it didn't appear to be a good one. More likely, Wild surmised, he was thinking about hitting the panic button.

Wild spotted Marsh shifting forward in her chair, gearing up for another salvo. He wondered exactly what she was after, but he never got to find out. A double knock on the door paused the interview and earned Ben Galloway a Medusa glare from the DI. Wild caught a glimpse of Galloway before the door closed him out. Pensive, that was the word. After a minute or so, Marsh re-entered into the room with Galloway trailing behind her.

Marsh continued for the tape, "DI Marsh has been called away on an urgent matter. DC Galloway has joined DS Wild, who will conclude this interview."

As she left the room she gave Wild a look he couldn't quite decipher. Galloway took the empty seat and passed Wild a folded piece of paper. What it lacked in words, it made up for in impact: JOHN DONNER SHOT DEAD.

Wild pressed back against his chair. He felt guilt coiling around his innards and something else — a malign sense of relief. "Okay, Adam, a couple of questions and then we're done. Do you know John Donner?"

Napier's eye twitched. A flicker of recognition was all Wild needed.

"He's very dead. Somebody shot him today — maybe he annoyed the wrong person. Maybe you know them as well?" He stopped short of naming Paul Maguire and instead went with, "I noticed a reaction when I mentioned John Donner's name. Before you heard he was dead, I mean. Can you think of anyone who might have cause to harm him? Sorry, I meant to say *reason* to harm him."

The solicitor came to life. "Excuse me, Sergeant, are you now questioning my client about a murder as well?"

"It just came in. For the benefit of the recording I am showing Mr Napier and his solicitor a piece of paper, handed to me when DC Galloway entered the room. Can one of you please read it aloud for the recording?"

Napier kept his hands back so the solicitor read the note, showed it to Napier and then recited four words. "John Donner shot dead."

Wild watched Napier scratch behind his left ear. An obvious signal, prompting the solicitor to call the interview to an end.

"My client has been extremely cooperative and I think that's enough for now. If you need to speak to him again you will need to make an appointment, not pick him up off the street."

"Oh, rest assured, we will. And in the manner you suggest — if it's just for a chat."

He threw in a two-second smile, closed the interview and left Galloway to mop up. As he left the room the tight ball of adrenaline in his guts burst like a water balloon, flooding his veins. He kept walking, slowly, deliberately, concentrating on each step as the sweat beaded at his brow.

Galloway's dulcet tones cut into his rhythm of thought. He kept walking. Only a few more steps now. He pushed the toilet door and angled his face away from the mirror. But some part of him wanted to look in the face of a man who could do what he had done. One glance sent him scurrying to the cubicle to vomit for England.

He heard the door creak open and roared, "Get out!" before Galloway could utter two words. Finally, when his stomach felt as empty as the rest of him, he emerged and ran a tap to drown out the hiss in his head. He splashed water on his face and then dared to look at his reflection. His sore eyes and emaciated face gave him a haunted look, which seemed about right. After straightening his shirt and jacket, he chewed on a mint and went out to face the world.

When he got upstairs he could see someone else with the DI in her office — DCI Garner on a royal visit. He forced himself to think about Donald Jacobson and Isabella Kimani, and felt his resolve harden. Donner no longer a threat and Jacobson's recording naming Paul Maguire were two reasons to keep breathing.

He sighed. No sense delaying the inevitable. He knocked, waited for admittance, and entered the lions' den.

CHAPTER 32

Marsh looked to the DCI and then nodded to an empty chair. Wild sat down.

"We want to reassure you, Craig, that no blame is attached to you regarding John Donner's death. You couldn't possibly have foreseen this outcome."

He would have asked if he could speak freely but he gave himself permission instead. "I didn't release him. That was procedure."

"Sure, sure," the DCI nodded slowly as if weighing it up. "Although some might consider the timing of visiting Paul Maguire in prison a lapse in judgement."

He felt the weight of Marsh's gaze, fixing him to the chair. "I was following a legitimate line of enquiry. It was an opportunity to gauge Maguire's reaction about his solicitor's murder and to probe Maguire's relationship with John Donner."

"That would seem to be the responsibility of the Bristol team."

"Sorry, with respect, sir, ma'am, am I getting a bollocking here? Jacobson rang me after all — for all the good it's done so far."

The DCI smiled. Marsh did not.

"Craig, don't be so bloody defensive. We are simply reviewing the facts."

Wild sought another fact for himself. "Where was Donner killed?"

The DCI replied. "In Clifton, near his home address. A bullet to the head at close range. The Bristol surveillance team were first on the scene, but the suspect is still at large."

Wild interpreted that as 'close but no cigar'.

"As you say, DS Wild, there's still Donald Jacobson's voice message. And if forensics can place Donner at the murder scene, that's a motive for killing *him*."

Now seemed a good time for a confession. "I, er, mentioned John Donner to Adam Napier at the end of his interview."

Marsh gasped. "You did *what*?"

"It seemed appropriate. You were out of the room so it's all on my shoulders. He knew Donner alright. Knew of him I mean."

DCI Garner sat back a little, like a mediator, and looked first to Marsh and then to Wild. "Naturally I have assured the Bristol team of our full cooperation and your availability for an interview. Thankfully, Sergeant, you have no further reason to interact with Paul Maguire."

Wild directed his comment to DI Marsh.

"Napier didn't deny knowing John Donner. He didn't have to — I could tell by the look on his face."

DCI Garner put him in his place. "That's hardly evidence."

"No it isn't, sir." He waited for Marsh to back him up. She didn't, so Wild laid it out for them. "If Napier knew Donner that's a probable link to Maguire. Napier finds out about Lee Rickard and like any good journalist he smells a story — and money. Or maybe he tries to sell the information directly to Maguire instead. Have we found any record of Napier ever visiting Maguire in prison?"

DCI Garner seemed unconvinced. "What if he did?"

Marsh rode in like reluctant cavalry. "If Napier told Maguire what he knew, it could explain why Lee Rickard wound up dead. At the very least it would connect Napier, Maguire and Donner."

Wild could have hugged her. "Exactly!"

The DCI still looked thoroughly unimpressed. Or maybe that was just his look.

* * *

Wild didn't mind the drizzle. It made the world feel fresh and cleansed. The world outside, anyway. He imagined Marsh and the DCI back upstairs, still discussing his involvement in the Lee Rickard investigation. Someone else would inform Juliette about John Donner's demise and in all probability he'd be taking a back seat from the investigation. Ben Galloway had suggested on the way out together that a Gable Cross team would take over in conjunction with Bristol. Then again, Galloway also believed in UFOs. Wild left him outside with one of the other smokers.

The words 'inter-team working' had made him shudder. He was contemplating whether to take something out of the freezer later or treat himself to a takeaway when he saw something under his windscreen wipers. His first thought was that some cheeky bastard from a pizza delivery place had leafleted all the cars again, until he realised his car was the only one. The plastic bag covering the note suggested premeditation. He removed the bag, got in his car and read the note carefully. He needn't have bothered — there was no mystery about the author. *We need to talk. Ring me.* Adam Napier had helpfully left his name and number underneath.

He thought about informing DI Marsh but the note wasn't much to write home about. Instead, he made a number withheld call, car key still in his hand.

Napier picked up on the second ring.

"Ah, is that you, Detective? I was starting to give up on you."

"Yeah, it's Wild. I've just finished my shift and saw your note."

"Fancy a Chinese? I think we ought to have a chat — off the record. It's about your wife."

Wild didn't bother explaining he was wifeless now. Mildly intrigued, he took some details and started the car. By the time he found his way to the Chinese restaurant he'd played a number of scenarios in his head and none of them ended well. He quickly crossed *helpful citizen* off his list and narrowed it down to selling information, retribution, or some sort of blackmail. The last option amused him. Maybe if Napier had researched a little harder he'd have seen the state of Wild's finances.

Before he got out of the car he searched through his new phone apps, the three that Marnie had installed for him, and activated the voice recorder.

The Jasmine Garden's green and yellow paintwork was hard to miss, as was the golden gong in the window. No stranger to Chinatown in London, Wild immediately felt at home. As he shut the door behind him a man in an immaculate suit homed in.

"Table for one, sir?"

"No, I'm, er, meeting someone — I thought he'd already be here." He scanned the room but no one fitted Napier's dishevelled appearance. "Only I don't see him."

"Ah, you're here for Mister Napier? Follow me please." The proprietor led him to a bamboo screen that obscured a side door. Wild felt his hackles rising.

"Where are we going?"

"A private area for special customers."

The suit showed him along a short corridor and then shooed him towards another door. He heard the nearby noise of the kitchens and a language he assumed was Cantonese, but only because he didn't know of any other Chinese languages. He tried to relax his shoulders, failed, and cautiously turned the doorknob.

Judging by its size, the side room may have once been for storage. Three people could have eaten at the table uncomfortably. Adam Napier sat against the opposite wall, facing the door. He looked smaller somehow, without a solicitor at his side calling the shots.

"Glad you could join me . . . Craig."

The manager loitered by the door and asked Wild for his order. He went with beef in black bean sauce because it felt like a special occasion. Not every day he avoided a beating and someone offered him dinner.

He sat down, noticed the circles on the table where a lager had stood, and tried not to fold his arms.

"You said on the phone . . ."

"We'll get to that once you've had your food."

Fifteen minutes of awkward conversation followed, where Napier shovelled chow mein into his face between sentences. Mostly he talked about news stories he had covered and trips to London.

Wild couldn't help being fascinated. It was like hearing a documentary delivered by a human cement mixer.

"In my line of work, I always found the Metropolitan Police to be very helpful — if you knew the right people of course." Napier smiled between mouthfuls. "You didn't fare so well with the Met yourself though."

Dinner arrived and Wild waited until the waiter left before responding. "The Logan Brothers' robbery? That is old news — even for you, Adam."

"I think we both know there's more to that story than ever saw the light of day."

Wild felt heat across his face that couldn't be attributed to the black bean sauce. He ignored it and concentrated on his food, chewing carefully to stifle the urge to ram his fork into Napier's forehead. Napier continued reminiscing, with a few more hints thrown in for luck.

When Wild set his cutlery down, Napier drew his own chair closer to the table.

"Like I said, I'm not bluffing."

Wild smiled behind his napkin. Only bluffers said that.

"I have historic information about DCI Stephanie Hutcheson that would not enhance her career prospects."

He paused. "When she returns from her maternity leave, I mean. And some of it might not reflect well on your reputation either."

He grinned a little but Wild smelled genuine fear there, and it wasn't of the police.

Wild upped the ante. "Steph is my ex-wife. What's it to me if you've uncovered something in her past?" He read Napier's rattish face. "I'm serious. And if you've done your research properly you'll know my reputation is hardly spotless." He stared hard into the windows of Napier's troubled soul. "With good reason."

Napier was sweating. "Look, I'm not asking for much — really. No, I'm not after money. I just want to be left alone for a while. I've a lot going on."

"Maguire not so understanding last time you saw him in prison?"

It was Napier's turn to burn up. "Don't underestimate me. I'll do it. I've been emailed documents — you'd want to know. It's all on my laptop — stuff that happened before your marriage ended."

Wild figured he was expected to react and denied him the pleasure. Glass houses and all that. "Tell you what, Adam. I'll make you a better deal. Whatever shit you're mixed up in, you talk to us and we'll help you."

"It's too late for that. If a man like John Donner isn't safe what hope have I got?"

Wild poured himself a glass of water, sniffed it and then took a sip. "If you're desperate enough to bring me here and try a cheap trick like blackmail, what have you got to lose?"

No answer.

Wild sensed that dessert wasn't going to lighten the mood any. "Time I was going."

Napier reached a hand across the table. "I'll get the bill."

"Don't bother on my account and don't get up — I'll find my own way out."

Napier looked so desperate that Wild half-expected to find a couple of heavies on the other side of the door. Then he remembered that the space beyond was within earshot of the main dining area, so probably not the ambience they were aiming for.

The manager zeroed in on him as he emerged, concerned at his early departure. He reassured him that it was a work thing and, despite some resistance, paid his share of the bill.

Out on the street Wild's bravado left him. His mind played tricks, half-convincing himself that Napier had figured out how Maguire knew where to find Donner. On his way back to the car he had two secular epiphanies. Firstly, he needed to check the prison visitors' log, to find out exactly when Napier had seen Maguire. Secondly, even if Napier was bluffing, he had to see what was on Napier's computer before anyone else did.

Fortunately, with Napier such a creature of habit it didn't take a detective to know where he'd be later that evening. Hopefully the laptop wouldn't be with him.

CHAPTER 33

Wild drove around the block twice, as if he were winding himself up like a toy. No sign of Napier's car, which overcame the first obstacle. He told himself he was being noble by protecting Steph's reputation, although she would've seen it as his ego over-extending itself.

The main door to the block wasn't locked — eliminating the second obstacle — so he proceeded. That was the deal he had with himself. If he could get in the building he would get into the flat somehow. He tiptoed past a baby buggy by a doormat that read *Home is where the Heart is* to reach the stairs. His muffled steps echoed in the cavernous stairway, but not enough to dull the pounding in his chest.

Someone had cooked spicy food and the aroma hung in the air, acrid and potent. Second floor, second door along, he reminded himself. He approached the door, relieved to see that all expense had been spared in its construction. A quick glance left and right and then he pressed an ear to the painted plywood. It felt rough against his skin. He stayed in position, opening his coat to retrieve an industrial-sized screwdriver. He took a deep breath, applied the blade to the gap between the door and the frame, and as he breathed out carefully exerted pressure until the cylinder lock gave way with a crunch. He grabbed the door by the letterbox and slipped the screwdriver back inside his jacket awkwardly with his left hand.

Once inside, he pushed the door closed and grabbed an old telephone directory nearby to prop it in position. Now in virtual darkness, he used his police torch to find the light switch, inhaling stale cigarette smoke down from the yellowed ceiling. Conscious of the flat next door, he moved slowly and deliberately along the hallway, poking his head into the living room before he stepped inside. He stood in the middle of the carpet and turned slowly, looking for signs of a laptop or a power lead. Finding only a printer, he tried a couple of drawers and searched a cabinet below the television. A film of grime tainted everything his gloved hands touched.

There was something almost sacrilegious about searching someone's bedroom, but he knew it had to be done. Ben Galloway was already in position at Napier's watering hole, ready to ring him the second Napier walked out the door. He had thought about having Napier stopped and breathalysed on his way home, but there was no need. He'd allowed a full ten minutes to get out, based on his own dummy run.

It hadn't been difficult to persuade Galloway to keep tabs on Napier, under the guise of the investigation. The DC was keen to impress *any* senior officer.

Wild paused at the bedroom door, hoping to God the laptop was there somewhere and not stashed away at another location. That would really be a pisser. As he turned the doorknob and eased the door he saw the body on the bed, slumped to one side, white foam seeping onto the pillow. He stared for two long seconds and then leapt across the space. He spotted the pills and whisky beside a bedside lamp, and an electrical lead on the floor that trailed into the darkness. Sure enough, a laptop glistened in the dark under torchlight.

Now he turned his attention to Napier. There was no pulse and of course his CPR kit was back in the car. Sod it, he'd have to do things old school. First he switched on the bedside lamp so he could see what he was doing, and then he scooped foam out of Napier's mouth with a gloved finger. One deep breath and then his training took over. He gave Napier mouth-to-mouth twice followed by thirty chest compressions. After two rounds he turned up the volume on his phone and dialled 999 so he could talk as he worked.

"Ambulance required. I have a man unconscious — suspected overdose. Get a move on." He made them wait while he tried mouth-to-mouth again and then gave them the address. Someone would be with him as soon as possible, and in the meantime stay on the line for instructions.

"No need. I'm a copper," he gasped, and went back to his work, sweat pouring down his face.

If Napier died then how the hell could he explain his presence? And if he lived . . . same question. Finally, when he started imagining Dr Bell's untimely arrival, Napier choked a little so he moved him into the recovery position whereupon Napier promptly vomited over the bedspread. The smell of whisky, lager and bile added to the foetid aroma of their earlier meal. Wild grappled with his own gag reflex, won the battle, and checked whether Napier was coherent. When he realised Napier wasn't fully conscious, he grabbed the laptop and lead and shoved them into his rucksack.

Napier mumbled something so Wild leaned as close as he could while avoiding the small lake of vomit. The patient coughed, half-opened his eyes and said, "Sorry," before closing them again. At least he was breathing on his own now.

Wild photographed the pills and spotted a corner of paper underneath the bottle. The note read: *Sorry, I had no choice*. Wild bagged it up. Jesus, this didn't look good.

Ten minutes later an ambulance crew arrived and announced themselves through the letterbox. Wild shouted from open bedroom door. "Just push it."

He recognised the crew from a previous investigation, where a discharged shotgun and a puncture wound to a suspect's head had warranted their presence. By the looks on their faces, they recognised him as well.

"What's the patient's status?"

"He's breathing unaided. He's thrown up and he slurred a few words."

One of the crew went over to the bed, looking over her shoulder to Wild as she whispered, "What's his name?"

"Adam Napier."

"Can you hear me, Adam?"

Napier groaned, although they got little sense out of him. Wild pointed to the pills but explained they were evidence in an ongoing investigation.

The medic turned back to Wild who was slumped on the floor, leaning against the wall. "He was lucky you found him."

"Before you take him away, can I check his pockets for keys so I can secure the property?"

He extracted house keys from Napier's trousers and stood back so the ambulance crew could stretcher him out. Alone in the flat Wild contemplated his next move. First, he tried to set the lock in place from the back and prop it shut again. Mission accomplished, he took the laptop out, opened it up and clicked the power switch. It chirruped into life and then confronted him with a password screen. He could have wept. How ironic that someone who lived so shambolic a life cared about data protection.

He considered trying variations of *Napier* with other characters, or *journo*, and then worried he might lock the machine up altogether. In the meantime he figured he'd better get to hospital and concoct an explanation that Marsh wouldn't tear to shreds in seconds.

He pushed the laptop back into his rucksack and managed to pull the door tight from the outside, so that it at least looked secure. Then he rang the neighbour's bell and a young man came to the door, sporting an unusual haircut. Shaved at the sides and curled back at the front in a way that suggested, to Wild, a media student trying too hard.

"Yes, can I help you?"

He flashed his warrant card.

The neighbour called behind him. "Dylan . . . Dylan, turn that down, it's the police."

The TV blared no more. Another male sidled up to the first and wrapped an arm around his shoulder.

Wild nearly nodded. He got it — they were a couple. *Thanks for sharing.* "Your neighbour, Mr Napier . . ."

"Oh, God," Dylan exclaimed. "What has Adam done now?" He made it sound like a terrible sitcom catchphrase.

Wild applied some discretion. "He's been taken unwell. An ambulance crew attended and I've tried to secure the door as best I can."

"Don't you fret, hun. I'll ring up the council and they'll probably send someone here first thing. Give Adam our love when you see him. Tell him the boys from number seven will keep an eye on his des res."

"Thanks." He thought about the missing car but clearly Napier hadn't wanted anyone to know he was home. This wasn't so much a cry for help as a one-way ticket.

CHAPTER 34

Wild broke the news to Ben Galloway by phone en route to the hospital.

"I'm sorry, Skip. You only said to ring you when he left and I've been waiting for him to show up."

"It's fine, Ben. I just wanted you to know. I'm heading over to the hospital for when he comes round . . . okay, thanks, that's good of you. I'll see you there."

Wild could almost see the news headline: police interview drives man to suicide attempt. His mind fast-forwarded to another investigation from an outsider like Stanton and the ignoble end of a less than glittering career.

His phone rang, mid-traffic. He took the call hands-free and tried to stay calm.

"Craig, it's Anthony Galloway. I've had a call about an overdose victim."

Wild tried to prepare himself for the worst.

". . . Ambulance on its way to hospital. I know the name is connected with your case. Would you like me to attend?"

He gulped. "No, that's fine. I'm going there now and Ben is joining me."

"Right you are, Craig, just thought you'd want to know."

"Thanks." He blew out a long breath and wondered what Ben Galloway might have said to his uncle about Napier.

* * *

As far as Wild was concerned, everything about hospitals was wrong. Far too hot, or too cold, dizzyingly bright lights, and every noise in the waiting area — especially the ones made by children — reverberated like a bastard. And those bloody seats. Five to ten minutes and then your arse slipped into a coma.

He watched the nurses gliding by and tried to avoid eye contact. They might have him pegged as the bad cop. Right now, the only cop. The rucksack containing Napier's laptop rested between his legs like a guilty secret, but at least he'd left the incriminating giant screwdriver in the car. He closed his eyes for a moment and thought back. Maybe bad cop wasn't so far off the mark. Had he been too hard on Napier in the interview? Or had Marsh?

"Excuse me, are you Sergeant Wild?"

He looked up in the direction of a gently smiling face as she walked towards him. A trace of an accent there — maybe Polish, he couldn't swear to it. Her ID read Iga Nowicki, staff nurse.

He held up his own ID, which she ignored.

"We have stabilised the man. He's feeling a bit sorry for himself but he's out of danger. We'll keep him in overnight and see how it goes tomorrow. He's been assessed by a mental health professional and they want to see him in the morning."

"Can I speak to him?"

Her face grew pensive. "I don't think he'd be up to talking right now."

"May as well be off then. Thanks," he read the badge again carefully, "Iga."

* * *

Caught between the devil and the deep blue sea, and with a laptop-shaped albatross on his back, he clutched at a straw.

"Marnie, it's Wild. How are things?"

"Things are pretty good, thanks. Leo is meeting Belinda again tonight, for a drink. The way he tells it, he went back to hers and cried on her shoulder! Hopefully it'll give him something else to think about until the weekend when he goes home. Not that he knows that yet!"

"Great." He said tersely. "The, er, reason I'm ringing is that I want to know how you get around a laptop password screen when you don't know the magic word."

She thought for a moment. "You should be able to open another account as a different user."

"Okay." He stretched the word out to a parody of okayness. "Will that give me access to existing files — docs, emails and all that?"

"No. You can always do that later when you've remembered your original account password. I imagine there's sophisticated software out there for that though — maybe our tech team can help you. Have you changed your home computer?"

"Not exactly. It's work-related." He winced. "Listen, don't worry about it. I'll think of something else."

"Sorry, Wild. Got to go. We're doing the rounds — for the sheds."

"Sure. Go keep our gardens crime-free!"

"That's the plan. See you."

The laptop might as well have been ticking. He thought about smashing it and then realised he'd still have to explain its absence. Unless . . . he *could* dump it, if he made it look like Napier's flat had been burgled after the ambulance left. Given the state of the place, it wouldn't take much doing. He nodded to himself. It was a shit plan, but at least it was a plan. And Steph never knowing the lengths he'd gone to on her behalf gave him a bit of a buzz.

He rehearsed it in his head again as he walked outside to the car. It should be easy. Shove the front door, mess the place up — *more*, and then drop the laptop in the river somewhere. What could possibly go wrong?

He heard a rush of footsteps, followed by deep breathing, and then a familiar face emerged from the shadows.

"Alright, Skip? Sorry I'm late, something else came up."

He was about to call off Napier's babysitter for the night when he realised that Ben would probably want to buddy up with him instead. Best to stick with Plan A.

"I'll leave you to it, Ben. The staff nurse reckons Napier is unlikely to talk tonight. Still, you could try using your charm. I've got some evidence to sort out from the flat."

As he walked away Ben Galloway called behind him, "Hey, you never know, Skip — you might get a commendation for saving his life."

He drove back to Napier's road and got out the car with the rucksack, taking the screwdriver along for the journey. After a moment's panic, he discovered the main door to the block was still unlocked. As he reached the second floor he slowed to a crawl. Television chatter filtered from the neighbouring flat. He reached Napier's door and stared hard at the shiny metal plate that sat above the lock, perfectly complimented by a new steel door guard. Bollocks.

He still had the keys in his hand, debating whether to try his luck, when he heard a nearby door opening.

"Dylan, it's the policeman. I thought I heard someone outside. It's good of you to pop back but there was no need — the council came up trumps."

Dylan popped his head out. "Yes, they fitted new locks, to be on the safe side. When you see Adam, tell him we have a spare set." He jangled them to make the point.

Wild commended them for being good neighbours, which clearly delighted them. Then he trudged back downstairs and let himself out the building.

Torchlight flickered across the patch of lawn outside of the block.

"Wild, what are you doing here?" Marnie lowered her torch.

"I needed to check something."

Sergeant Galloway moved closer. "Evening, Craig. Marnie, could you give us a minute?"

She glowered but stepped away to let the boys have their little chat.

"Glad I caught you here, Craig. I wanted to thank you — for what you did for our Ben." He mimed smoking a cigarette, and Wild knew exactly what type.

Wild was taken aback because a) that was at least two months ago and b) why the bloody hell would Ben share that anecdote with his uncle? "We're a team. It was only a bit of grass, and besides, I heard about it after the fact."

Galloway nodded. "Hearsay. An unfounded accusation and soon retracted."

"Exactly."

"Well, we're much obliged. If there is ever anything I can do for you . . ."

Wild glanced longingly at the block of flats and then thought better of it. "Where's Marnie gone?"

Galloway radioed her.

She sounded out of breath. "Call came in to me . . . suspicious activity in a back garden . . . on my way now."

"Wait for backup. That's an order, Marnie."

"Sorry, Sarge, didn't get that. Over."

Sergeant Galloway got on to the station and then he and Wild put in an Olympic sprint. They approached a large corner house with a side entrance to the garden, and no sign of Marnie outside. Wild unlatched the door and Galloway reached into his jacket, pulling out a small metal cylinder as well as his torch. "Ready?"

Wild tried to adjust to the lack of lighting. The moon was on strike. The sky had clouded over and the only light came from the dull glow of underactive garden globes. He closed the gate behind him, taking care to step over the gravel to grass. A straight path led to an oblong shape in one corner of the garden that could only be the shed.

He heard a scrabbling sound and then the crunch of footsteps. Marnie's voice sounded clear in the semi-darkness as her torch beam struck a stranger's face. "Police officer. Stand still."

Her words had the opposite effect. The figure darted off to one side, into the undergrowth. A second figure, emerging from the shed, wasn't so lucky. As Marnie moved forward to contain him he swung a fist, and she dropped him to the ground with a well-placed block and follow-up sweep of her leg. She drew her taser, warned him, and added, "I dare you."

Sergeant Galloway rushed to the gate to cut off the escape route, which left Wild free to check the shed for anyone else and then assist Marnie. Not that she needed any assistance, with her prisoner cuffed, secured, and sat on the ground. Feeling surplus to requirements, Wild ranged his torchbeam until it found the second burglar. The miscreant raised a club and ran towards him full pelt. Another torch converged on him, along with a bright red dot, accompanied by the words, "Armed police."

Suspect number two immediately dropped the weapon and fell to his knees. "Don't shoot — I'm unarmed."

Sergeant Galloway was grinning as he approached. "Hands behind your back then. There's a good lad."

He might have been disarmed, but his tongue was still engaged. "Lucky you had a gun, copper, or I would have sorted you out no bother."

Galloway turned him around. "Gun? You must have misheard me. I said, 'Aw please.' Isn't that right, Sergeant Wild?"

Wild forced a straight face. "Absolutely."

They sat the two burglars back to back on the grass under Marnie's control while they searched for any discarded items.

Wild sidled up to Galloway in the shed. "I saw the red dot."

"Oh that," Galloway laughed. "Light pen," he winked. "Saves time sometimes."

"Risky."

Wild was struck by the chaos in the shed and did some digging around. In the back of a cupboard he pulled out a tin. Inside was a clear plastic bag containing smaller bags, each of which appeared to contain drugs. He was still smiling when he stepped back outside.

"Congratulations," he said to Marnie. "You've either caught yourself a pair of burglars in search of a stash, or two dealers with a novel way of hiding their merchandise." As he said it, both suspects slumped forward.

Sergeant Galloway turned to Marnie. "Best get the shed secured and we'll go through it properly in daylight, in case Sergeant Wild missed anything. "Okay, over to you, PC Olsen."

"Oh, right." She radioed for transport for two suspects and helped one of them to his feet, keeping a careful hold on his wrists behind his back. Galloway followed suit with the other suspect and Wild acted as bagman to carry the evidence to the street. As he pulled the gate behind him he noticed that the houselights were still off. Maybe the owners were heavy sleepers or this was their second home. Either way, there were no witnesses to tonight's escapade.

CHAPTER 35

Wild drove back to the police station to complete his statement about the two dealers Marnie and Sergeant Galloway had apprehended. Adam Napier's laptop remained in his rucksack in the car boot but he could feel its presence keenly.

Halfway to his destination he picked up a phone call from Ben Galloway.

"Alright, Skip?"

He knew that tone. "What's up?"

"I got a bit of a funny situation. You were right about Adam Napier . . ."

Wild didn't interrupt, as he had no idea where the conversation was going.

"You said to stick around in case he wanted to talk? Well, there was a bit of a commotion and one of the nurses came to fetch me. Napier was trying to sneak out of hospital without being discharged. He assaulted a member of hospital staff when it all kicked off but luckily I was on site to intervene. I'm waiting to find out if he's fit, you know, *mentally*, to be detained in a cell."

Wild knew he had to think fast. "Better to let him stay there overnight if they can keep him safe."

"He's fine now, I think. Very apologetic, and a bit weepy. Hold on a sec . . . right, they do want to keep him in and they may not press charges.

"Did you see an assault happen?"

"Yep."

"Bollocks to them then, we'll charge him in the morning. Get statements. You're a diamond, Ben."

"Cheers, Skip."

By the time Wild reached the police station he'd exhausted every scenario and the only option that played out remotely well in his head was the truth. He'd speak to Marsh tomorrow and lay a version of the truth at her feet, like a sacrificial offering.

* * *

"Well, you're bright and early this morning, Craig. Something on your mind?"

He didn't tell her he'd been awaiting her arrival for forty-five minutes, bolstered by coffee and fast food.

"I'd like to talk with you."

"You'd better come through to my office."

Reverend Houghton might have thought confession good for the soul — if she wasn't Church of England — but Wild found nothing to recommend it. Marsh listened in silence for a full ten minutes of explanation, justification and obfuscation. Finally, he was all out of words.

She drew a long breath. "Right, stop me if I've misunderstood. You went round to Napier's flat — out of concern for his welfare, after a private meeting with him?"

"I wouldn't call it private exactly. We had dinner together in a Chinese restaurant."

"Was anyone else there with you?"

"Not in the actual room, no."

"What is it with you, Craig? Do you have some sort of self-destruct button?"

He took this rhetorically and said nothing.

"Napier could say anything took place and you'd have nothing to refute it."

He pulled out his phone, pressed play, let it run and then stopped it after his ex-wife got a mention. "It's all there."

She nodded gently. Good boy. But he wasn't off the hook.

"Don't you think DCI Hutcheson can take care of herself, especially as you're out of her life?" She sucked a thoughtful tooth. "This is a mess, Craig. A steaming mess."

Now seemed a good time to mention the laptop.

"Jeezo, you don't do things by halves! Where is it now?"

"I booked it in as evidence last night after assisting Marnie and Sergeant Galloway."

"Well at least you did something right. What else have you got planned? That's a serious question."

"I'm still waiting on the prison visitor logs. I asked Harris to sort it out . . ." He saw Marsh shaking her head. "If they show a pattern of visits from Napier to Maguire, surely that's grounds to check his laptop for anything incriminating?"

"I hope so — for your sake. You realise if he has anything on you or your ex-wife it will all have to come out into the open?"

"I know. It was stupid to think otherwise."

"And there's nothing else you want to tell me at this juncture?"

"Nope."

She threw him a half-smile. "Unofficially, it's not the worst thing I've seen a police officer do out of desperation or incompetence. Officially though, I credited you with more sense than that. Right, off you go then and chase up the prison visitor logs. And start praying Napier appears a few times on the list."

* * *

An hour later and Wild could have sworn the reverend had put in a good word for him with the Man upstairs. An administrator for the prison apologised for the delay, said the request had got lost in transit, and sent over a spreadsheet showing four visits for Paul Maguire and all with Adam Napier's name against them, spread over a three-month period. Wild printed it off and all but barged into Marsh's office.

She rubbed her hands together. "Okay, now you have your link. This doesn't prove anything though."

"It's a step in the right direction. Like I told you, Galloway is bringing in Adam Napier for assaulting a nurse. It's fortuitous that Ben was there to see it happen."

"Lucky for you, you mean! Here's how things will run. Ben will interview him about the assault — with me — and then DI Stanton and I will ask him about Paul Maguire, in relation to Lee Rickard's death. If we have reasonable cause I will ask the techies to get into his laptop and you can go and search his flat — properly this time. But understand me, Craig, if he is squeaky clean you could be packing your bags."

Wild prodded the air. "He isn't. I could smell the desperation on him at the Chinese. He knows something and he's keeping it from us."

He left the office with a spring in his step. This called for fresh coffee. He climbed the stairs to the canteen at a gallop, wondering what Napier would have to say for himself. Not being present in the interview seemed like a small price to pay for the chance to turn Napier's flat over.

He spotted Marnie, hugging a mug of tea as she stared out the window. He grabbed a coffee and approached her.

"How's life in the fast lane?"

She looked up, startled. "Morning, Wild. I'm just waiting for Sergeant Galloway and then we're back to the garden shed for a thorough search." She set her mug down. "Sorry, I wasn't implying anything."

He sat down and smiled, waving a hand to show he wasn't offended. "You have a point. Always better to conduct searches in daylight."

She pursed her lips. "I was thinking about last night's arrests. Really, you were the one who found the drugs."

"Only because you caught the genius twins in the act. Otherwise, your Sarge and me could have missed the whole thing. So, taking a step back, it might be worth revisiting other break-ins on your list . . ." He left it there in the hope she'd join the dots, and enjoyed watching her puzzling it out.

She lifted her head. "You mean . . . you mean search the other burglary sites again because previously we weren't looking for anything hidden there."

Wild felt caffeine rolling through his veins, like a wave of joy. "Sounds like a reasonable hypothesis. Maybe once you've searched Tweedledum and Tweedledee's homes first, in case they made a list of what was hidden where. You can never underestimate the stupidity of the criminal classes!" He caught her scowling. "I'm kidding." Except he wasn't.

CHAPTER 36

Dylan and the other one, whose name Wild hadn't bothered to learn, came to the front door together.

"Hello again, Detective. How's our Adam doing?"

"He's, er, on the mend. I can't discuss it — you understand. I've come for his keys."

Dylan looked pensive. "We can pop in now and get some of his clothes for you. I can leave a casserole in his freezer as well."

"Best not. I need to enter his premises to execute a search." He held out an open hand. "I can sign a receipt."

The couple looked at one another, adjusting to the lack of bonhomie, and then Dylan disappeared into their flat to fetch the keys. He returned and stood there with his finger in the ring. "I think I'll give Adam a call — no offence, but he's not a great fan of the boys and girls in blue."

Wild stared deadpan. "He won't answer — we have his phone. Look, I'm trying to be diplomatic here. And incidentally, is that cannabis I can smell in your flat?" He took a step forward.

The keys magically became available. Dylan's face paled. "That's fine officer, here you go. Just post them through the letterbox when you're done."

Wild closed his hand like a clam. "I think I'll keep them for now."

The door closed and he imagined pills being flushed down the toilet or plants going out the window. Napier's new locks needed some persuasion, but he was good at that. He started with the bedside cabinet, despite the smell of stale vomit from the duvet. Napier's imprint was still there like the ghost of overdoses past.

There were a few receipts and a couple of loose pills, but nothing that looked like a password. The pillows, greasy to the touch, hid an old tissue and a book by Carl Jung: *Man and his Symbols*.

He stared at the cover, vaguely aware of Jung, and less aware of the meaning of symbolism, although he knew someone who would be. There was nothing else within easy reach of the bed that had writing on it, not even under the bed. A wallet in the drawer held no surprises and nothing of interest. It went straight into the bag with the mobile phone.

In the living room he found a box file with more receipts, stored chronologically by category and listed out on a piece of A4 paper. Very handy, come tax-return time. He scanned through the paperwork and sure enough the list recorded travel dates and Bristol prison visits.

In the absence of a better plan, Wild rang Marnie. He filled her in on his problem and returned to the bedroom, walking and talking.

"There's a book under his pillow. Maybe he has got some sort of code from it to remember his password?"

Marnie sensed his anxiety and let him down gently. "Doubtful. Think about it logically. If you wanted an easy way to recall your password, wouldn't you rather have a prompt?"

"Like those online questions — mother's maiden name, that kind of thing?"

"Sort of." She sounded doubtful.

"Well that's the only book in the bedroom and the only psychology book in the flat. Maybe one was enough! What's so special about Jung?"

"Well, you pronounce the first letter as a Y for one thing. Right . . . he first studied . . ."

"Marnie, I'm not interested in a history lesson right now. I need a bloody password."

"Erm, okay," she floundered. "Let's think. Jung was into archetypes . . ." She read the silence at the other end of the phone. "You might call them universal characters found in different cultures and myths." She was talking to herself now. "No, archetype is probably too long a word. And anima/animus is too easy to confuse, especially if you're pissed!"

"Any danger of you using words I'll understand?"

She clicked her fingers. "Got it, possibly. Jung talked about the shadow — the suppressed or unexpressed aspects of the self. Try shadow as a password, and maybe use a zero for the letter O."

"Is that with a capital S?"

"Probably not. More chance of typing it in wrong."

"Thanks, Marnie. I'll call you back."

He rang Marsh next. She sounded unimpressed, until he explained the source of his inspiration. She left him on the line and he heard footsteps as she travelled around the building to the technical support office. Cue some muffled conversation and then a *Windows* fanfare sounded in his ear.

"Excellent work."

"Thanks, boss."

"I meant by Marnie," she chuckled. "Right, collect whatever evidence you can find — including that box file — and get your bahookie back here."

Ten minutes later, Marsh rang him again.

"I have good news. There's no sign of any documents containing Paul Maguire's name, which scuppers any notion of Napier writing a book about him. Even so, best to check the flat again for a USB flash drive or printed pages."

He stood for a moment, taking in the hallowed atmosphere of the flat, as if Adam Napier were there in spirit. A different spectre came to mind. *What if Napier hadn't been bluffing about the file on him and Steph?*

"Where have you put it, you bastard?"

The room didn't answer, and Napier's ghost wasn't giving away any clues. And then Wild thought again. Marnie always said that the home was a reflection of the person, which probably explained why *he* still had half his possessions in boxes.

He went back to the bedroom. The laptop had been there after all. He started at the room's perimeter, partly because the carpet was threadbare at the edges but mostly to keep his distance from the foetid smell of the bed. No conveniently loose floorboards or hidden compartments. No face mask to wear either. He went to the *business end* of the bed where vomit had seeped into the duvet and stained it. Cursing Napier as he felt under the mattress, he worked his way around to the opposite end nearest the bedside cabinet.

When he made contact with a flat corner of something, he raised the mattress and heard liquid trickle on to the carpet. He braced with his other hand and felt a spring digging into his palm, and pushed against it to expose a brown cardboard cover. Inside were half a dozen pages, one containing colour copies of photographs — all of them Steph, showing her enjoying a cosy dinner for two, hands entwined on the table. He recognised the dress and that hairstyle from their days of wedlock. He recognised the other person too — Inspector Laghari, who he'd met for the first time several weeks ago in London.

He didn't dwell on the pics, acutely aware that if someone had taken a similar level of interest in *him* they might have created a companion photo collection. Albeit with less focus on fine dining and more on an enterprising use of his refreshment breaks. All stagnant water under the bridge now.

He flicked through the remaining pages and read his own name in an opening paragraph. Later he'd tell himself it was an instinctive decision, which was no decision at all. He took the page and folded it into his pocket, declaring to the empty room, "Steph, you're on your own."

As he lifted the soiled mattress again he noticed a silver object about the size of a battery. He grabbed the USB flash drive, replaced the cardboard file and tried to figure out what to do about it. The idea came out of the blue. A very dark blue. He had just boiled a kettle and filled a mug with hot water when his phone rang again. He nearly jumped out of his skin.

"Hello?"

"It's DI Marsh. Everything okay? You sound on edge."

He leaned across and gave the flash drive a sea burial. It sank with a small trail of bubbles, as if breathing its last. "Yeah, everything's fine, ma'am. I've searched high and low. No sign of anything else."

"Napier's laptop is a treasure trove, and also a prosecution lawyer's dream come true. The techies have dug up old emails between Napier and Jacobson, setting up prison visits. We'll need to cross-check everything for dates and build a complete timeline. Hold on a second . . . say that again . . ." Her voice faded.

Wild fished out the flash drive, shook water from it and then wiped it vigorously on his trousers. While he was waiting for Marsh to finish her more important conversation he returned the flash drive under the mattress. He used the rest of the time wisely, cooling the kettle with cold water and then emptying the mug with a quick rinse of cold before returning it to the grubby wooden mug tree with green mould on its base.

Marsh caught up with him again in Napier's armchair, glancing through Napier's scrapbook.

"Are you sitting down, Craig?"

"Ma'am?"

"I'm looking at emails back and forth between Adam Napier and Lee Rickard. It's all here in black and white. Napier arranged to meet Rickard at the literary festival. Oh, Jeez. He even mentions grabbing a coffee together."

Wild stared at a younger Adam Napier receiving a journalism award. A spiky-haired rake in need of a good dinner, glass trophy in hand, steely eyed and straight-backed — a lifetime away from the man in the pub still chasing a story he could live off.

"I'm going back now to put all this electronic evidence to Napier. I can't see he has anywhere left to go. It's a good result for the team, Craig. There'll be a drink for you on your return."

The call ended and he closed the scrapbook on the past.

* * *

Wild returned to the police station. He pushed the swing door and entered a hive of activity. There was a change in atmosphere. He dumped the evidence on his desk and muttered to himself, "Smells like team spirit."

"Craig, er, Sarge," Harris called across to him.

A small cardboard container came sailing through the air. Wild caught it and opened the box of Cadbury's Heroes. A nice touch.

"Marnie has gone out for cakes."

He resisted the urge to mention the words, 'Great use of a pool car,' and instead went with, "Where's the DI?"

Harris caught the chocolates one-handed. "She rang up and said she'd be with us shortly. DCI Garner requested her presence."

By the time Wild returned from cataloguing and booking in his evidence, DI Marsh was back in her castle — judging by the light through the blinds. He was halfway across the carpet tiles when the blinds rattled and someone banged on the glass. He knew a summons when he heard one.

"You seem to be the man of the hour. Your DCI is *very* happy with you, as am I."

He narrowed his eyes and lingered by the door.

"Well sit down, man. You could look a little more pleased!"

Only he wasn't, not even when Marsh produced a bottle of malt whisky. Before he could say a word she lifted a small tray from under her desk, containing two tiny steel tumblers like oversized thimbles. These she filled with practised ease and then replaced the cap.

"We are still working, after all. Your health, Craig."

He raised his drink. "Yours too, Morag."

"Come on then, out with it. What's eating you?"

"Why did Napier kill Lee Rickard?"

She took a sip of whisky and smacked her lips. "You were pretty much on the money. Napier said he found out more than he'd bargained for with Rickard and smelled an opportunity. He says he befriended him, and once he knew a few details — the prison sentence for one — he started building a file. We found some hidden stuff on the laptop. Deleted but still there somehow." She waved her hands in the air, hocus-pocus. "It's beyond me."

His mood hadn't lifted, despite the excellent malt. "What about the victim's mobile phone? We never found it. Did he take it?"

Marsh looked up and filled another tiny beaker. "Come in," she called.

DI Stanton joined them. He took a seat and shook hands with Wild. "A great result all round."

Wild was starting to feel queasy with all the bonhomie in the room.

"Ma'am, the victim's phone?"

Marsh talked over him. "How did you get on, Gareth?"

Stanton smiled like a dog that had just woken up with two dicks. "Hair follicle tests confirmed Lee Rickard had been on SNRI anti-anxiety medication since he came out of prison. His GP had a repeat prescription waiting for him."

Wild turned so fast his neck cricked. "What about Juliette Kimani's meds?"

Stanton threw him a pitying look. "She's on SSRIs. Similar, not the same. Even without a reaction with Rickard's meds that amount of ketamine in his system meant a death sentence. And we all know where it must have come from."

Wild downed the last of his whisky before it evaporated. "I s'pose you'll be leaving us soon, sir, now that NCA is in the clear."

"Oh, I'll be around for a few days. Still a few threads to tie up." He and Marsh shared a look that Wild couldn't decipher. "Anyway, I'll leave you both to it."

Once he'd gone, Marsh put her tray away. "You can be a real arse. Now, this phone you're going on about. Napier says he took it with him, when he left Rickard."

"Left him to die, you mean."

"Quite so. And he dumped it in a panic. Can't remember where. What is your problem with DI Stanton?"

Wild dodged the question-shaped bullet. "If we get the number from Isabella — because there's no way she wouldn't have it — we can find out where and when it was last active. Tie up one of Stanton's *loose threads* for him."

Marsh touched the whisky bottle lovingly and then consigned it to her desk drawer. In its place she set a cardboard box.

"You've been with us for over three months now, and I'm minded to keep you. This is an unofficial team-warming present. You can open it now."

He delved inside and retrieved a black plastic and glass module.

Marsh watched him, one hand resting over the other. "It's a dash cam with a built-in motion detector. I gather your car was vandalised not long after you arrived here. Some people in your position might have spoken to their superiors about it, but you must have tackled it another way. Once you've installed this and people see it — people in general, I mean — it's unlikely to happen again."

He laughed. "Nothing gets past you, does it?"

Marsh smiled. "I'll ask one of the techies to install it for you, unless you'd rather Marnie set it up?"

"No need to disturb Marnie while she's on duty. Could you make the call now?"

CHAPTER 37

Wild made it to Keynsham police station ahead of the 10 a.m. briefing. He wanted to savour every minute of the day that Paul Maguire got what was coming to him. Good of Marsh to arrange his ticket, but she probably still felt bad about him missing Napier's confession. He certainly did.

DC Grazia Kelley came out to meet him. She exemplified discomfort. "This way, Wild," she said needlessly as she took him staff-side.

He moved slowly, expecting another mouthful about the drugs search on Stuart Hoyle's home, and stalled her in the corridor. "Go on then, get it out of your system."

"I . . . I wanted to apologise. Stuart eventually told me about his problem with Maguire, and how you promised him a way out."

He aimed for magnanimity. "You weren't to know. And being Family Liaison, it seemed wrong to burden you. Did you report his connection to Maguire's organisation?"

She shook her head. "I've only Stuart's word for it — and I think their family's been through enough, don't you? Come on, you're guest of honour."

Kelley steered him through the corridors and stairways to a briefing room where four people were waiting. She patted his arm and left him to it.

"Ah, Craig, isn't it? This is DI Barlow and DS Nellister. I'm DCI Rouse."

There was something familiar about her though he couldn't place it. Unfortunately, he didn't have to.

"Let's shoot the elephant in the room, shall we? I've met DCI Hutcheson a few times in London. You probably won't remember, but we met there once as well."

He nodded. Nicely done, avoiding the words *ex* and *wife*. The DI and DS looked none the wiser.

"We have recorded testimony from the late Donald Jacobson," she dipped her head in Wild's direction, as if he'd done something clever. "Plus there's the link to the late John Donner, and that investigation is still ongoing." She thought for a moment and pointed Wild to a table containing refreshments. "Adam Napier's visits give us a conduit for information, while Napier's confession in Wiltshire names Maguire as a prime mover in Lee Rickard's death. One way or another, Maguire is implicated up to his neck." She passed around some blown-up photocopies of a man's ring. "Craig, I believe this is what you're talking about?"

He set his tea down. "Yes, ma'am."

"Call me Pippa, please. We don't stand on ceremony among our own here. We checked with the United Grand Lodge of England and confirmed Donald Jacobson's initiation date. If the ring inscription checks out, that's a direct link to Jacobson, post-mortem." Her face hardened. "Okay, we'll confront Maguire in an interview. If he's wearing the ring, that makes our job easier. We'll also be having his cell searched during the interview. We might get lucky with DNA on the ring but it could have been cleaned several times."

Wild piped up. "I doubt it, Pippa." He tested the name and enjoyed it. "That Masonic ring is Maguire's trophy and he doesn't know I saw it previously on Jacobson."

DI Barlow reminded Wild why he was a DI. "We also have information about where Maguire hides his burner phone — from an undisclosed source."

Wild would have tipped his hat. Cody Faulkner must have got his deal after all.

They travelled in one car. It wasn't far. DS Nellister drove and Wild rode up front, so the seniors could discuss strategy together. He had that Christmas morning feeling he remembered from childhood, when something good is definitely going to happen. This, he reminded himself, was why he signed up. Maybe it wasn't true justice for Lee or for Donald — nothing could be. It was the next best thing though: holding the right people to account.

Nellister came into the prison with them and then went his own way. DCI Rouse broke off from her conversation with DI Barlow to give Wild some advice. The same advice Marsh had bestowed on him the previous day: *don't let him bait you*.

Wild led them into the interview room. Maguire's opening words bounced off him like sand.

"I see you've bought along more friends this time."

He played ignorant, often his strongest suit. "These senior officers will conduct the interview. I'm mostly here as an observer."

DI Barlow's head practically swivelled towards him. Maguire cracked his knuckles and light glinted off his recently acquired Masonic ring. Wild paid it no attention.

The solicitor, Stephen Kershaw, walked the tightrope between professionalism and obstruction. Wild got the distinct impression that he didn't much care for his client but was lumbered with him. The words payment and piper came to mind.

DI Barlow started at the far horizon, working his way steadily closer, reconfirming old facts and checking his understanding. Maguire sat stony-faced, occasionally rolling his shoulders or rubbing the back of his neck. Eventually his impatience and confidence collided.

"Why are you really here today, coppers?" He grinned like a mobster, albeit one with a West Country accent.

Barlow gave his best impression of 'puzzled'. "You've had four visits from Adam Napier. What can you tell us about them?"

For a moment Maguire faltered and then the mask of a smile slipped back over his face. "He's a journalist." He leaned back contentedly. "He wants to write a book about me."

Barlow nodded as if he gave a shit. "And how did that come about?"

"He got in touch through my solicitor." Maguire looked straight at Wild. "My previous solicitor."

Wild snapped back at the speed of spite. "When he found out about Lee Rickard?"

"Is that supposed to mean something to me?"

Maguire's solicitor decided to join the interview. "My client has no knowledge of a Lee Rickard."

The DI shot Wild a cautionary glance, but didn't intervene.

"Sorry, that was his new name. You knew him as Jordan Hughes. Did Jordan ever come up in conversation?"

Maguire laced his fingers together. His face suggested he could break the table with them.

Wild took a back seat now he'd ratcheted things up a notch. The DI read from DI Marsh's summary.

"Adam Napier denies talking to you about a biography and a search of his computer and home found no evidence of any notes. Not a trace. In addition, Napier tells a very different story. He says he came to you because he discovered Lee Rickard used to be Jordan Hughes." DI Barlow looked Maguire in the eye. "You've already confirmed you knew Jordan very well. He testified against you."

Maguire's solicitor was sweating. "Are you asking my client a question?"

The DI massaged the bridge of his nose. "I'm happy to clarify that. Mr Maguire, did Adam Napier discuss Jordan Hughes with you?"

Maguire's knuckles whitened. "He may have mentioned him, as part of the book."

"The book Napier denies was ever discussed. He says he first came to see you to offer information about Hughes. After that he sought to get details from you to blackmail Hughes. And when Hughes called his bluff and said he'd contact you directly, Napier tried to appeal to your better nature. And then he — or you — decided Hughes was too big a threat and had to be dealt with. Ketamine was a nice touch, by the way, given it's not part of your previous product range."

"I never said a word against Hughes and you can't prove otherwise."

"Of course not," Wild pitched in. "Because there were things Jordan knew about your business that he never revealed — according to Napier's testimony, you understand. Your old solicitor, Donald Jacobson, was the messenger and set up the meetings."

Maguire relaxed his hands. "Well, unfortunately he's not here to corroborate that."

Wild was on a roll now. "No, when he found out you had John Donner commit arson to scare a girl into silence, Jacobson confronted you and told you he'd had enough. Did you know his daughter died in a fire years ago?"

Maguire blinked slowly. This was new information.

"You underestimated Donald Jacobson's courage. I can see that amuses you. Sure, you sent John Donner to kill him, but Jacobson was an extraordinary man. Here, I'll prove it." He turned to the DCI. "Ma'am?"

DCI Rouse cued up Jacobson's parting words. "I am now playing Paul Maguire and his solicitor a recording of a telephone message left for DS Wild on the night Donald Jacobson died."

Everyone sat perfectly still when a dead man started speaking.

"*Wild, it's Donald . . . After the interview . . . in prison . . . I told Maguire I was through . . . I won't be party to firebombing children. John Donner came here, attacked me — said Maguire ordered it. Wild, it's bad . . .*" Donald's laboured breathing filled the room. "*Oh God, they're coming back . . . Get them, Wild. Get them for me.*"

Maguire looked to the door and the prison warden in the room. Wild smelled the blue touch paper burning.

DCI increased the volume on the player. "And here's the second part of the recording."

"*Are you sure he's dead, John?*"

"*Take a closer look if you want . . . This isn't my first time. Chalky wanted him to suffer and wanted him to know why. No one walks away. You'd do well to remember that, junior. Right, have you found something suitable? Chalky loves his little trophies. Let me just take a picture to send to him.*"

Wild thought they'd done an excellent job of cleaning up the sound levels. Both voices were more distinct. He studied Maguire's face as John Donner tightened the metaphorical noose around his neck.

DI Barlow handed Maguire and his solicitor a transcript.

Maguire picked up the page, glanced at it and then slapped it face down on the table. "This is bullshit. That could be anyone."

Barlow smiled. "It could, but Jacobson's phone was found hidden in his sock and DS Wild's number was the last one he called. Imagine that. Knowing he was dying and still managing to incriminate you in his final moments."

As Wild pushed his chair back, he could sense a change in the room. The DI made the arrest for incitement to commit murder. And while Maguire was still reeling, Wild played his final card.

"We'll need your ring — by which I mean Donald Jacobson's ring. Guildford Lodge?" He shook his head. "I thought you were smarter than that."

Maguire glanced at his ringed hand. Wild read the thought, yelled, "Now," and hurled himself across the table, landing on Maguire as his colleagues worked their way around. It took three of them — including a prison officer — to subdue Maguire, so DCI Rouse could prise the ring from his finger.

"You're dead!" Maguire roared, spittle flecking the air as he strained against the three men pinning him down. Maguire laid eyes on his solicitor who sat there traumatised. "And you're dead as well."

Maguire was brought under control and escorted from the room. Wild picked his chair up and got his breath back. A couple of minutes later another prison officer entered the room with DS Nellister.

Nellister held up a clear plastic bag. "We found a burner phone in Maguire's cell."

Wild placed it on the table and laid a hand on the bag in benediction.

CHAPTER 38

Wild had already rung the reverend twice without leaving a message. Although he'd been the bearer of difficult news many times in his career, this one felt different. Marnie had teased him that his empathy skills were improving. He wasn't so sure.

Uncertain of the workings of the clergy, he'd checked out the Lincolnshire church online and aimed for ecclesiastical downtime.

"Jane Houghton speaking."

"Hi, it's Craig Wild — from Mayberry."

"Hello there. You've done well to catch me. It's been non-stop soul saving today."

He laughed briefly and then summoned his work voice. "Listen, I'm ringing with news. We have charged a man with Lee Rickard's murder . . ."

She cut in quickly. "Don't tell me his name, I'd rather not know. I find it easier to try and forgive a stranger."

"If it helps any, the man in custody said he was in fear of his life and acted in desperation."

"That's two lives wasted then."

"We've also arrested someone else from Lee's past in connection with his death."

After a pause, she said, "Thanks for letting me know."

He decided to keep talking. "I also wanted to tell you that drugs we found at Lee's flat were probably planted there. So it looks as if he was turning his life around, and you were part of that. You made a difference."

She changed the subject. "How's Isabella?"

"It's early days. She's resilient though."

The silence stretched out like a canyon.

"Craig, it's probably not the done thing, but how would you like to attend Lee's funeral? I can show you the sights of Lincoln too."

It caught him unawares. "Come up to Lincolnshire?"

He tried to tune out Marnie's two thumbs-up practically jabbing him in the face.

"Of course, Craig, I quite understand if you're busy."

Marnie opened her hands, as if you say, 'When are you likely to get a better offer?'

"Actually, yeah, I'd like that."

"Brilliant! In that case I'm doubly glad you rang. I'd also like your advice. Lee left instructions — not to be opened unless — you know . . . I'd misplaced the letter. Genuinely. Anyway, he wanted any money left in his account to go to Conor Hoyle's family. I thought maybe you could speak to them?"

"I reckon it'd be better coming from you. I'll contact the family liaison officer in Bristol to check they're happy to hear from you. I'll text you my home number and catch up with you soon."

That left one more thing to take care of. He rang Sergeant Galloway.

"Anthony, it's Craig Wild. Listen, I'm here with Marnie. Can I borrow her?"

He could see that same eagerness in her face.

Galloway chuckled. "I suppose so. She can take an extended break, on account of her recent successes. Don't be all day though."

"We won't. And it is work-related."

Marnie followed him out to his car. "Where are we going?"

"It's only right that we tell Isabella — and Juliette — in person."

"So, what, I'm the caring face of Wiltshire Police?"

"Not exactly. You were in at the start of this, I thought you'd like to be there at the end — as far as Wiltshire Police is concerned. Plus, I was hoping for a couple of minutes alone with Juliette."

"What about her husband?"

He didn't answer immediately. "Went back to London and his play, as soon as John Donner was cold."

There was only one topic of conversation in the car.

"Be honest, Wild. You never took to Juliette. That was as much your class prejudice as any detective's instinct."

He didn't argue the point. "I don't like being lied to." He knew that look. "Okay then, taken for a fool. She wasn't straight with us from the very start."

"Is anyone ever?"

"She hampered the investigation by withholding information. If she'd been more forthcoming maybe Isabella wouldn't have been placed in danger." He changed tack and asked her a question. "How did Napier put a tracker on Rickard's car? I mean, how did he know which car — and when would he have seen it?"

Marnie's jaw slackened. "Oh, Wild, surely you don't mean . . . Juliette?" She couldn't come up with a better explanation. "Are you going to tell Isabella? She'd never trust her mother again. Juliette couldn't possibly have known what Napier would do."

He thought about it for a long minute. "She's an author, remember? They're supposed to have good imaginations." He frowned. "Are you really sure this is the career for you?

"Without a doubt."

If one of the highlights of the job was catching villains, then this surely qualified as a lowlight. Whether it was making the fateful knock on the door to say their loved one was never coming home, or informing a family that the person who ruined their life was now charged and in custody, it never brought real closure, only pain. Their pain and his paperwork.

Juliette opened the door before the bell had ended. No doubt Isabella had seen their car pull up. Juliette let them in and sat next to her daughter on the sofa, a motherly arm around her shoulders. Wild remained standing, took a breath, and dived right in.

"I'm here to inform you that we have someone in custody for the death of Lee Rickard, and another man has been arrested for incitement to commit murder."

Isabella started crying, burying her face in her mother's shoulder. Wild turned to Marnie. "Could you put the kettle on please?"

She stared daggers at him but did as he requested.

Juliette asked questions that might have satisfied her curiosity but wouldn't ease her daughter's pain. He told her what he could, which wasn't much, and gladly took over tea-making duties when he heard the kettle click from the open doorway.

There was no easy way to separate mother and daughter, so he didn't look for it.

"Mrs Kimani, can I speak to you in private?"

Isabella looked up suddenly.

Marnie held out a hand. "Why don't we go and have a chat upstairs?"

Wild sat down and waited for the bedroom door to close.

"Adam Napier pleaded guilty to killing Lee Rickard. At first I couldn't work out how he managed to follow Lee home all the way to Lincolnshire, and then he mentioned a tracking device. Someone would have had to put it on Lee's car."

He expected her to cave. He was wrong.

She stared at him defiantly. "You don't have children, Sergeant. You cannot appreciate what Isabella has been through — what we've all been through."

He always set a low bar when it came to hearing justifications and he was used to being disappointed. Even so, he let her say her piece.

"We felt so blessed when a compatible donor came forward through the church network. I wanted to know everything about him, especially when they became friends. That was my right as her mother. Imagine my horror in finding out that the man who saved Isabella — who she became *entangled* with — was a killer."

"He made a bad choice with unintended consequences, much like your decision to have Adam Napier dig into Lee's life. Napier wanted to exploit him, only Lee was too smart so Napier killed him." He left out any details that might have softened the blow.

"Is that everything you came to tell me? You've done your job, now you can go."

He could feel the chill in the room. "Not quite. Isabella also became friends with the vicar in Lee's parish — part of your church network. The Reverend Jane Houghton is conducting Lee's funeral in a few days and thinks Isabella will want to attend. My advice?" He answered himself. "Let her go. Let Isabella mourn the person *she* knew." He got up. "One more thing. Call it a favour. Don't write about this — don't be like Napier and try to profit from someone else's tragedy."

Juliette's piercing gaze never wavered. He started walking.

"When Marnie comes down, tell her I'll be out in the car."

* * *

Marnie heard the front door close and watched Wild from the upstairs window.

"I have to go."

Isabella remained sat on her bed. "Do you think Lee really loved me? He said he was meeting someone at the festival — some sort of business deal — and then he was coming to see me. As long as Mum wasn't around, of course. We had even swapped copies of our front door keys."

Marnie put a piece of the puzzle into place. "When's your birthday?"

She smiled sadly. "In a few days."

"And your parents never knew you were running away with Lee?"

"Not running away. Going away. Only he never arrived. I thought he'd got cold feet, or maybe Mum had argued with him, because my app showed him travelling back to Lincolnshire." She scrolled through her phone and tapped an icon named *playlist*. "I disguised it so Mum wouldn't find it."

"Can I take this with me? I promise we'll return it as soon as we're finished."

"Sure, let me unlock it," she passed it over. "Makes no difference now."

Marnie glanced to the closed door and then sat back down beside Isabella, taking her hand. "Yes, I'm sure he loved you."

* * *

Wild offered Marnie a wine gum after she'd put on her seatbelt. "Everything okay?"

"So-so. Isabella gave me her phone, so I've got Lee's number. She thinks he had a Samsung — definitely something Android."

"We'll set the wheels in motion as soon as we get back. Harris should be able to confirm the service provider through his direct debits. I'm surprised he hadn't spotted that already."

"There's something else. Isabella has an app on her phone. One of those *where-are-you* locators that lets couples follow each other's movements."

"So much for trust."

"In their case, I think it was meant to be romantic."

Wild slammed on the brake before they reached the end of the drive. "That's it! That's how the arsonist did it. I couldn't figure out how Donner knew where to find Isabella after she left Lee's flat. I mean, exactly where to find her. He must have had Lee's phone to track her location."

"Does it matter now?"

"I'm not sure. But it means Adam Napier met John Donner, or whoever started the fire. So where's the phone now?"

CHAPTER 39

Midnight... the witching hour. A motorcycle slows in a quiet, non-descript terrace. The rider dismounts, takes the small petrol bottle from its fastening and casts an eye along the road. No mistaking the only Ford Focus among the row of cars.

He stretches across the roof and pours carefully, as the cloying petrol fumes seep into his motorcycle helmet. He coughs softly, but he doesn't stop, now dribbling fuel across the top of the windscreen, and then finally smashes the bottle between the front wheels. Undeterred by the cacophony of glass he stands back, ignites a match and lights a strip of rag. The cloth catches and he throws it onto the car where the flames quickly multiply.

He gets back on his bike, unzips his jacket and draws the gun. It doesn't take long, less than a minute, although time seems to stretch. After the whoosh as the fire catches hold, a front door bursts open and a man in a dressing gown rushes out, fire blanket in hand.

There is only time for one shot and then time speeds up. The shooter sees the look of horror as the victim falls backwards. He secures the gun and he's away before the body hits the ground, echoes of a scream drowned out by sixty horsepower.

CHAPTER 40

Wild woke up in a sweat, pulse hammering through his ribcage, eyes open, rigid with fear. A rhythmic banging, insistent and shrill, played nonsensical Morse code in the distance. As his muscles softened he focused on the sound and picked out shouting in the mix. He climbed into his jeans and grabbed his trainers by the bed, along with a piece of aluminium tubing. It could have been a wardrobe rail, only it wasn't.

"Alright, I'm coming."

He looked down from the top of the stairs to see the letterbox flap forced back by four fingers.

"Hurry up, mate, your car's on fire."

He met a middle-aged couple on the doorstep, still in their nightclothes. As he followed them along the terrace he caught the acrid stench of burnt rubber. His Ford Focus, still partially alight, looked like war footage. A woman was crying outside the house opposite his car, cradling a man on the ground.

She looked up plaintively. "He's been shot — somebody call for an ambulance."

Wild told the couple to dial 999 and to get the police as well. Nothing to gain from his own warrant card.

The fire engine arrived first. Marsh and Galloway were on the scene a few minutes later. By then Wild had collected some details about the shooting victim and walked along the road to the end of the terrace. There were no clues to be had.

Marsh found him in the street, blood on his hands and a vacant look on his face.

"Wild," she called him towards her car.

He was slow to respond. She met him at the kerb.

"The team is on their way. Why don't we let them deal with all this and go and have a chat inside?" She turned back to Galloway and gave him his orders.

Wild opened his front door and kept walking. "I'll put the kettle on." He got cups from the drying rack and took milk from the fridge. If Marsh spoke again he never heard her. When he drowned the teabags he remembered she was in the house with him and turned to see her watching from the door.

"I'm okay, really."

"Which is more than you can say for your car!"

He laughed for a couple of seconds and then went back to tea-making. "Is he going to be alright?"

Marsh glanced towards the door. "The victim was still conscious when they took him away, which is always a good sign."

"It should have been me."

She took a cup, added three sugars and passed it back to him. "Aye, I know. Finish your tea and pack some things. You can't say here, it isn't safe. I'll get someone to drive you."

He looked up, suddenly alert. "The dash cam in my car — I had it set for motion."

Marsh held out her hand. "Keys. Right, stay here."

He did as she asked and was still sat there when she returned, clasping his cup of untouched tea.

"Ben is taking the SD card to Technical Support. The lack of street lighting doesn't help but no doubt they'll do what they can. I don't want you going outside. Do you understand? I have things to do but I'll get someone to sit with you. Drink your tea."

She left him and he heard noises in the distance. When he looked up again Marnie was in the room. She gave him a nervous smile and then looked away.

"Hiya Marnie," he blinked a couple of times. "I'm fine. Just a bit shook up."

"Jesus, Wild. Someone nearly shot you."

The room snapped back into focus. "You want a brew?"

She said yes, just to give him something to do. He carried on talking as he moved around the kitchen.

"Did I ever tell you, Marnie? I met this bloke once, Irish fella, ex-Army. He'd know how to deal with something like this. It was a while ago now but I might still have his number somewhere." He glanced to the ceiling, grasping for a memory.

She sat opposite, saying nothing. His rambling ran its course and he fell silent again. They drank their tea quietly.

Marsh returned, entering the room softly like an usher at a funeral. "Everything's under control. Your car is evidence, Craig, so a recovery vehicle is on its way. Not that you are ever likely to drive it again."

He smiled for an instant when he thought about filling in an insurance claim.

Marsh was still very much in charge. "We'll contain the story as much as possible but the local TV and newspapers will want some sort of statement. We're not releasing the identity of the victim — orders from above."

He looked confused for a moment and then nodded. "Did we miss something?" Even in his hazy state he knew it was a stupid question.

"Come on, Craig — get your bag. You can't stay here while this lunatic is at large."

He looked her in the eyes. "Where am I going?"

Marsh came forward and laid a hand on Marnie's shoulder. "Just till tomorrow."

Marnie felt the weight of expectation bearing down. "You can stay at mine for a couple of nights, now that Leo has gone."

Wild thought for a moment. "He went back to his wife?"

"Yeah, guilt-ridden and with his tail between his legs."

Even though she tried to make light of it he could see she was troubled.

"Okay," Marsh strangled the word. "Let's get you out of here. We'll talk again tomorrow morning. I'll have Ben Galloway drop you off."

* * *

Marnie helped him in with his bags. "Right, well, this is us. Just give me a few minutes to check the spare bed."

When she returned he was sitting in the lounge, eating from a packet of custard creams. "Sorry, I'm ravenous. What time is it?"

"Nearly two in the morning. We're expected at nine, so I'm gonna brush my teeth and say goodnight." As she clicked on the bathroom light she heard him call behind her.

"Thanks, Marn."

She didn't answer.

Wild surfaced around eight. He felt like shit, although he figured he was doing better than the shooting victim. He grabbed his own towel from the bag and took his turn in the bathroom, breathing in steam and fruits of the forest. The soap smelt girly but as he'd forgotten his own, beggars couldn't be choosers. He wasn't keen on the fancy toothpaste either.

Marnie sat on the couch, staring intently at the local news, a bowl of cereal in her hand. She looked up as he put in an appearance.

"There's muesli in the jar or some rye bread for the toaster."

"I'll settle for tea and grab some proper food in the canteen."

She glanced towards the kitchen and passed him her empty bowl. He took the hint. He made tea with one quarter cold water to save time, and stood at the doorway behind her.

"Anything on the news?"

"Not yet. I'd be surprised if one of your neighbours doesn't post something online."

"What, and risk DI Marsh's wrath? Never!" He downed his tea in three guttural gulps, like a cow at a trough. "Cheers again for putting me up. I can't remember much of last night — apart from the obvious, I mean."

She turned off the TV. "You were on one, talking about some squaddie you met who was a vigilante. Must have been the shock talking."

"Hmm, sounds about right." He ditched the cup in the sink, checked again that he had his warrant card, phone and all the other fun stuff he got to use at work, and declared himself fit for duty.

Ben Galloway was waiting outside at eight forty on the dot. "Morning, campers."

They were late getting in, which wasn't entirely down to Galloway's careful driving. Wild went straight up to the canteen and managed to beg a bacon sandwich. When he came back downstairs he found the main office sparsely populated. Marnie was waiting at his desk.

"The DI would like us to join her in the briefing room."

He licked ketchup from the side of his mouth and finished his sandwich, wiping his hands and mouth with a paper napkin. "I s'pose they have you down as chaperone."

Marnie didn't seem to share the joke. "Looks that way."

CHAPTER 41

The room fell as silent as a crypt when Wild turned the door handle. One of the whiteboards had been cleaned and two photographs now sat side by side in the centre — the unlucky neighbour, who Wild had met for the first time earlier that morning, and an old picture of Wild from his days in the Met.

Marsh got up without a word and began filling in the blanks.

"Ian Reynolds, aged thirty. Married, no kids. Former soldier, hence his willingness to get stuck in with a fire blanket. He's lived on the terrace for about six months. They're taking him into surgery today, all being well."

Wild frowned as she turned back to the board and carried on speaking.

"Ben, as soon as that bullet is removed I want you to liaise with the National Ballistics Intelligence Service."

Galloway nodded and made a note for himself.

"What about my dash cam footage?"

"Thank you, Craig — I was coming to that. Seems the heat from the fire damaged the unit. Our techies are using . . ." she made speech marks with her fingers, marker pen still in hand, "'advanced software' to repair the SD card. It's another high priority."

Wild spoke to the room. "What do you want *me* to do?"

Marsh's answer hit him like a slap in the face. "Stay out of sight. If we can keep a lid on the victim's true name and status, the shooter has no reason to come back. Officially *you* remain on the critical list and under protection."

She gave the impression she was mulling something over. However, he knew her better than that. He sat down and awaited her judgement.

"Didn't you say you'd been invited to Lee Rickard's funeral in Lincolnshire? Maybe it's a good time to get away for a few days."

He felt the chip on his shoulder scalding his skin. "Is that an order, ma'am?"

"No it bloody isn't, and it's not an invitation to start a fight either. You have to leave this to us, Craig, so either make yourself scarce or strap yourself to your desk."

He heard Marnie choke on her breath and recalled that he hadn't mentioned the funeral to Marsh. Marnie had been there though when he'd taken the call.

Harris cut into the gap. "What about CCTV?

"Nothing as yet."

Now was not the time for a public falling-out, so he answered Harris instead. "There are back lanes behind the terrace, and waste-ground, so we'll need to study the map carefully. If someone knew what they were doing they might not surface on CCTV until they were some distance away."

Marsh's pen pointed at Harris. "That'll be you then, once you've checked with the techies again." She turned to face Wild. "They've been here since dawn at my request."

Harris left the room, phone in hand and stepped back inside a minute or so later.

"Someone is bringing down prints."

It wasn't long before a timid knock announced a visitor. Wild always got a sense that the good folk in Technical Support preferred the company of machines to people. He'd met Sharna three times since arriving at Mayberry and shared about as many sentences.

She had a deferential air that really grated on him, as she crossed the floor and handed some A4 colour prints to DI Marsh without a word. Marsh glanced at the pages before passing them around. Sharna was left to make her own way out.

"Looks like we got lucky. The gunman took off past the windscreen."

Wild and Marnie shared a couple of pages, which he supposed were the best of them. Like looking through a bonfire and only a partial number plate. Maybe not so lucky. Marnie wrestled a page from him and studied it more closely.

"Ma'am, that's a classic bike." The image was a little fuzzy but she knew the badge. "It's a Triumph."

"Certainly is!" Harris piped up.

"No," she snapped. "A Triumph motorbike — looks like a Bonneville. Could be a T100 or a T120. That's seven thousand pounds of classic engineering." She stopped talking, aware that everyone was looking at her. "I've, er, seen them at exhibitions."

"That's a good start," Marsh addressed the team. "Ben, liaise with the hospital — we want that bullet. Harris, follow up Craig's insight on the local area. And Marnie, seeing as you're our motorbike expert," she said with a smile in her voice, "see if you can narrow down the model and then search for registered owners. Okay then," she clapped her hands twice rapidly, "off you go."

Marsh sat on the edge of a table, watching until everyone else had left. In two sentences she conducted the world's shortest risk assessment for attending the funeral and wished him a good journey. His temporary departure was a done deal.

The good reverend was delighted he could come up early and Ben Galloway agreed to lend him his car. He spent the rest of the day getting up to date with paperwork. After that, a funeral seemed almost a pleasure. Marnie sprang for a takeaway that evening and they watched a *Lord of the Rings* film. Apparently she was a fan — who knew?

CHAPTER 42

Wild set off early doors, on the road by six thirty. He reached Lincoln before ten, with a little flexibility on the speed limit. Jane Houghton took his update call and suggested they go out for lunch, once he'd dropped off his bags.

"I know a nice little pub, just off my patch."

"Doesn't sound very ecumenical." He hoped he'd used the right word.

"We're very broad-minded in the C of E these days. See you when I see you."

He tried to read between the lines and found only spaces. Hard to believe he used to be good at this, or so he thought. When he stopped for petrol outside Lincoln — he wasn't made of money — he picked up some overpriced chocolates and kidded himself he was being a considerate guest.

* * *

"Do you want a cuppa first, after all that driving?"

He shook his head and put his sports bag down in the hall. He liked her jeans and Stonehenge sweatshirt combo — but didn't know how to say so without sounding awkward.

"Right then, shall we?" She rattled her car keys and twenty minutes later they were waiting for lasagne and a shared salad.

"How did you end up as a vicar then?" He was never big on small talk.

Jane laughed. "I'd always been a bit religious. You know, Christmas service, trying to lead a decent life." She glanced skyward. "Although I took a detour in uni — all that real ale and revolutionary talk went to my head!"

It made a nice change to have a conversation without a solicitor present, or a microphone recording two copies. The arrival of the food didn't slow the casual chat.

"And what about you? Didn't you say you'd been married?"

He smiled. He hadn't, well played. "Yeah, to another copper. Separated now, awaiting the divorce." He paused for effect. "I know, doesn't put me on good terms with Him upstairs. She's in London and I'm in Wiltshire. Not exactly amicable."

It seemed to him that her demeanour changed once they set foot back inside the vicarage and he smiled to himself as he grabbed his bag. Such was the power of hallowed ground.

"I'll take you to the guest room. It's this way." She walked back past him outside.

He followed her across the drive and up the street to a house a few doors along.

"I've been really lucky," she explained. "The study and my office just needed a deep clean. I spent three days in a B&B and then one of my flock was going away for a fortnight so they let me use their home. How amazing is that?"

He wiped his boots a little too enthusiastically on the mat. "I hope your neighbours won't think you're moving a man in?"

She smiled and turned sharply. "They know me better than that. You're in the back."

It was a nice room, a bit chintzy for his tastes. The bed felt solid enough though. Once he'd unpacked, he used the facilities and then joined her downstairs with the box of chocs under his arm.

He mumbled, "These are for you."

"Ah, thanks, Craig. That's really kind."

She patted his arm, which felt like Morse code for *no*. They returned to the vicarage, where he made himself at home in the study while she did whatever vicars do between services. He imagined there were still some preparations for Lee Rickard's funeral and he didn't intend to ask.

He was happily browsing a well-thumbed copy of Adrian Goldsworthy's *The Complete Roman Army* when Marnie's text came in.

How is it going?

He rang straight back. "Hi, it's quicker to call. How is the investigation without me?"

She would have said, 'It's only been half a day,' but she could tell by his tone that it wouldn't be well received.

"I've checked Bonneville T100 and T120 owners — I still can't be sure of the model, and the partial number plate doesn't match anything on record."

"Fake then," he added, with a hint of irritation.

"There are three owners within a hundred-mile radius, of which the nearest is a woman in Haydon." She spoke for him. "I know, too close for comfort. We are doing a drive-by today to check for CCTV in the area."

He heard the excitement in her voice. "What about Ian Reynolds?"

"His surgery is scheduled for this evening."

"Okay, keep me posted."

"Enjoy the rest of your leave and try not to give Juliette Kimani a hard time."

"Yeah, if she turns up." He figured he'd said enough so he cut the call.

CHAPTER 43

Marnie returned DI Marsh's handset across the desk. "He's arrived safe and sound, ma'am."

"Aye, it sounded like it. Let's see how he feels when DI Stanton arrives for Lee's final journey." She went to her door and clicked her fingers to summon DC Harris.

Marnie had noticed that Harris had yet to achieve first name recognition from the DI, unlike herself and Ben Galloway. Harris held up his car keys in lieu of conversation and Marsh nodded.

"Let's get it done then."

The four-mile journey was mostly conducted in silence, Marsh exuding a presence that Marnie remembered from her school days. Unsurprisingly for a B road, cameras were thin on the ground, and with two roads to choose from Marsh announced they'd be making their return by the other route.

"Harris, take us around the area — see if we can get an eyeball of the bike owner's address."

He did as he was told, Marnie watching from the back seat, showing a level of attention that she'd only witnessed before in a driving lesson. Marsh directed Harris according to a prearranged schedule that he wasn't party to. When he drove past a small parade of shops and the entrance to a modern housing estate Marsh flicked her head to one side and instructed him to pull into the next gap.

"Walk up there and take a look at the garages. There's no way they would leave an expensive motorbike out on the street."

As Harris got out the car she handed him a fiver. There should be a newsagent on the estate, go buy a local paper. And leave your car keys in case we need to move."

Harris had barely crossed over before Marsh turned to Marnie. "We passed a property rental place just before we stopped. Can you head up there and ask about garages for rent. Make sure you get a business card from them. When you get back, climb in the front — it will attract less attention."

The aluminium and glass door pinged as Marnie pushed it open. A middle-aged woman looked up from her desk and smiled. A faint scent of essential oils, probably a plug in, permeated the space.

"Can I help you?"

Marnie faltered. "I'm, er, looking for a garage to rent — for storage."

"We are mostly homes and commercial properties, and to be honest garages are like gold dust around here. Some people do rent out privately. If you want to leave me your details I can ask around." The woman waited. She looked bemused. "If it's for storing commercial goods you'll need to have your own insurance."

"Yeah," Marnie knocked the edges off her speech. "Nothing expensive, just market goods. Can I take your card and get back to you?"

"Sure." The woman handed it over.

As she headed for the door Marnie added, as an afterthought, "It's all legit."

The woman nodded and smiled, as if she had just caught her out.

Marnie stood outside for a couple of seconds and pretended to read the card. Wild was right when he'd said: *always get your story straight before you open your mouth.*

She got into the front passenger side.

"Everything okay?"

"I think so." She showed Marsh the card.

"You keep it for now. It's different isn't it, this kind of work? Harder in a way."

Marnie didn't answer for fear of incriminating herself.

Marsh stared out the windscreen, looking pensive.

"Marnie, I owe you an apology. I shouldn't have mentioned Craig's funeral invitation in Lincolnshire. Do you think he put two and two together?"

"I'm sure of it."

"Oh well, it's done now. He'll get over it."

Yes, Marnie thought, *with you anyway.*

Harris appeared in the distance, walking at a pace. As he approached, newspaper in hand, he blinked at the incomprehensible scene of Marsh and Marnie in the front seats, before consigning himself to the back of the car. He gave them his report, such as it was.

"There's a row of garages around the side of the maisonettes. One was open and empty but they aren't numbered." He stopped talking.

Marsh pulled out into traffic and waved ironically at a van driver who'd only let her out because he was indicating for the parking spot.

"I've marked the map, Marnie. See if you can add any CCTV on the way back and then the two of you can work through it at Mayberry. I need to see DCI Garner at Gable Cross."

* * *

Harris, Ben and Marnie sat in the briefing room. Harris grabbed the map, glanced at it and then thrust it back at Marnie.

"You better get on with it then. Only don't get too comfortable in CID. I'm nipping upstairs for a coffee. Call me if anything comes up."

Galloway said nothing until Harris had let the door slam shut behind him.

"Don't mind him. His nose has been out of joint since DS Wild joined the team."

Her eyes widened. "What, Harris has passed his sergeant's already?"

Ben chuckled. "No way. He was well in with DS Thorpe though."

Marnie re-checked the map and passed it over. "What actually happened to him?"

"No one knows. Honest. Not even my uncle and he's a fellow sergeant. One morning DS Thorpe wasn't here and the boss announced that he'd left the team. End of story, no forwarding address." His brow furrowed. "We'd be better working at desks — you can use the skip's."

It seemed to Marnie that Harris, Galloway and Wild were on a continuum. Harris, on the current showing, did the bare minimum. Galloway did more and was eager to please, although he seemed a bit lacking in initiative. As for Wild, he lived for the job. Collectively they were like the three unwise monkeys.

"What do you want me to do then, Ben?"

He thought hard, like a child counting mentally on its fingers. "Tell you what, do a full check on the bike's owner, Raquel Beaumont. I'll start with the Highways Agency and see about footage from the cameras you've marked."

Galloway's voice became increasingly louder as he exhausted all avenues to get camera footage. Marnie, meanwhile, learned that Ms Beaumont had no previous convictions and also owned an ageing red Peugeot. Clearly, she'd spent her money on the bike. Marnie waited until Galloway banged the phone down again and then raised a hand to attract his attention.

"There are some filters I can't use. Might be a CID thing?"

Before he could reply, the office door swung in at an alarming speed. DI Marsh entered with a face like thunder.

"Can you believe it? No one at Gable Cross is free to help us and the Surveillance Support Unit is tied up for the next two weeks. We'll have to make do." She stomped off to her office, pausing by the door. "I don't suppose either of you has had Covert Surveillance training?"

She peered over the desks like a cat above a birdbath. "Where's Harris?"

Marnie tried changing the subject. "I think DS Wild has done the training, ma'am. He mentioned surveillance work in London."

Marsh couldn't have looked less impressed. "In that case you'd better get Craig on the phone. And if Harris isn't back here in the next five minutes I will personally hunt him down." She shut the door behind her slowly and deliberately.

Marnie grabbed a phone. "I'll get Harris down first and then see how Wild is doing."

"I'd have left Harris in the canteen."

"Hardly conducive to teamwork though."

Ben grunted. "Harris isn't exactly a team player, is he? Why do you think I'm so keen to move on?"

She thought about that as she dialled. The way Wild told it, Galloway wanted a new challenge. She didn't waste time on niceties. "Harris, you better get down here. The DI is back in her office." That was the easy call.

Wild picked up before the third ring. "Hi, Marnie. Everything okay?"

"The boss wants you to ring her urgently. What time is the funeral tomorrow?"

"The church service is around lunchtime. Now you mention it, I don't know if it's a burial or cremation afterwards. Is there a problem?"

"Best you talk to the DI. But if I were you, I wouldn't make plans afterwards. Gotta go, bye."

He mulled it over, decided Marnie had been asked to play the good cop, and then rang the bad cop. "Ma'am, it's Craig Wild." He heard a drawer close at the other end of the line.

"Your leave is cancelled the second that funeral is over. Understood?"

He didn't waste time with reasons. "Clear as day. I'll be back by six p.m."

"Good, I'll see you here tomorrow then."

CHAPTER 44

Reverend Houghton took the news about him leaving early better than he'd expected, much to his disappointment. They joked about the similarities between their jobs, which she insisted were both *vocations*, and assured him she understood.

She made pasta that evening, describing herself as a *pasta fiend*, and he sprang for a bottle of wine. Nothing ostentatious, although not the cheap stuff either. They ate on trays, watching one of her history DVDs — on excavations of Roman Colchester. In many ways he couldn't have been happier.

"Do you know what, Craig? I think you're the first bloke I've spent time with in a long time — years, probably — who didn't find the vicar thing . . . troubling." She touched at an invisible dog collar. "Typically, it's a challenge, a turn-off or a turn-on!"

"Blokes, eh?" He grinned to try and stop himself blushing.

They killed most of the chocolates and sunk the rest of the wine. By ten thirty he was all in. Later, in the tiny kitchen, there was a moment where they nearly collided as she crossed by him to put a pan away. She grabbed his arm to steady herself and they stood together, almost swaying.

"Tell you a secret, Craig . . . you're the sort of man I should have met in university. There's a kindness in you."

She nodded wisely and then puffed out a breath. "Don't mind me — too much pasta and too much wine!"

He put his hands on her shoulders and she snaked her arms around him, and they hugged for what seemed an extraordinarily long time.

"Thanks, Craig, I needed that. Goodnight my friend, see you in the morning. Sleep well."

Which was nigh on impossible for the first hour, as he kept thinking about her and whether there'd been a moment where something might have happened, and then judging himself for even thinking it.

* * *

Wild waited until he heard Jane moving about the house before he got out of bed. For one thing, he didn't know where the iron was, and for another he still felt sheepish about fancying his chances with a woman of the cloth.

After the world's feeblest shower he joined her downstairs, phone in hand for updates. During breakfast he picked up two texts on the bounce. Both made him eager to get back to Mayberry.

The surgeon had removed the bullet and the patient was responding well.

Marsh had made a statement the previous night for the newspapers and local news to put out that morning.

"You seem busy, if you don't mind me saying so."

He looked up and felt that tingle again. "Yeah, just work stuff," he said unapologetically. "It seems that Lee's case isn't as over as we thought."

She left at eight thirty for her office. He ironed and packed, ready for a fast getaway. On the walk over he lamented the missed trip to Lincoln cathedral and wondered whether staying an extra day would have been a good thing after all.

As he walked across the drive he heard a vehicle pull up behind him. A spotty youth got out of a small white van, opened the back doors and extracted a funeral wreath.

"Excuse me mate, are you with the vicar? Any chance you could take this in for me? I'm running late."

"Sure." He signed a slip and then carried the rosette of white flowers at arms' length.

When he put it down in the doorway he couldn't resist checking out the card: *In deepest sympathy — Kath, Rob and family.* He was still crushing the lump in his chest as he went through.

"Some flowers arrived. I signed for them."

"Thanks." Jane looked up from her desk. "Well, don't you look smart! Oh, I meant to say, Gareth Stanton should be here shortly. I expect you two have lots to talk about."

Wild figured she meant well, but the use of DI Stanton's first name suggested a familiarity that rankled. He arrived fifteen minutes later. Wild went out to meet him. "Sir," he held out his hand.

"Gareth's fine, while we're here. Your DI tells me we have a situation?"

Wild took it as rhetorical and merely nodded. A good call.

"I spoke with her last night and we agreed that I'd brief you before we go back to Mayberry."

Wild knew when to keep his mouth shut.

"Let's, er, take a walk."

Wild pointed him to the nearby graveyard. Given the occasion, it seemed appropriate. Stanton talked and he listened, turning it over in his brain.

". . . The news statement says the gunshot victim is still critical, and no official confirmation whether they're a serving police officer — which should be enough to reassure the shooter. Also that the police are urgently seeking a person of interest." DI Stanton lit up a cigarette, offered one — which Wild declined — and blew smoke across a headstone. "We now have CCTV showing the bike out and about in the early hours. Fake plates but it's a distinctive model. Any questions?"

Now seemed a good time to show willing. "If this bike's owner is as innocent as the database suggests, who else has access to it?"

DI Stanton took another drag. "There are no flags for Raquel Beaumont and nothing relevant on her social media. If it's not her, we're in the dark. Hence the surveillance, under DI Marsh's careful tutelage."

He smiled, and Wild smiled back as if he shared the joke. As soon as Stanton wandered off — presumably to make a private call — Wild rang Marnie.

"Are you still working with CID?"

"Not today," she gave a leaden sigh. "Tomorrow though, apparently. Why?"

"Any chance of a favour when you're on lunch? Can you search social media accounts for Raquel Beaumont and get back to me later. Thanks."

* * *

There were more people in the church than Wild had expected. The local congregation had done the vicar proud. She had a sort of glow about her, so different from the woman he'd shared pasta with the previous evening.

She welcomed everyone to the sad occasion and explained that as Lee had no family, he would be mourned as a member of the community, and by those closest to him in life. Everyone stood when the coffin entered the church and they remained standing until Isabella Kimani and her mother sat down in the front row. No Mr Kimani, Wild noted.

He was glad to be at the back because it meant he wasn't so close to Isabella. Poor kid, she was in pieces — so much for first love. He felt for Juliette as well. What a penance to be cast as the grieving in-law. *Morning has Broken* was a nice albeit traditional touch, which neither the electric organist nor the mourners managed to completely murder.

The reverend's eulogy closed with a quote from the Bible, for which Wild forgave her.

"As we say our farewells to Lee, let us finally reflect on these words from the Book of Matthew, chapter 25: 'For I was hungry and you gave me food, I was thirsty and you gave me drink, I was a stranger and you welcomed me.' Let us remember Lee in our kindness to others." She took a deliberate breath. "We will now hear a song chosen by Isabella, who knew him best."

Wild braced himself for some hip-hop monstrosity, but what he heard was Green Day's 'Wake Me Up When September Ends'. There wasn't a dry eye in the house.

He lingered in the church long enough to offer condolences to Isabella, who seemed to brighten a little when she saw him. Not so her mother, who gave her best fake smile and told him how much her daughter appreciated his being there.

The reverend asked for a private word next door so he said his goodbyes, told DI Stanton he'd see him later, and followed her into the study.

"I just want to say," she froze for a moment and then deftly removed her dog collar. "Have a safe trip home, Craig, and keep in touch — if you want." And before he could think of a reply she leaned forward and kissed him.

He thought about that a lot on the drive home.

CHAPTER 45

Wild resisted the urge to ring Marnie as soon as he was on the road. He lasted about an hour.

"I'm not your assistant, you know! Look, I can't talk long. I looked into the matter we discussed . . ."

He figured someone was nearby, hopefully not her sergeant or that weasel Harris.

". . . The only thing that caught my attention was a photo taken outside a pub called The Crown."

"Right," he was already starting to lose interest. "Pretty popular name for a pub."

"Yeah, about twenty in the west, mostly concentrated around Bristol and Bath."

He felt a rush of blood and started looking for a lay-by. "Send me the pics when you can. I've had a brainwave."

Long ago, about the time Wild joined CID in fact, he gave up on the idea of coincidence — as far as investigations were concerned. More often than not, things that seemed related *were*. You just had to find the connection and make it stick. He listened to the lorries roaring past, which chimed with the roaring in his head. If he was right, they were one step closer to nailing the shooter. Something he'd like to have done with a hammer. He dialled Stuart Hoyle's mobile.

"Stuart, it's DS Wild. A quick word, okay?"

Stuart cleared his throat. "Nah, mate," he said over loudly. "Can't meet you for a drink later, I'm chillin' with my family."

Wild got the message. "One question and I promise I'll never contact you again. Was the pub you were summoned to in Bristol called The Crown?"

Wild felt the tension in his jaw.

"Yeah, roight first time. Cheers then!"

Only when the A420 welcomed Wild back into Wiltshire, over two hours later, did he face the prospect of returning to his house. And, more importantly, his neighbours. It'd be safer to stay away. He hoped Marnie would see it that way too, until he got something else organised. Time to find out.

"Marnie, are you free at the end of your shift?"

"For your information my shift finished half an hour ago, and DI Marsh already asked me the same thing. She wants to discuss the plans for tomorrow. We're all waiting for you."

"Okay, but I'd also like a private word. See you when I see you."

He updated Marsh with his ETA and got a curt reply that DI Stanton had already arrived. Of course he had.

* * *

Wild joined the throng in the briefing room just as Marsh announced, "Thanks everyone for staying on."

She'd sprung for cakes although, he noted darkly, not much of a celebration this time. Marnie hadn't met him outside, so he went into the meeting blind.

"Okay team, the good news is that I managed to beg a favour for today from our colleagues over at Gable Cross." Her lips squeezed together as she waited for the tribalism to subside. "They provided four hours of surveillance, which DCI Garner kindly wrote off as team training."

She gave a signal to Marnie, who was acting as photo monitor. A series of time-stamped pictures showed a supermarket home delivery at 09.42.

DI Stanton gave an alpha male murmur, in lieu of beating his chest, and everyone turned to see what he had to say.

"It might be interesting to see what she ordered."

Wild nodded to him, *great minds and all that* . . .

"On page two you'll see Raquel Beaumont leaving the maisonette at 11.45. She drives her Peugeot to the Cockleberry McDonald's, treats herself and then drives straight home."

Ben put his head into the lion's mouth. "What about the afternoon?"

"The Gable Cross team signed off at lunchtime and went about their normal duties."

Harris mumbled something monosyllabic and Marsh was on him like a wasp.

"Speak up man."

Never one to avoid playing with fire, he repeated himself. "I said she missed breakfast."

Wild wondered whether he was expected to put Harris in his place, as the DS, or if Marsh would let it go this time. She managed to smile, or she'd found an agreeable way to bare her teeth.

"Good point, Harris. You can follow that up tomorrow, and the supermarket order too. We'll reconvene here at seven forty-five tomorrow. Ben, you and DI Stanton will observe the home address. Craig and Marnie will support you and respond if Raquel goes mobile again. Any questions?"

Wild tried — and failed — to get Marnie's attention. As he drifted to the door to wait for her outside, he heard Marsh calling him back.

"Just a quick word, Craig."

He always knew when he was in the doghouse by the way she mangled his name. He held out Galloway's car keys to him.

"Thanks. I'll drop you off when you're done — see you downstairs."

Harris followed Ben, so clearly this was a table for four. The trio were huddled together like conspirators. DI Marsh touched Marnie's shoulder as if she were a possession.

"Marnie tells me she's been helping you with some online research on Raquel Beaumont? Ben's already looked into that."

"I know. I thought it was worth a second look."

Marsh didn't argue the point. Wild knew why. Galloway was diligent but he lacked *nous*.

"And?"

He was feeling generous. "Marnie found a social media pic of the motorbike owner outside a pub where I think some of Maguire's people used to drink — in Bristol."

DI Stanton gave Wild a quizzical look and then turned his attention to Marnie.

"It's The Crown, sir."

"I'll speak to one of my NCA colleagues. When was the picture posted?"

Stanton took a step towards the door. "Shall we check it now?"

Wild didn't like his tone and clearly nor did Marsh. "Tell you what, Gareth. Why don't you and I do that in my office and these good people enjoy the rest of their evening?"

Outside, Galloway was still looking at the bodywork. He shot up as Wild and Marnie approached. "It's, erm, a bit low on petrol . . . and you might have cleaned it."

Wild reached into his wallet. "I have been to a funeral."

"Oh yeah, right, I was forgetting. Come on then, let's get the two of you home." Galloway said it without malice, but Wild still felt a sting.

* * *

Marnie opened her front door, went straight to her bedroom and closed the door.

He stowed his bag in the guest bedroom with the rest of his stuff, and wondered when to mention using the washing machine. As he lay on the bed — shoes off — he let his mind drift back to the funeral service. He felt the weight of his eyelids pushing him into the duvet and was on the point of dropping off when he heard Marnie rapping on the door.

"What are we going to do about food tonight? Do you fancy pasta?"

He forced himself off the bed. "Anything but that."

"I've got some sort of fish pie in the freezer. Will that do with veg?"

He opened the door to find she had retreated into the living room.

"Sorry to land myself on you again. I promise to get something sorted soon."

"Sure." She sounded as if she'd never been less sure.

He followed her out to the kitchen where she hunted out their frozen dinner. "Leo left a bottle of white wine in the fridge, if you want any?"

He passed. He'd never quite forgiven white wine for that time Steph took the piss out of him because he couldn't pronounce Pinot Grigio. Forty-five minutes and an obliging oven later they sat like a distant couple, talking at opposite ends of the sofa.

"You never said how you got on in the east." An arched eyebrow suggested she already knew the answer.

He could have pleaded the fifth, or talked around the edges, but it had been a very long day and he couldn't be arsed. So he laid out the entrails of his trip and invited her to read the omens.

Part way through his confession she looked at him earnestly and declared, "This calls for wine," and promptly raided the fridge.

Wild considered himself open to new experiences and Sauvignon Blanc combined with dark chocolate Hobnobs was definitely a winner.

"Do you think you'll see her again?"

He crunched the last quarter of a biscuit, hoping Marnie hadn't noticed the crumbs by his feet. "Not sure what the point would be. I mean, we live in different worlds. And then there's God, of course."

She tipped her wine glass to him. "That's some serious competition! Oh, I nearly forgot. DI Marsh gave me some photos of your poor car — for your insurance claim."

He softened the blow with more wine and wondered whether God was getting his own back.

CHAPTER 46

Marnie leaned over the steering wheel to stretch her back. "Do you think they've tapped Raquel's phone?"

When Wild didn't answer she glanced left and saw him dialling. As he was already sighing heavily she left him to it.

He turned to the door. "Hello? No, that's brilliant. Let me just get my policy number." With that, he let himself out the car and nudged the door shut.

She adjusted the volume on her two-way radio. DI Stanton alerted the team to a postal van that had pulled up near the target address.

"The driver has the correct uniform and I can see her staff number. Noting it now for checking. She's delivering a parcel to the target . . . just being signed for . . . Craig, can you stop the van when she comes back out to the main road."

Marnie swallowed. "Will do. Sorry, I didn't think to flag it on the way in."

"Well there are two of you."

"Sir."

She watched intently until the red van appeared. Without thinking, she dashed across the street and blocked the side road, arms spread wide, vaguely aware that Wild was shouting behind her. She held up her warrant card and the driver lowered her window.

Marnie coughed as she fought to get her breath. "You made a delivery a few minutes ago — I need to check some details."

The van pulled in and the driver made a call to her boss. Satisfied, she gave Marnie the information she needed and was allowed on her way. Marnie was walking back to the car when her radio gave a couple of bleeps, followed by Galloway's voice.

"Target has opened the upstairs curtains at the rear. Hang on, she's coming out the back door."

Stanton cut in like an angry surgeon. "Did she lock the back door?"

"I dunno. I . . . I think so. Looks like she's on the move. Should I follow her?"

"Absolutely not. Craig and Marnie, stand by."

Marnie started running, dodging traffic to get back to the car. Her colleague was still on his phone.

"Wild, get in the car — *now!*" She pulled the door behind her, staring daggers. "Is she on foot, on her bike or driving, over?"

Galloway sounded as cool as a cucumber. "S'okay. Got her. She's gone to her car."

Marnie started the engine in the surveillance car. "Ready, over."

The Peugeot emerged and joined the main street.

Wild leaned towards the gearstick. "Not too close now."

"I can drive without instruction."

"Yeah, but the way you stopped the postal van wasn't exactly covert. You basically stopped traffic."

Marnie nudged the car out, prompting a taxi to brake sharply. She waved behind her and swiftly moved off.

Wild reported as he watched the Peugeot, two vehicles ahead. "We're on the move, over." He clicked the button. "I'd come down a gear if I were you . . ."

Marnie glared. "Do you want to drive? Say the word and I'll pull in." She spoke to the windscreen. "What you fail to realise is that this is your day job. Mine involves community policing, warring neighbours and the occasional grievous bodily harm. I'm desperately trying to create a positive impression and you leave me hanging to go and sort out your bloody car insurance!"

He saw Raquel indicate left, considered mentioning it, and then thought better of it. "Look, Marnie, I *promise* I will speak to DI Marsh again. In the meantime, if the target goes to the burger place again I'll buy you a milkshake as a peace offering."

She wore out the faintest of smiles in seconds. DI Stanton checked in and Wild responded.

"Target is following the same route as yesterday, sir. We're three cars behind now as a precaution." He signed off. "Happy now?"

"Strawberry," she replied. "I want a strawberry milkshake."

Wild picked up again to provide a running commentary, the sort where not much happened. Finally, the traffic conga reached its conclusion.

"Back to McDonald's, over."

"Park at a distance and one of you go in after her."

Raquel Beaumont took her time getting out the car. Wild couldn't be certain but he'd have bet money that she was talking to her phone. She walked purposefully, not confidently — a woman on a mission. He waited until she had her back to him and then slowly exited the car, closing the door softly. Marnie wound down her window.

"Strawberry."

He mock-saluted and scanned the car park as he walked. A heavy-set bloke, who filled half a sports car, proved incapable of waiting until he got his fast food home. Wild imagined the grease marks over the upholstery and shuddered.

Elsewhere, a little girl practised pester power by leaning out of a backseat window and yelling at the top of her lungs, "Happy Meal!" while her mother scurried off.

Wild reached the door first and let Happy Mum in ahead of him, earning a grateful nod as she sailed past. He waited in line, observing. The target did nothing extraordinary, said nothing, only the body language marked her out as a person on a tight leash. He scooted in a little closer to listen to the target place her order. Again, measured and casual — to a point. Every word pronounced clearly, almost as if she had another audience.

"Two quarter-pounders and two fries, please."

He avoided eye contact when a nearby order point became available, requested a strawberry milkshake — he was a man of his word — and an apple turnover thingy for himself, mostly to try and delay his departure. As he turned to leave and watch the target walk out the door, he spotted a familiar if unexpected face staring over at him.

DI Marsh's finger exerted its own gravitational pull. "Remain in the car park. I'll come out."

The target was mobile before Wild reached his car. He ignored her driving by, turning to look at the sky instead. In their car, Marnie had moved to the driving seat.

"Come on, we need to get moving."

"Stay put — Marsh is coming over."

Marnie looked across. "She's brought a friend. If Harris is anyone's idea of a friend."

Marsh and Mr Popular joined them in the car. Marsh started speaking before she'd closed the door.

"Harris was out the back with the manager, checking yesterday's order."

Harris almost swelled with pride. "Double burger and fries."

"Same as today," Marnie chipped in.

Wild clung to his phone theory. "So unless she's a big eater, there's someone waiting at home. The question is, who?" He wasn't done talking. "I thought maybe she was talking, when she got out the car. Only I couldn't see a phone in her hand."

Harris played detective. "So she's an accomplice?"

He shot him down gently. "I didn't get that impression. She held it together pretty well in there but I think she was bricking it — and not because she was on to us."

DI Marsh's far off gaze acted like a do-not-disturb sign. Even Harris knew to keep schtum. A phone call pulled her out of it.

"Yes?" She did not like to be disturbed. "Uh huh." Her mood lifted a scintilla. "That's great news, Ben. Thanks for following it up. Report in when the target gets back." She jabbed her phone into silence. "We have confirmation from Ballistics Intelligence that the bullet pulled from your unfortunate neighbour is a match for the one that killed John Donner."

Wild felt like he and Marsh were the only two people in the room, albeit a room on wheels. "A professional hit?"

"Hmm, not very professional where you're concerned. Should we assume that Raquel is at risk?"

Harris's words spilled out of his mouth. "Can't be that much at risk if she goes out every day."

Wild saw Marnie's face twitch.

"Coercive control comes in many forms. She might have a job, visit family, even socialise. None of that means she's free."

Marsh shifted towards Harris. "Did you hear back about Raquel's food delivery?"

Marnie's shoulders sagged. "I'm so sorry, ma'am. I haven't chased up that parcel." She reached into her pocket for the note.

"Give it to Harris. He can go there after he's visited the supermarket manager. On you go, Harris, I'll get a lift back with these two."

Judging by Harris's face, he didn't know whether he'd been rewarded or chastised by the DI. Wild sympathised: *been there, my friend*. Marnie extended a tentative hand towards her milkshake and the DI smiled benevolently.

* * *

No one said a word in the briefing room, even though DI Marsh and DI Stanton hadn't put in an appearance yet.

Harris was still writing on the whiteboard, his marker pen squeaking out his findings.

The supermarket order included lager, razor blades and aftershave. It all pointed in one direction, although Harris had helpfully asterisked the items. He had also earned more brownie points by his contact with Royal Mail. Not only did they now know who had sent the package — a mobile phone company — but the obliging manager had confirmed there was another delivery on the way.

Wild could hear Marsh and Stanton having a private conflab outside the door. It sounded like a DI version of *Top Trumps*. The voices ended abruptly, followed swiftly by the door handle. They walked to the front of the room together like a double-act, although that didn't fit with what Wild had overheard.

"Right, team," Marsh looked momentarily at DI Stanton. "Here's the situation. We have good reason to think there's an unknown male in Raquel Beaumont's home, and that he is responsible for the murder of John Donner and the attempted murder of our own DS Wild."

Wild sat straighter at the sound of his name. Since bedding down at Marnie's he'd thought about the shooter as an abstract scumbag. Now, in the room, it all felt very personal. He tuned back to Marsh's Glaswegian drawl.

". . . There's no indication that Raquel Beaumont is involved so her safety is our top priority. We also don't know whether this unknown male has other firearms. After much discussion with DI Stanton," she paused for a nanosecond, though long enough for Wild to get the gist, "we have decided to make contact with Ms Beaumont to try and get some intelligence, ahead of more direct action."

Marsh returned Wild's stare. "A third consideration is Craig's theory that Ms Beaumont is always on the phone — and therefore under scrutiny — whenever she travels. If he's right, that presents us with a problem." She brought her hands together like Pontius Pilate. "We'd like Marnie to make the initial approach to Raquel tomorrow — as a female biker. We need to move swiftly on this. Harris has excelled himself by getting agreement to delay the parcel delivery . . ."

For some reason Wild couldn't fathom, Harris saw this as kudos and not sarcasm.

". . . So we have a two-to-three-day window to lock this down. Any questions?"

She glared at Wild so he knew to back off.

"Okay, Marnie, Harris and Craig, stay on. The rest of you, about your business until tomorrow morning."

Wild wondered whether DI Stanton had business to be about. Apparently not. Wild put his mouth in neutral and moved to the front of the room.

CHAPTER 47

Wild was instantly awake. Something had clicked — a light switch or a door. He listened hard for sounds of movement. His first instinct, to grab a makeshift weapon, faded when he remembered he was at Marnie's. He put on joggies and advanced to the door. As he teased it open he heard a tap running in the kitchen. He followed the sound and light show.

Marnie stood by the sink, glass in hand and shrouded in a dressing gown. "I couldn't sleep."

He didn't bother pointing out the time. No doubt she'd seen the symmetry of ten-to-two on the kitchen clock. He figured he ought to say something though.

"Busy day tomorrow . . ."

She nodded and drank more water. "Do you think I'm ready?"

"Yeah, I'm sure of it. Try to get some sleep." He led by example and left her to it.

"Thanks, Craig," she called after him, tipping the rest of her glass away.

* * *

Wild was absolutely clear about one thing. He'd never say it was a shit plan. And under the circumstances he didn't have anything better to offer. He still didn't like it though — too many unknowns.

Raquel Beaumont left her home around ten thirty. She drove within the legal limit, obeyed the Highway Code, and she periodically tilted her head towards the central console — as if in conversation.

Marnie watched the Peugeot pass in her bike mirror and then slipped in behind the surveillance car that contained Wild and Marsh. Harris would already be there.

She parked up near the target's car, not *too* close, removing her helmet to walk the rest of the way unobstructed. Every step seemed to echo against her ribcage.

The target stood two ahead in the queue with her back to Marnie. She waited until the target reached the counter and then moved her helmet from one hand to the other. Wild took the signal and prompted Harris to act suspiciously, not much of a stretch in Wild's opinion.

Marnie *happened* to glance out the window.

"Hey," she announced. "Has anyone got a red Peugeot 205? Some bloke is looking it over." She dumped her helmet with Marsh, who sat near the door, and rushed out shouting, "Oi, what the fuck do you think you're doing?"

Harris ceased his loitering and scarpered. Marnie made a pretence of looking around the car and then marched back. Raquel met her halfway across the tarmac.

"Is it your car? Bloody creep. I only spotted him 'cos my bike is nearby—" she pointed, "—and I like to keep an eye on it."

Raquel looked ashen.

"Are you okay? I couldn't see any damage. Probably chancing his luck." Now came the tricky part. "Do you live locally?"

Raquel froze and then pulled herself out of it. "Yeah," she said weakly.

"I could ride behind, in case he's waiting to follow you. Or maybe we should call the police?"

"No," Raquel yelped. "No police. I don't want any fuss."

"Okay, suit yourself. I'll just collect my order and my bike helmet, if you hang on."

"I'll be fine, thanks. I'm running late anyway." Raquel started walking.

Wild watched it all from the comfort of his binoculars. Marnie went inside, certain that the red Peugeot was already on its way. Now it was a waiting game.

Once Raquel made it home she drew the curtains, or somebody did, and there was no sign of movement for the rest of the day. DI Stanton ran the surveillance rota through the night with the same result. Unless he planned on tunnelling out, the mystery shooter had dug in.

Raquel never showed up for burgers and fries the next day, although she did open the curtains. Marsh approved the parcel delivery for that afternoon and although a long lens picked out Raquel signing for it, it told them nothing else.

Wild was privy to another tense conversation between Marsh and Stanton.

"We can't wait indefinitely, Morag. She could be being held against her will. My recommendation to your DCI is that the Armed Response Group is deployed now."

DI Marsh rejected the idea out of hand. Partly, Wild thought, because DI Stanton had called her Morag in front of her sergeant.

"No, Gareth. It would be impossible to evacuate the neighbours without creating a scene. And Raquel would be in there with him. He's killed once already — the risk is too high."

"Then what's your alternative?"

Wild fancied that Marsh looked to him for inspiration.

"What if I died? I mean, if the local news announced it. Maybe that would force the shooter to act. He might make a break for it, especially as there's been no indication we're on to him."

Marsh looked unimpressed. "It could put the two of them under greater strain, with unpredictable consequences."

Stanton seemed more amenable. "Imagine the PR disaster if we delay taking the initiative. Your newspaper friends would have a field day: *Police allow gunman to hide in the community for days.*"

Marsh opted for a stalemate. "We'll go and discuss it with DCI Garner then."

They walked past Wild and he turned to follow them.

"Not you, Craig. This one's for the grown-ups."

Marsh told him later that the DCI had agreed with him. He tried not to look too pleased about it. She certainly wasn't.

CHAPTER 48

Wild had always understood the importance of timing. Another cadet intake, a different police station, and Stephanie Hutcheson might have been no more than a pretty face in the crowd. Instead, she now owned that empty spot on his ring finger. Like his Nan used to say, destiny turned on a sixpence. Even that stupid dalliance — well, several dalliances — that made him take his eye off the ball with The Logan Brothers' raid in London had been down to one ill-judged decision.

He thought about that as he waited in the car park, stomach on a knife-edge and two-way radio resting between his legs, awaiting the bleeps.

Stanton sounded gleeful. "Target has left her home. Armed Response Group is standing by. We await your intel."

Wild looked out to Marsh's car that faced him across the tarmac. He couldn't see Marsh's face clearly at that distance and was glad of it. Maybe sending Marnie back to make contact was too high a risk. No other choices came to mind. He checked again that his driver's door was unlocked, felt his pocket for his warrant card, and counted down the moments.

Raquel parked in a different spot, which threw Wild a little. Truth be told, she was nearer Marsh now, but the DI paid her no attention whatsoever. Raquel behaved differently, a casual facade of glancing around at the rest of the car park before she moved. Marsh carried on with her phone conversation — to Wild, who pretended to check his watch as they played along.

Marnie arrived, got off her bike and went straight inside, Raquel watched her and slowly followed her in. Marsh moved into position now, leaning against her car, phone still at her ear. Marnie exited first, burger in hand. Raquel emerged a few minutes later, with what Wild assumed was her usual order. The rest of her day would be anything but usual, which he figured she would eventually look back upon as a blessing. In the meantime, she was about to be forced down a rabbit hole.

Marnie, alerted through her earpiece, lowered her burger and turned. Wild watched her reciting the script.

"Oh, hello again."

Marsh zeroed in behind the target like the final actor in the opening scene of Macbeth. She tapped her on the shoulder, and a finger on the lips met Raquel when she turned. Now Marnie moved around, behind Marsh, all under Wild's watchful gaze.

One by one, Marsh went through a series of question cards, inviting yes or no answers without words, Marnie filling with covering chatter all the while. Finally, Marsh signalled Wild over. He took out his warrant card and made silent contact. He only had one question, plus a pen and paper.

WHAT IS HIS NAME?

Raquel's hand shook as she scrawled it out. Marnie stopped gabbing. Two words emerged: JONAS FAULKNER. Marnie motioned for the car keys and immediately got into the Peugeot's passenger seat. Marsh sent Raquel off to join her.

It seemed a good time to let the DI know how he felt. "I don't like this at all."

"We're in touch with Marnie all the way. Get the house keys to DI Stanton."

He grabbed them and ran to his car. On the drive he rang Harris to text him the target's landline number. He figured it might buy a few seconds if they were needed. As soon as he was off the call his phone rang again.

"Yes?" he snapped.

DI Marsh didn't waste time on intros. "So Cody Faulkner has played us all — even Paul Maguire."

"It's looking that way. I'll ring you when I see DI Stanton."

"Okay, I'm following them. It'll be okay, Craig."

He spoke from the gut. "It better be."

CHAPTER 49

Marnie gave encouraging glances to Raquel, who had taken out her mobile phone and placed it in the central console.

Jonas Faulkner's voice filled the car, even though he never raised his voice. "What's keeping you?"

"Sorry, Jonas. The woman with the motorbike wouldn't stop talking." She blushed and Marnie smiled.

"Make sure she isn't following you."

"I've checked — it's clear."

They heard a big breath and then, "Check again."

Marnie listened as Jonas told Raquel that they needed to get away, and her motorbike had to be destroyed.

"But Jonas, I love my bike — I've spent every spare penny on it."

His silence became her silence, and then he said, "The copper's dead. I'll get you a new one once we're settled. We'll pack our bags tonight."

Raquel swallowed. "Yes, Jonas."

"Right, call me when you're here."

The line went dead.

Raquel stumbled on the words, "What's going to happen?"

Marnie touched her arm. "You're safe and we'll keep you safe. My colleagues will handle it from here."

Wild had driven like a man possessed, without the hindrance of conscience. He met DI Stanton and handed him the door keys. Stanton was already briefed, thanks to Marsh's update in transit. Wild watched the keys pass from Stanton to a member of the Armed Response Group — two pips for a fellow inspector. Wild knew he wouldn't figure in the conversation.

A few minutes later, Ben Galloway reported in. "Target vehicle in sight. She has parked up and has a phone to her ear."

* * *

"Where are you, Raquel?"

"I'm just walking up. I'll be with you in a couple of minutes, Jonas. I had to park somewhere different."

Marnie heard movement on the phone before he spoke again.

"What do you mean?"

Marnie checked Raquel's progress with a hand on her shoulder. She looked panic-stricken so Marnie did the only thing she could think of, dropped the call and then reached into her jacket for the radio. "I think he suspects."

Stanton alerted Armed Response. "You have a green light, Inspector."

Three armed officers made their way to the front door, and another two to the rear gate. Wild exchanged a few words with Stanton and then started dialling. He imagined the landline ringing upstairs in the flat where Jonas was hiding.

The answering machine kicked in. Wild waited for the beep and hoped Jonas would bite.

"Jonas, it's Sergeant Wild. I'm still alive, you fucking idiot. Pick up now, if you've got the balls." He heard a faint echo and then the phone clicked.

"Still alive? That's easily remedied."

Wild heard a distant sound through his phone, like a front door opening. Then a reciprocal noise, as if it closed again.

"Raquel! Get up here. Goodbye, Sergeant."

The line fell silent but Wild and Stanton had an open radio channel to hear it unfold in real time. Wild put it together in his head — a stair creak, soft footsteps, a warning call, a rush of bodies, and a door giving in.

"On the floor — do it now. Face down, arms wide — do it now. Where is the weapon?"

Wild felt his blood rush as he listened in. Jonas complied — because three Heckler & Koch submachine guns make a persuasive argument. He couldn't relax until he heard the magic words.

"Suspect detained, weapon neutralised. There's no one else present. The scene is contained."

Wild contacted Marnie. "Everything okay with you?"

"Yeah, all good. Raquel is a bit shell-shocked. We're fine. DI Marsh is with me now."

She signed off and steered a quivering Raquel towards the DI's car.

"I'm so sorry, I panicked. I thought maybe Jonas could see your officer and me. I thought he might . . ."

Marsh nodded softly. "Don't you worry about that now, Ms Beaumont. Let's get you back to the police station and put everything in writing. And then we'll have a chat."

Marnie had a feeling the UK Protected Person's Unit would be receiving a call.

Jonas seemed to think his handcuffs were malleable. Wild watched him struggling in vain from the safety of the surveillance van. Stanton leaned closer.

"Your DI and I will interview him. I'm sure you can find some other way to make yourself useful. We want more information about how the crime group operates."

Wild gave him his best smile, as if to say, 'Good luck with that, sir.' He radioed Ben to accompany Marsh and asked Marnie to meet him at the front door. Armed Response had been so quick there'd be little footage of their entrance on social media, although no doubt some scrote had hit *send* as soon as Jonas came out with a blanket on his head. The public didn't like to see police with guns, apparently. Not unless the bad guys had them, anyway.

Marnie followed Wild inside, gloves and shoe coverings at the ready — thanks to him. They knew the pistol had been recovered at the scene, so this was secondary evidence gathering. Even so, she was wary.

Wild watched her take a few steps into the living room. She faltered, staring into space. He'd seen the way that shock stalked a person until it caught them unawares. He thought back to when his car got cremated.

He took a couple of steps towards her and stalled. What was the protocol between mates when one was a woman?

"You did really well out there . . ."

Her face softened. "Thanks. I was worried that Jonas had heard me in the car with Raquel. I thought he might be able to see us together, out the window, and make a break for it. Or take a shot."

"I think my phone call distracted him."

"Huh?"

"I rang her landline and told him he was a fucking idiot."

"Nice."

"Yeah, you'll learn stuff like that when you get your sergeant's."

She laughed and he gently patted her back a couple of times, the way someone does with a horse they're a little afraid of it. Then he slipped back into work mode.

"Look for the biker's jacket — from the dash cam. They're a bugger to clean, if he bothered, so we may find some gunshot residue. The bike's being collected as well."

Finding the freezer empty, he tried the washing machine and the laundry basket. The latter provided currency in the case, literally. A stack of notes, wrapped and sealed in a plastic container, along with Jonas Faulkner's passport and his old phone in pieces.

The Holy Grail though, was the motorcycle jacket hanging up in the closet. He could go to his bed a happy man. And speaking of beds . . .

"At least you'll get your flat back to yourself."

Marnie didn't look him in the eye. "You could stay until the weekend — if you wanted."

He understood. After a brush with death, real or imagined, the last thing you wanted was time on your own to reflect.

"Thanks, Marnie. That'd be great. Could you pop back to mine with me to pick up a couple of things?"

She waited in the car. No neighbours came calling and there was no 'sorry you were nearly shot' card through the letterbox. The house felt empty, and it no longer felt like home. He got his things together and stood in the front room for a few seconds, eyes closed. He remembered the sense of finality when he'd first arrived, months earlier. Kidding himself he would put down fresh roots.

"Not here," he told the room, with its half-filled boxes still lining the wall.

He walked past Marnie in the car and knocked at his neighbour's. She asked who it was before she'd open the door, and he had to show his warrant card at the window. She peeped out from the curtain, mobile phone in hand. Finally reassured, she opened the front door no more than a foot.

"Yes?"

"I just wanted to say how sorry I am about your partner. I gather he's making good progress in hospital."

"Yeah. I don't want to talk about it." The door slowly closed.

CHAPTER 50

The word around the police station was that Cody Faulkner's solicitor had been inexplicably unavailable to represent his brother Jonas. Someone from Santers would be leaping into the breach instead.

Wild sent Marnie up to the canteen, so he could book in the evidence they'd collected and have a private word with Sergeant Galloway about her. Meantime, the forensics team were all over the biker's jacket like a rash. A quick word with Technical Support and then he headed upstairs to try his hand at tea and empathy.

He took a seat at Marnie's table without so much as a glib comment. Her hands were moulded around a mug of tea. She barely looked at him as she spoke.

"Remember when we were in London that time, after the firearms team had picked up Tony Weston? I wasn't worried at all about Jackie."

Wild touched the back of his head, much as Jackie had with a cosh.

"Today was different, I see that now. It was me in the firing line." She smiled darkly at her own joke. "How do you . . . how do you do it?"

He broke off a piece of biscuit, dunked it in his tea and then consumed it. "There's no magic trick. I focus on the job at hand. I take refuge in probabilities, I suppose. We had armed officers front and back of their flat. If he had stuck a gun out the window someone would have plugged him." He realised the conversation had taken a decidedly dark detour.

"Shouldn't you be downstairs for when the DIs come out?"

He took out his phone and put it on the table. "Harris said he'd call me. He's in Marsh's good books right now so he's a happy bunny. It'll be first name terms next."

"It's Harry. His name is Harry Harris."

He took a swig of tea. "Parents can be cruel bastards sometimes."

"It's not entirely their fault. *Harrison* Harris is named after his grandfather. Some sort of family tradition, so Sergeant Galloway told me."

"No wonder he's always a bit chippy with his colleagues." He offered her a whole biscuit and crunched on the partial one. "The main thing is, we got our man today."

Marnie finished her tea and shifted her chair. "Yes, there is that. Oh well, back to uniform for me tomorrow, I imagine."

"Well, after you've written up your notes!"

She finished her tea and left him to it. He gazed out at the pale sky and wondered whether he had the strength of his convictions. One conversation at a time, he told himself.

The letting agent's singsong voice quickly lost its melody. "Why would you want to break your lease?"

"Have you seen the news lately?" He filled in some of the blanks.

"Perhaps you'd like to come in and discuss it?"

"Yeah, let's do that." He made an appointment and then picked up the mugs for the return journey to the counter.

By chance he saw DI Stanton heading out to the car park and made a mad dash to catch him before he drove away.

"Sir!" he doubled over, hands on his knees to give his lungs a fighting chance.

"Don't worry, Craig — this isn't goodbye. I'll be returning in a few days. I need to report back and attend a case meeting."

Wild could almost feel heat at the back of his neck and when he turned he saw DI Marsh staring down at him. Her crooked finger reeled him in.

"Have a safe drive, sir, and perhaps we'll finally have that pint when you get back?"

He meant it, but he couldn't tell whether Stanton knew that. He didn't give it much thought on his way back inside. DI Marsh's office door had been left open. Wild crossed the threshold and closed the door on them. Marsh's first words surprised him, on a day when he'd thought that couldn't be possible.

"How's Marnie doing?"

He sat down and crossed a foot over his knee. "She's coping. I think we pushed her too far."

"You mean I did."

He saw no reason to contradict her.

"She could have said no, Craig."

He went with hollow laughter. "What, and disappoint you? That was never going to happen. Don't worry, me and Sergeant Galloway will get her through it." He could sense the brick wall ahead so he changed direction. "How did the interview with Jonas Faulkner go?"

Marsh seemed to relax a little, or maybe they just had a common enemy. She walked him through it by the numbers. A senior solicitor with marginally more scruples than his client. A masterclass in no-commenting, despite irrefutable evidence — the gun at the scene, transference of gunshot residue to the motorbike, and the unexpected Christmas present of trace evidence emerging that linked Jonas to Donald Jacobson's office.

"It's a testament to teamwork and the diligence of everyone involved with the case."

The word *everyone* threw the switch for him.
"Can I speak plainly, ma'am?"
"When have you not?"
He took that as an invitation.

CHAPTER 51

Days later, an hour before Cody Faulkner's scheduled arrival from prison, Wild found himself in another tête-à-tête with DI Marsh. She walked him through developments.

"Jonas Faulkner may be cut from the same cloth as his brother, Cody, but he's also a survivor. No surprise then that his earlier no-comment interview technique underwent a seismic shift once the noose tightened sufficiently."

Wild nodded. He'd seen it so often he could mark the beats. Some idiot thinking that saying nothing could make it all go away, or at least be harder to prove. And then reality bit them on the arse, usually through forensic evidence or CCTV. After that, they'd rat out their own grandmother if they thought it would lessen their culpability.

"What did he admit at the second interview?"

Marsh smiled. "Well, let's just say it helped that Cody's solicitor still wasn't picking up his messages. Jonas swore blind that he spoke with Paul Maguire to receive his orders. When confronted with evidence to the contrary, seeing as Maguire had earned himself a stint in solitary for his behaviour, Jonas passed the poisonous parcel to his brother. And Cody, as you know, only agreed to speak with us today if he got a day trip down to Mayberry."

Wild began to wonder when DI Stanton would put in an appearance. Marsh saved him the bother of asking, when her phone rang. She took a brief call, stabbing the red button with a look of great satisfaction.

"Cody has just left HMP Bristol. Gareth Stanton is on board. Now, while we've a little private time, we need to have a talk . . ."

"I know," he tried to cut her off. "Say nothing in the interview unless I have your express permission."

She smiled. "That's perfectly true, although not what I'm referring to. I've assured Gretchen Lambert you will give her a story for the Chronicle. Liaise with a press officer first and then run it past me."

His breath caught in his throat. "And why would I agree to that?"

"Two reasons." She chopped her desk with the edge of her hand. "Firstly, as penance for the way you spoke to me about Marnie." Another chop. "Secondly, Gretchen told me in the strictest confidence that Napier posted some papers to Norman Easton, the day before you saved his life. He duly passed them on to Gretchen, who has agreed to spike any story about you. As to the former Mrs Wild — DCI Stephanie Hutcheson — that's neither my business nor my concern."

If he wasn't mistaken that was empathy radiating across the desk. "You bought Gretchen off — for me?"

"Don't talk pish. I did it for me, for my team. But mark me, Craig, although I have given you a certain latitude while you settle in, consider yourself settled now. Here on in, you will follow the chain of command. Are we clear?"

"Ma'am."

"Then go grab yourself a coffee and leave me in peace till I need you."

He took her at her word, closing the door quietly behind him. He could hear her dulcet tones on the phone as he walked away. Perhaps he ought to have been surprised to find Marnie on a break, but nothing surprised him lately in this nick. DI Marsh had the place sewn up tighter than a drum.

Marnie beamed at him. "DS Wild, can I get you a coffee?" She got up before he'd had a chance to reply.

After he sat down she presented him with a mug of steaming caffeine and a bar of chocolate.

"What's the occasion?"

"DI Marsh got the green light for my secondment."

"That's fantastic. Shouldn't I be buying the drinks then?"

"The DI told me what you said to her—"

He hoped he didn't have to hear it again. He hoped wrong.

"—If she didn't get me on the team after all I'd done, you'd ask DI Stanton or use your contacts in London to find me an opportunity out of county."

He was glad she'd skipped the part about him telling Marsh to shove his job otherwise, or maybe Marsh had missed that bit out.

"As soon as Ben moves over to Gable Cross, his desk is mine!"

* * *

Cody Faulkner's eyes never settled. Wild watched him on the monitor upstairs as they booked him in. He oozed menace. Only DI Stanton, standing sentinel, appeared immune. He looked as if he could wait all day.

The prisoner had little to say in the interview, after confirming his name. True to his word, Cody never went *no comment*, but he was hardly forthcoming. All perfunctory answers, some after a brief exchange with his reluctant solicitor. A cynic might have suggested he was merely playing the clock.

Marsh and Stanton led from the front. Wild sat in the room with them, as silent as revenge. Cody kept him in his malevolent gaze though. Wild deflected his attention by counting his tattoos. Every accusation seemed to ricochet off him in his brother's direction. It was, to all intents and purposes, a Cain and Abel rematch. Cody said — through his solicitor sitting next to him — that he knew nothing about

Jonas's involvement until Paul Maguire told him. Then added that he'd personally played no part in commissioning or inciting the shooting on the street where Wild lived.

He paused to look directly at Wild.

"Believe me, Sergeant Wild, if I wanted you dead, you wouldn't be sat there now."

The solicitor leaned forward suddenly, as if he'd just unexpectedly shat himself. "What my client means . . ."

Marsh didn't need help with the meaning. "Are you threatening one of my officers, Mr Faulkner?"

Cody didn't blink. "It's a statement of fact."

Marsh let their evidence do the talking, courtesy of DI Stanton. Even Wild was impressed at his industry. No wonder he'd been away for a few days. Phone records for a burner phone, triangulated in the prison vicinity, linked to Jonas's old mobile that Wild had recovered from Raquel's flat. A search of the entire prison wing had been instigated, once Cody's secure transport had left the prison.

Cody refuted nothing, admitted nothing, just sat there and took it. After the interview sign-off and the end of the recording he stood up, flanked by police officers. He looked down at Wild the way a hawk observes its next meal.

"You know I'll be out at some point, DS Wild. And so will Jonas and Chalky. Be seeing you, Detective."

Wild's legs turned to lead. He couldn't have stood if he'd wanted to. Stanton got to his feet.

"You've said your piece, Mr Faulkner, and there's nothing on tape."

Cody smiled and his solicitor, still seated, shrank back. Stanton stared Cody Faulkner down and sucked at a tooth.

"Now let me say mine. Imagine if word got out to Paul Maguire that you'd tried to stitch him up and helped us find his burner phone. That'd be a pretty tense situation, especially if your prison transfer got lost or delayed. We can both think about that on the drive back to Bristol."

* * *

DI Stanton made it back to Mayberry for a celebratory drink, partly to recognise their team effort on the investigation but mostly to mark Marnie's forthcoming secondment. Even Harris played nice.

Wild only stayed for one drink and then made his excuses, which DI Marsh generously let pass. Marnie walked him out to his car.

"You okay?"

He spared her a recital of Cody Faulkner's patter. He figured she'd had enough to deal with in the past few days.

"Yeah, I just need to start going through my stuff again. Downsize a bit this time."

"Still can't believe you're moving again. I'll keep my eyes open in case there's anything suitable near me."

"Cheers."

It was stupid, defying all logic, but he took the long route home and looped a roundabout in case someone had followed him from the pub. Finally, he parked the replacement Ford Focus at the other end of the terrace, away from his own front door. A couple of curtains twitched. He ignored them.

A small white envelope awaited him on the mat indoors. No writing on the front, the card within unsigned. The outer message read: *Thinking of you at this difficult time*. He put it on the mantelpiece. Maybe his neighbours weren't the uncaring bastards he'd imagined them to be.

Around ten p.m., as the old house creaked and groaned, he thought about that card again. Why wasn't it signed? Not even a scrawled name or a house number. The room suddenly felt very chilly.

After that, he was a man on a mission. It took him nearly an hour to find what he was looking for, stuffed in amongst his London memorabilia. The stark white business card was plain apart from a name and a phone contact. He grabbed his mobile phone and dialled the number carefully, squeezing the phone to stop it shaking.

The call connected after four rings. He'd expected a machine at that hour but he remembered the voice on the other end well.

"Hello? It's, er, Craig Wild. You probably don't remember me. I wasn't even sure if your number would still . . . Oh, you do." He took a breath and leaned against the mantelpiece. "You did say, if I ever found myself in a difficult situation . . ."

He stopped talking because he didn't have to say any more. The more he listened, the easier he felt. It might not have been the traditional interpretation of 'keeping the peace' but it meant he'd be able to sleep at night.

It was time for him to speak again. "Well, I'm hoping it won't come to that. A warning should suffice. I'll see you in London at the weekend then. Same place? Text me a time. Thanks, Karl. You're a lifesaver."

THE END

ACKNOWLEDGEMENTS

Special thanks to Warren Stevenson and Sarah Campbell, the College of Policing, the Ministry of Justice, and the Comms Centre Inbound Team at Avon and Somerset Police.

ALSO BY DEREK THOMPSON

DETECTIVE CRAIG WILD MYSTERIES
Book 1: LONG SHADOWS
Book 2: WEST COUNTRY MURDER

THOMAS BLADEN THRILLERS
Book 1: STANDPOINT
Book 2: LINE OF SIGHT
Book 3: CAUSE & EFFECT
Book 4: SHADOW STATE
Book 5: FLASHPOINT

Thank you for reading this book.

If you enjoyed it please leave feedback on Amazon or Goodreads, and if there is anything we missed or you have a question about, then please get in touch. We appreciate you choosing our book.

Founded in 2014 in Shoreditch, London, we at Joffe Books pride ourselves on our history of innovative publishing. We were thrilled to be shortlisted for Independent Publisher of the Year at the British Book Awards.

www.joffebooks.com

We're very grateful to eagle-eyed readers who take the time to contact us. Please send any errors you find to corrections@joffebooks.com. We'll get them fixed ASAP.

Printed in Great Britain
by Amazon